Award-winning author **Elizabeth Rolls** lives in the Adelaide Hills of South Australia with her husband, two soccer-mad sons, two dogs and a cat. She also has four alpacas and two incredibly fat sheep, all gainfully employed as environmentally sustainable lawnmowers. Elizabeth enjoys reading, walking, cooking and her husband's gardening. Elizabeth loves to hear from readers, and invites you to contact her via email at books@elizabethrolls.com and visit her website at www.elizabethrolls.com.

**Michelle Willingham**'s parents hauled her to antique shows, she entertained herself by making up stories and pondering whether she could afford a broadsword with her allowance. Currently, she teaches American History and English, and lives in southeastern Virginia with her husband and children. She still doesn't have her broadsword. Visit her website at www.michellewillingham.com or email her at michelle@michellewillingham.com

Just like one of her fictional heroines, **Marguerite Kaye**'s fantasy has become reality. She has published history and travel articles, as well as short stories, but romances are her passion. Marguerite describes Georgette Heyer and Doris Day as her biggest early influences, and her partner as her inspiration. Marguerite would love to hear from you. You can contact her at Marguerite_Kaye@hotmail.co.uk

Still involved in the fields of marketing, advertising and public relations, **Ashley Radcliff** has also finally found time to pursue her first love: writing fiction. Now settled in a small Appalachian town, she draws creative inspiration from the untamed landscape of the Smoky Mountain foothills.

**Bronwyn Scott** is a communications instructor in the Puget Sound area, and is the proud mother of three wonderful children (one boy and two girls). When she's not teaching or writing she enjoys playing the piano, traveling—especially to Florence, Italy—and studying history and foreign languages. Readers can stay in touch on Bronwyn's website, www.bronwynnscott.com, or at her blog, www.bronwynswriting.blogspot.com.

# Delectably Undone!

## ELIZABETH ROLLS
## MICHELLE WILLINGHAM
## MARGUERITE KAYE
## ASHLEY RADCLIFF
## BRONWYN SCOTT

TORONTO NEW YORK LONDON
AMSTERDAM PARIS SYDNEY HAMBURG
STOCKHOLM ATHENS TOKYO MILAN MADRID
PRAGUE WARSAW BUDAPEST AUCKLAND

ISBN-13: 978-0-373-29636-1

DELECTABLY UNDONE!
Copyright © 2011 by Harlequin Books S.A.

The publisher acknowledges the copyright holders of the individual works as follows:

A SCANDALOUS LIAISON
Copyright © 2010 by Elizabeth Rolls

PLEASURED BY THE VIKING
Copyright © 2010 by Michelle Willingham

THE CAPTAIN'S WICKED WAGER
Copyright © 2009 by Marguerite Kaye

THE SAMURAI'S FORBIDDEN TOUCH
Copyright © 2010 by Ashley Radcliff

ARABIAN NIGHTS WITH A RAKE
Copyright © 2010 by Nikki Poppen

Recycling programs
for this product may
not exist in your area.

# CONTENTS

# A SCANDALOUS LIAISON

Elizabeth Rolls

## Author Note

Writers are often asked where their ideas come from. I suppose, like our dreams, they come out of the well of our subconscious. But how do we fill the well? As a child, I loved Greek mythology, but I also longed to draw and paint really well. An aunt had books of mythological paintings, and I'd sit in the corner of my uncle's study for hours imagining all the stories they told and dreaming about them. Finally, I realized—older brothers are harsh critics!—that my drawing skills were nonexistent and I needed another way to tell stories.

Names are essential. Without the right names I can't write the story, *because I don't know who the characters are.* So there I was, contemplating erotic paintings and all those Greek gods chasing nymphs around the Mediterranean Basin, and in strolled Evelyn, Viscount St. Austell.

Evelyn (pronounced *Eve-lin*), was originally a man's name. Like Jocelyn, Hilary and Shirley it has crossed genders and become predominantly a woman's name. But in the early nineteenth century, Evelyn was still a man's name. I've no idea why my scandalous viscount insisted on being called Evelyn, but I wasn't prepared to risk an argument on the subject and have him stroll back into my subconscious with the story!

*This story is for Anne, who answered so many questions about painting murals, and for Tony, whose long-standing friendship is unshakeable, even to the extent of answering my very nosy questions about dreams.*

*And it's for Smokey,*
*who snoozed by my desk for so many years and stories.*

*I miss you, old friend.*

She glanced back over her shoulder, smiling, face half hidden by the hood of her cloak. No words, just the beckoning smile, part innocence, all invitation. His breath came in hard and fast as he reached for her, touched the billowing cloak… His fingers passed through it like smoke, and with a soundless sigh the cloak dissolved, taking with it the fading vision as he lunged forward. He tried to cry out but could not. And there was nothing except loss and yearning…

He awoke into darkness with a jolt, his breath shuddering as he sat bolt-upright. He'd had a hell of a dream; at least he thought he must have. Sweat cooled on his body and his heart hammered. Yes. Something about a cloak. Only…he couldn't remember. Just that he had dreamed… that he had wanted something and it had been taken from him. The cloak had taken it…or had he lost it? He lay down again and closed his eyes. As he drifted back toward sleep the thought flickered…something? Or someone?

Evelyn Fitzhugh, Viscount St. Austell, stared mutely at the murals adorning the bedchamber walls of his Grosvenor

Square mansion. A line from Lionel Trehearne's letter asking for the commission sprang to his mind: *You may find, my lord, that the style of these pictures differs somewhat from your expectations.*

He'd been so shamed by that cold "my lord" that he'd scarce noted the content. *My lord*…from Lionel of all men. And the letter signed with a cool *Trehearne*. He deserved it, though, for what he'd done, so Evelyn had swallowed it with as good a grace as might be, and gone ahead with the commission. Despite the gulf of class between them, son and heir of a viscount and son of a schoolmaster, Lionel had been like an elder brother to him once, and Evelyn had repaid that with a betrayal of trust so base that even now he burned with shame to think of it. Youth might explain folly; it did not excuse a failure of honor.

Now, faced with the murals he had commissioned, he recalled the content of that letter; Lionel's style *had* changed. Fundamentally. Oh, the technique was recognisably his, the same economy of line that suggested shape and bulk with a few simple strokes of charcoal. But six years ago Lionel's work, while brilliant, had not left Evelyn this short of breath. Yes, it had been erotic, but this—this aching sensuality—was new. He swallowed, looking again at the slender nymph gracing his bedchamber walls. Who was she? Only blocked and roughly sketched in charcoal as yet, even complete her identity would remain a mystery. In each of the five pictures her face was hidden, shadowed by a cloak in one as she looked back over her shoulder… in farewell? Her back was turned in the next as she melted into her lover's embrace and he bent to take her mouth. A veiling of soft tresses hid her face in the third painting— how, with only a few strokes, had Lionel conveyed the silken glory of her hair…? Evelyn swallowed. Lionel had entitled that one *The Nymph, Worshipping at the Feet of the God, Administers the Kiss of Venus to Apollo.* The cascade of curls might hide the actual moment, but the naked god's head flung back in imminent ecstasy, the taut corded muscles and the hand sliding through the tumbled locks to stroke the nymph's throat, a gesture at once possessive and tender…there was no doubt as to what she was doing. Evelyn's mouth dried and his heart hammered a slow, heavy rhythm. He hardly dared look at the next picture—the nymph surrendered in passion to her immortal lover.

In the final picture she lay sleeping and sated in her lover's arms, her face shielded by his tender, caressing hand…. Evelyn shut his eyes and felt the cool fire of her tresses slipping through his fingers, the softness of her cheek against his shoulder, her quiet breathing a caress. He wouldn't lose her again. He couldn't….

A rumble of carriage wheels down in the street jerked him out of the daydream to gaze again at the reality of what he had commissioned.

Who was she?

Dammit! Lionel was the last man alive he would have chosen for this commission! Six years ago Evelyn had accepted Lionel's ultimatum that he was to remain out of their lives. He'd done so. Only by chance had he heard through a mutual friend that Lionel had gone to Italy. He could only suppose that his friend had doubted his promise to keep away. After that Lionel had dropped out of sight, communicating with no one. Evelyn wouldn't even have known the man was back if he hadn't received the letter asking for the commission and submitting a series of pen and pencil sketches. He had no idea how Lionel had heard about it, although he supposed it was common knowledge that rakish Viscount St. Austell had asked for a set of murals to adorn his bedchamber walls in his Grosvenor

Square mansion to celebrate taking possession after the exit of his last remaining paternal great-aunt to a cousin's country home.

He could, of course, have lived here even with Great-aunt Millicent in residence. However, the thought of being subjected to a catechism every time he failed to come home, or did anything even remotely scandalous, had been enough to keep him in lodgings since he had inherited his father's title four years earlier.

To make matters worse, Millicent had roundly condemned his interest in art. At least, not his interest precisely, but certainly his taste. That was one thing, but when she had taken it upon herself to slap a coat of scarlet paint across one of his favorite nudes, which he'd hung in a little-used guest chamber, it was the outside of enough.

This, then, was his revenge. Great-aunt Millicent, fond of extolling the virtues of her saintly father, the fourth viscount, was likely to have apoplexy when she heard what was now adorning the deceased saint's bedchamber walls.

Half a dozen painters had submitted sketches for Evelyn's inspection; he'd rejected them all. Very well, he'd asked for explicit, but none of them had looked anything but tawdry and lewd. His main aim might be to annoy Great-aunt Millicent, but that didn't mean he wanted to live with boring paintings. Except for Lionel's entry none had so much as caused his pulse to flicker. He might still have rejected it; even six years on, salt rubbed into a still-raw wound could sting. But the address given, a shop down by Westminster Bridge, suggested that Lionel was struggling. This was the only way Evelyn could help him and perhaps make amends for the carelessness that had broken their friendship.

That was what he was telling himself, anyway. He took

another look at the worshipping nymph, and his body hardened. But he'd written back, suggesting terms for the commission and omitting all mention of their falling out, only writing politely at the end that he "hoped they were both well?"

Even now the memory of Loveday Trehearne shamed him. An endless regret for youthful, selfish folly. Mention her name in a letter to her brother he would not. Especially in a letter over this particular commission.

Lionel's reply had dealt only with the commission, agreeing to his terms with one stipulation: their only contact should be by letter. Payment for the work should be made directly to an account at Hoare's Bank. There would be no meeting. Which suggested that Loveday was still with him.

Evelyn turned back to the murals. The blocking was done. He owed Lionel money, which had to be paid before the actual painting would commence. And the sooner it was done, the sooner Lionel could finish the paintings and Evelyn could move back into the family mansion.

He ought not to be here. No contact. So why the devil, having bribed the shopkeeper for the address, was he standing in the rain on the Strand at the entrance to Little Frenchman's Yard, about to break that agreement? He'd paid the money owed at Hoare's. There was no possible reason for him to be here. Except…

He just wanted to see Lionel, dammit. Nothing else. Perhaps make amends. He wasn't going to dishonor himself again. Although judging by the dank, malodorous passage that led into the yard, it seemed unlikely that Loveday was still with Lionel. He would never have permitted his sister to live in a place like this. She could have married, or… *Married.* Evelyn forced his suddenly clenched fists to relax.

It was none of his business if Loveday had married. He was considering a betrothal himself. Not that he'd met Miss Angaston yet, but delicate approaches had been made by his aunts to the lady's family. It was considered an excellent match by all concerned. Her wealth and beauty, his wealth and title. It was the sort of marriage he was expected to make; that had been dinned into him from childhood. In his world marriage was made for social advancement, for wealth, for convenience, to oblige one's family. He had never questioned that. He recalled his father's calm voice; suggesting possible brides, but assuring Evelyn that there was no hurry…that if he wished to sow a few wild oats first, it was perfectly understandable…. It had all made perfect sense at the time. It was the way of the world.

But his father had been gone for four years now. At twenty-eight, even without his aunts' less-than-subtle prodding, he knew that it was time to settle down. He had woken several months earlier, on his birthday, with a mouth like the bottom of a birdcage, and had wondered who the stranger in the mirror might be, and if he even liked him. He had responsibilities, people who depended on him; in short, he'd grown up.

Now… Evelyn hesitated at the mouth of the passage. Something down there was snoring. His nose wrinkled at the sourness oozing from the passage. Six years ago Lionel Trehearne had lived in a decent set of rooms in Blooms-bury, with Loveday to keep house for him. Nothing fancy, but they had been comfortable on Lionel's earnings as a painter. Why was Lionel now living down here? Evelyn stepped into the darkness and, as his eyes adjusted, realized that the snoring came from a bundle of rags and newspaper at the far end.

Trying not to breathe deeply, he traversed the passage with its damp walls. Stepping over the snoring bundle and its reek of gin, he came out into the yard. Hemmed on all sides by shabby buildings that leaned on each other in haphazard support, with just that one passage leading in, the yard seemed to repel what little damp, gray light was left in the day. Hard to imagine that even in the blaze of high noon the place would be anything but dank and drear. In the dying light of a rainy day it breathed despair.

A boy watched from the mouth of an open door. As Evelyn approached, dull eyes sharpened with wariness.

He stopped. "Good afternoon. I'm looking for Lionel Trehearne."

The child shrugged.

A battle-torn ginger cat slunk past, jaws weighed down by a rat nearly its own size.

Narrowing his gaze, Evelyn slid his hand into his coat pocket and jingled a few coins. "That your tongue the cat's got?"

A shake of the head. A flicker of what might be humor in the eyes. "Nah. Ut be a rat. Big un."

"So it is," said Evelyn. "And you can talk. Now—Mr Trehearne?" He jingled the coins again.

Straightening, the child pointed to a door over the passage, reached by rickety steps. "Up there. Leastways, I s'pose that's who yeh mean. Nowt else here for a toff like you."

Evelyn flipped a shilling piece to the boy. "Thank you."

The coin vanished, snatched in midair and tucked away in the putrid rags.

Evelyn mounted the steps warily. They were just as rickety as they looked. Every one creaked in protest and he tested each tread, keeping his weight to the sides, telling himself that the structure would probably survive a few more minutes.

The door at the top was as makeshift as the staircase. He knocked, hoping that Lionel would let him speak before flinging him straight back down the stairs. Listening, he waited, and eventually heard soft footfalls on the other side.

Then "Who is it?"

His stomach plummeted. Not the baritone rumble he'd expected. Not even a male voice. Soft, musical, the light cadences fell sweetly in a familiar pattern. Words thickened on his tongue, unformed like his thoughts. Yet one word, one thought, cut crystal bright.

*Loveday.*

One thought twisted clear of the tangle…and with it, anger.

"It's me—Evelyn. Open the door."

A bolt scraped back and the door opened.

"I see six years have not robbed you of one iota of charm," said Loveday Trehearne.

For a moment all he could do was stare at the woman in the misshapen doorway, and try to reconcile her with the girl he remembered. Long-lidded tawny eyes, the red-gold hair, the firm chin. A small, reddened hand came up in an achingly familiar gesture to push back an errant curl.

So much the same…and yet where the golden eyes had once held the joy and bubble of laughing innocence there was the hard edge of wariness, and with it something darker—despair? Where once her bright curls had been bundled into a loose knot with bits forever escaping, now it was confined severely—just that one shorter lock tumbling down to tempt a man's fingers. And her mouth, once so soft and quick to smile, looked as though it had forgotten what a smile was.

"Dammit, Loveday," he said, stepping past her. "What in Hades is Lionel about, bringing you to this…dump!"

Her eyes sharpened to blazing daggers. "Did I invite you in, *my lord*?"

The icy tones slashed deep, touching hurts he'd rather forget.

"If you didn't intend to invite me in, why open the door?" he demanded. And wanted to bite his tongue out. This was *Loveday*, and she had every right to want his hide for a hearth rug.

Her fists clenched, and her mouth flattened. "Good question. Easier to push you down the stairs with the door open, do you think?"

He dragged in a breath and forced a lid on the roiling ferment within. He had deserved that.

"I'm sorry. All right? I never meant to hurt you!"

"You didn't *mean* anything!"

Lord! Where had that frozen whip come from?

"I made a mistake. I never should have touched you."

"*You* made a mistake?" Her teeth were clenched, eyes narrowed., "How unfortunate for you." And as quickly, the blaze was extinguished in a cool smile. "You were told not to come here. That was part of the agreement, as I recall."

"Did you make that stipulation?"

She shrugged. "Why would that make a difference?"

It shouldn't.

"Where is he? Lionel made good money as a painter. Judging by the sketches he sent me, he still could. Why are you living like this?"

The delicate brows rose. "Like what? In squalor? Fashions change, my lord. In art…as well as women."

"Don't do that!"

"What? Stop speaking the truth?"

"Stop 'my lording' me as though I were a stranger!" He fought down hurt and anger. "For God's sake, Loveday—let me help you. Let me give you some money. I can—"

"No!" It burst from her.

"Dammit, Loveday! It's just money. It doesn't mean anything!"

Her lip curled. "Easy to say when you've plenty of it. Anyway, money for what? Money for what we did six years ago?"

*Money for...* His hands balled to fists as her meaning slammed home, and the cool speculation in her eyes scored deep. He closed his eyes, reaching for control.

Opening them again, he found her still watching, her face a mask. His own control shredded, he gritted his teeth against the rising tide of fury...and saw, really saw, the stacked canvases around the dingy room.

"Paintings," he heard himself say.

"I beg your pardon."

No, that should be his line, but the blank mask had at least been replaced with a puzzled frown.

"I'll buy paintings." Surely if he bought enough paintings it would help Lionel get her out of this...this *hell* without trampling their pride in the mud. Without making her feel that she had been paid off like a whore, albeit belatedly.

"*What?* You haven't even looked at any of them!"

He didn't really need to; they were Lionel's. "Easily remedied." He strode past her to a stack leaning against a battered table, and crouched down, flipping through them backward and forward. Mountainscapes; Italian, he supposed. Beautiful, evocative, painted by the old Lionel. Any or all of these could grace his collection. Evelyn put one aside...and his breath stopped. The next canvas glowed. A lonely shore with a single, distant figure standing bathed in golden light where the sand met a dreaming sea... Silently, he set it aside, and kept looking through the stack until he came to the last one....

His hands shook as he drew it clear. He knew this one. Not the painting; he'd never seen it before. But the subject—the young girl curled up reading in that shabby old wing chair she'd loved, one hand caressing a tabby kitten asleep in her lap, red-gold tresses tumbling over her shoulders, glimmering against the dark, cracked leather.

Lionel must have painted it just before or after...as a reminder?

"How much for these three?"

She stared. "You want those? Even the seascape?"

"Yes. Especially that one. How much?"

The mask had crumbled. Instead there was panic in the wide golden eyes and parted lips. "I...I don't know."

"Fifty, then?"

"Fifty? For three?" Some of the spark rekindled and she scowled at him.

"Fifty each."

"But that's too much!"

"No, it isn't. They're good. Better than good." They were, too. Especially the beach scene, which must have been painted after whatever cataclysm had transfigured Lionel's style; it had the same quality of yearning that infused the murals.

"What happened to him, Loveday?" he asked, without looking up from the painting.

"What...what do you mean?"

Glancing up, he tapped the beach scene. "The man I remember didn't paint this."

She paled, eyes huge. "What—"

"Something must have changed him," said Evelyn, watching her. "Oh, the technique might be his, but the rest isn't."

Her expression eased very slightly. "Oh. Well, nothing, just…just Italy. Yes. Just Italy." She finished in a rush, her face now red and her hands, those expressive hands, twisting together. "We've all changed, my lord."

"I see." She'd never been able to hide a lie. He let it go. For now. "I'll take these three today, deposit the money at Hoare's with the rest, and come back tomorrow for the other paintings."

Her jaw dropped. "What other paintings?"

"The other paintings I'm going to buy. I'll look at them now."

Loveday watched, heart and stomach inextricably tangled, as Evelyn worked his way through the stacked paintings. Dear God in heaven—what now was she to do? He was putting so many paintings aside!

Looking down, she discovered that her hands were twisting in her paint-smeared apron. Sweet Lord! If he noticed *that*! Trying to be unobtrusive, she tugged off the apron and stuffed it into a drawer.

He was absorbed in the paintings, though, and didn't so much as glance up. She watched, imprinting every detail on her mind, renewing and overlaying memories. He crouched, flipping through canvases, and she knew the easy strength it took to hold the position, could see in her mind's eye the taut stretch of muscles hidden by the elegant trousers. Her trembling fingers remembered the ripple of muscle under warm skin in his broad back as he set one painting aside and reached for another. Icy fingers of fear clenched to a fist in her gut. How close was he to realising the truth?

As if catching her thoughts, he looked up, frowning. Her mouth dried.

"I'll have to bring a carriage tomorrow," he said. "What will you tell Lionel?"

She took a shaky breath, her brain scrambling for coherent thoughts, for an honest answer.

"When did I ever tell Lionel anything but the truth?"

The deep blue eyes held hers, searching. "I know, but he refused to see me, so—"

"That was me…that is—" She floundered. He looked as though she had struck him, straightening slowly, face rigid.

"You didn't trust me."

"No! I mean—yes. That is…" She fought to steady her restless hands. "I made such a fool of myself!"

His mouth twisted. "Loveday, you didn't make fool of yourself. The fault was mine."

"Not entirely," she muttered.

He looked as though he was about to disagree, and she hurried on. "Anyway, I was embarrassed."

"Then Lionel won't come looking for me with a gutting knife when he hears I called?"

*Oh, God!* "Lionel forgave you long ago," she whispered.

"Did he?" said Evelyn. "But you didn't."

She gathered the remaining shreds of pride around her. "There was nothing to forgive. Like you, I decided long ago that I had made a mistake." A mistake in thinking the daughter of a schoolmaster could ever mean something to him. She lifted her chin. "I didn't care to be reminded of it."

A muscle tightened in his jaw. "In that case I'll remove myself from your presence." He bent to pick up the paintings.

"Wait!"

He looked an enquiry.

"It's raining. They'll need to be wrapped. I have some oilcloth to protect them."

The oilcloth was in the drawer where she had stuffed the apron. She drew it out, trying to steady her hands. When she turned, he had set the paintings on a chair, and stepped back.

Clutching the oilcloth before her like a shield, she moved forward. The paintings needed protection. *Think of that.*

Kneeling beside the chair, she lifted the first one, the portrait Lionel had painted of her before they had left for Italy. Before everything. She remembered how he had chatted casually doing it, full of laughter, plans. She remembered the kitten, poor little Oliver. Biting her lip, she covered the painting with the cloth, reached for the next one. It was the mountainscape, peak after peak piled up in a wild jumble and celebration of what he had seen. He had said once that it was the immensity of the mountains he had tried to paint, that it was important to know why you were painting something. Heat stinging behind her eyes, she folded it into the cloth and reached for the last painting.

A choking lump seared her throat as she looked for the last time at the lonely beach with the solitary figure caught between land and sea, lost, always wondering…. She jerked the cloth over it and let out a breath she had not known she was holding. It was better to let these paintings go. Especially if the rent was to be paid and food put on the table. She could trust Evelyn to care for them.

She stood up, lifted the paintings and held them out.

He was frowning.

"Is something wrong? Have you changed your mind?" she asked.

He shook his head. "No. I'll look after them for you."

Her throat tightened—he had always been able to echo her thoughts—but she shrugged. "If you don't, then you'll have wasted your money. Here." She steadied her voice as he came toward her. "Take them."

Heat jolted through her as he grasped the paintings and their fingers brushed. He was close enough that she could see each separate eyelash, the faint shadow where he had shaved that morning, and smell the lemony tang of cologne. Once, her world had been built of that fragrance, and she'd dreamed that one day he would realize she was no longer a child, imagined the gentle touch of his hands and the caress of his cheek against hers…. Sometimes dreams came true, but left a bitter taste.

Everything in her tensed as the dark lashes lifted and his blue gaze stabbed her.

"Loveday—you need to let go."

She had done that. Long ago… Then she understood. Looking down, she saw that she was clutching the paintings as if she would never release them. One by one she relaxed her fingers, allowing him to take the canvases, feeling as though part of her had been ripped away.

He tucked them under one arm and held out several gold coins.

She scowled. "What's that for?"

"A down payment." He frowned, glancing around the room. "Is money safe here?"

She bit her lip. "I have a safe place." No need for him to know she kept money stuffed in her stays.

His brows lifted, his gaze straying to her breasts, and she blushed again. Trust Evelyn to guess exactly where that "safe place" might be! She lifted her chin and glared, daring him to comment.

He simply held out the coins.

She took them. Five sovereigns. She'd forgotten how heavy even one sovereign was. Her fingers closed tightly on the coins. She would be able to buy dinner. Keeping her expression blank, she looked up at him.

He was watching her, a puzzled frown on his face. "What time will suit you tomorrow?"

"Five o'clock?" That gave her time to get home and make sure anything that needed to be put away was put away.

"Five o'clock then. Will Lionel be here?"

"No. He won't mind about you coming, but he won't be here."

The deep blue eyes searched her face and she kept her expression, her mind, empty.

Evelyn nodded and turned away. Only to stop at the door and look back, holding her gaze. "Loveday, I did write to ask, and Lionel assured me that you were not...that there were no consequences, but—tell me the truth. Did I give you a child?"

Her heart pitched. "No, Evelyn. You did not. I swear it."

His eyes searched hers, then something in him seemed to relax. "Good." He bowed slightly and left, closing the door behind him.

She shut her eyes tightly to hold back the tears. It wasn't as if that door hadn't been closed before.

*Thank God for that.*

She hadn't deserved to pay that price for his stupidity. He'd told Lionel that if there *were* consequences, then he would do the right thing. Lionel had written back, assuring him that there was no child, and...*no need for such a sacrifice on your part, Fitzhugh.* Evelyn had not believed that Lionel would conceal such a thing, but seeing Loveday again, he'd had to ask. His conscience, despite its spectacular lapse in allowing him to seduce her, had insisted on asking.

More to protect the paintings than for any other reason,

he hailed a hackney, and sat lost in thought and regret as it rumbled over the streets back to St. James. He would see her again tomorrow when he collected the rest of the paintings. He frowned. And what the hell was he to do about that? Every tenet of honor and decency demanded that he keep his hands off Loveday Trehearne. But one look into those golden eyes had been enough to warn him; he still wanted her. Just as he had six years ago when he'd called on Lionel one evening and found Loveday there alone, heartbroken over the tabby kitten who had come to grief under the wheels of a passing carriage. He'd meant only to comfort her. Just to hold her for a moment. But he had underestimated his growing desire for her, overestimated his own decency and control.

He forced the memories away.

And he'd said that he would go back tomorrow. Well, he'd take a footman to help carry the paintings out to the carriage. And he was leaving town the following day, anyway, to go down to Steynings for the house party his aunt Caroline, Lady Drummoyne, had insisted that he host. She had arranged for Miss Angaston to attend. If he were courting Miss Angaston, he couldn't be seducing Loveday. He couldn't be seducing Loveday, anyway; honor and decency forbade it. As they should have done six years ago. He didn't much like the careless young fool he'd been then; damned if he'd repeat his selfish folly.

By the time he returned to town the paintings in his bedchamber would be complete, and there would be no need to see Loveday Trehearne again.

She was like smoke in his arms, winding around him, her hair a fragrant veil. It had been so long since he had held her…. He hardly dared believe she was really there, her soft lips trailing fire on his jaw, her breath the sweetest caress. His body ached, burned with the need to claim her, to make sure that this time she was *his*. He turned his head to capture and devour her mouth…one touch, one taste, and the mist drifted between them. He clung, and she slid through his fingers; he tried to cry out, but tears glazed her cheeks and she was gone, the mist triumphant…and he woke, reaching out, his voice finally breaching the prison of his throat.

Evelyn fell back against the pillows with a groan as sweat chilled on his shaking body. Was he ill? His eyes adjusting to the dark, he reached out for the glass of water by the bed. He'd woken like this several times in the past few weeks, his erection like iron. Aching with arousal from whatever he'd dreamed about. Something about a mist… But it evaded him. Shivering slightly as he cooled and his arousal eased, he settled down again to sleep.

Loveday reached home the next day just as the bells of St. Clement Danes pealed four o'clock. An hour to change out of her work clothes and tidy up. Make sure everything that should be away was away. She ached all over. Back, arms, legs and neck. But she forced herself through the chores, ignoring the aches and the longing for a cup of tea. She couldn't afford tea. Cleaning paintbrushes, she treasured the thought that tea was possible again. Along with better lodgings. Except that respectable landladies didn't much like indigent artists. And landlords…well, she wasn't going to think about landlords and what they liked. Nor would she think of all the other things that no amount of money or good fortune could bring back. She was going to be all right. Safe. Secure. Successful.

More pealing bells broke into her thoughts. Five o'clock. He could be there at any moment. Her hands shook as she worked faster, rinsing brushes. But six o'clock pealed without bringing him. He was late, and her rumbling stomach suggested that it was time and more she went to find some dinner. It wouldn't occur to Eve—to *St. Austell* that other people couldn't just ring a bell and eat when they felt like it. No.

She tamped down the bitterness at once. That was unfair. After all, he had paid for last night's dinner and the dinner she would eat tonight. She had the paintings stacked, ready for him. He'd take them and leave. Then she would be free.

He might not even come himself. He might simply send a servant to collect the paintings. There was no need for him to come at all. Beyond the paintings there was nothing here for him. It would be safer for her if he did not return.

She bit her lip. No. *She* was safe enough. He'd been clear about that. It was her heart that would be safer if he did not come. Six years. Surely that should have been long enough for the foolish organ to learn some common sense?

The way her pulse leaped at the knock on the door assured her that common sense was in short supply. She cast a final glance around the bare, gloomy room, checking for anything that might betray her, and with a steadying breath, opened the door.

Relief punched through him at the sight of her as the door opened. He stared at her, dazed, stunned at the release from a tension he had not realized was there. As if at some deep level he had a memory of her vanishing and had expected her to be gone…but there she was.

"Good afternoon, my lord. Your paintings are ready. Do you need help taking them out to your carriage?"

*For God's sake—call me Evelyn!*

He'd always been Evelyn to her. But he had destroyed

that friendship, and she was right to remind him of it. Of the gulf between them that he ought to have remembered all those years ago.

"No." He gestured to the footman behind him. "I brought help." Clearly she wanted him gone from her home as quickly as possible. He couldn't blame her for that. "We'll get out of your way." Evelyn winced inwardly at the coldness of his own voice.

For a moment he thought she flinched, but she said only, "Thank you," before turning away. He watched as she wriggled her shoulders, as though they were stiff, and fought down the urge to go to her, knead the slender arms and rub all the soreness out. Only he wasn't alone with her. With a muttered curse he turned back to the waiting footman.

They carried the paintings out to the carriage under the watchful gaze of several of the yard's denizens.

He hadn't intended to return. But he found himself dismissing the coachman once the paintings were loaded. Of course, he had forgotten to assure Loveday that the money was in the bank. He could tell her that and then leave.

The door was open as he trod up the steps. He frowned. Surely she should keep it shut. He raised his hand to knock anyway, unwilling to enter without her permission…and his hand froze in midair.

She had her back to him, but he could smell the turpentine and knew what she was doing—cleaning brushes. How many times had he seen her at that task?

"Loveday?"

She swung about with a gasp, still clutching a brush. "Oh! I thought you'd left."

"Without saying goodbye?" That was exactly what he'd intended. He thought they'd been good intentions, but in the end it had felt shabby. "I forgot to tell you that the money is in the bank."

"But we didn't agree on a price."

"Fifty pounds each, wasn't it?"

She stared. "For the three you took yesterday. But—"

"Including those, I bought twenty paintings. I deposited one thousand pounds."

She dropped the brush, scarlet flooding her cheeks. "That's too much! Especially for—" She broke off, the color ebbing, leaving her blanched. "Some of them were not...not Lionel's best work."

Evelyn nodded. "No, they were not. Some of them were his older work." He bent down and picked up the brush. "The way he painted before. Like the mountainscape, the portrait." *Before what?* "But the others, that seascape—" He drew breath. "What happened to him, Loveday? Something changed him."

Their eyes met and Loveday felt herself drowning, falling into the deep, deep blue just as she always had. She had always known he would see the difference. Even if he didn't yet quite know what he had seen.

"Things happen. People...change, Evelyn. That's all." She held out her hand for the brush.

People did change. And she lied by evasion.

He gave her the brush and she took it, fumbling, and turned away to hide the tears. There was a muttered curse, and his arms came about her, drawing her back against the comfort and strength of his body. She shook as his fingers closed over hers and gently removed the brush, to drop it in the basin.

This was madness. The heat and strength surrounding her were temporary at best, and illusory at worst. *He was not for her.* If she had not known that six years ago, she knew it now. She should pull away, before all her hard-won common sense dissolved. And yet she remained.

The length of his body pressed against her, warding off the chill. His cheek rested on her hair, his breath warm in her ear. Her heart hammered as heat stole through her. It had been like this that other time. He had offered comfort, and she had lost her head, reached up and kissed him clumsily on the jaw.

She slammed the door shut on the memory. Of his shock. And then his eyes darkening as he drew her closer and showed her what a kiss could be.

Now he held her helpless before him, one arm close about her waist, his other hand lifting to touch gentle fingers to her face and throat. She quivered, her soul crying out in silent delight, her breath coming in soft gasps as her pulse danced and an ache blossomed in the growing dampness at her core. There was a reason…somewhere there was a reason she must refuse him, but she had forgotten what it was as her body, alive and yearning, melted against him. Warm lips brushed her ear, and his hand stole up to cover her breast, kneading lightly. A moan escaped her trembling lips as heat stabbed, a golden shaft from breast to that growing secret ache, and his arms tightened. Her head fell back against his shoulder and one hand rose to cover the tormenting fingers at her breast, pressing them closer, wanting more. The fierce ridge of his erection rode hard against her bottom and she moved her hips, wanton, enticing.

With a harsh groan he pulled away, stepping back, leaving her bereft, torn apart. Summoning every fading ounce of resolve and courage, she turned to face him, her cheeks scarlet. His eyes blazed into hers, hot and dark.

"Evelyn?" She held out her hand. Not knowing why, only that she must.

He flinched, looking down at it. And she saw what he must see: the frayed cuff of her sleeve, smeared with paint, and her hand, roughened and paint-stained, reaching across an unbridgeable gulf; the schoolmaster's daughter and painter's sister, and the aristocrat.

"You still clean his brushes. He's been home today, then?"

Her hand fell. Time to step back from the edge. As he had done. "Brushes need to be cleaned, my lord. Or they become useless."

He frowned. "So he came home, left you with his brushes, and went out again? Why? Because I was coming?"

"He had to be…somewhere else." Crimson scorched her cheeks again at the lie. So far she'd been able to avoid direct lies. Not this time.

"It used to be something you did for him while he made a cup of tea for both of you and talked about his day, his work. What he had planned for the next day."

She turned away to hide the pain. How many times had Evelyn been there while she did just that? Sometimes he'd helped her. A novelty for the viscount's heir, to play at a dirty manual task.

"Loveday?" His very gentleness sliced at her. "Did I destroy that, too? Your friendship with Lionel?"

"No!" Shocked, she spun around. "He was angry, upset, but what you—" She broke off. That was unfair. It had not been just Evelyn. She had known what she was doing. It would have taken only a word, a gesture, to stop him. She had not spoken that word or made the gesture, because she had not wanted him to stop. Any more than she had wanted to stop just now. She ached with the pent-up yearning of six endless years. "What *we* did," she corrected herself, "did not cause any falling out between Lionel and myself." She dragged in a breath. "It's different for us. It's not as though I disgraced an ancient name, or anything like that."

"Dammit, Loveday!" Evelyn caught her wrist in a fierce grip. "Don't cheapen yourself like that, as though your innocence was of no account! You're still his sister, and he was right to be furious with me. And even if you had no brother to be furious, I still should not have taken you." His voice had gentled and his clasp on her wrist eased. "I don't want to think that it made a difference between you."

Unthinking, she laid her other hand over his. "Evelyn, I promise you, it made no difference."

Slowly, he nodded and released her. "Very well. I'll wait."

To her absolute horror, he went and sat down on a chair.

"Wait?" Her tongue felt frozen.

He gave her a level look. "You can hardly expect me to leave you here alone at night. I'll wait until Lionel returns. If he doesn't wish to speak to me, I'll go as soon as he's back."

She nearly choked. "But…you can't!"

"Yes, I can."

Panic fluttered in her throat. "But—" She cast about for a way to be rid of him. "Your dinner. I…I've no food here for you. Indeed—" this would shift him "—I must go out to get my own dinner."

He stared at her, clearly stunned. "You were planning to go out by yourself? At this hour?" He rose.

"You're leaving, then?" She tried not to sound relieved.

His gaze narrowed. "Not exactly. I'm taking you out for a meal," he said.

"What? No!"

"And if Lionel isn't back by then," he continued, as if she hadn't spoken, "I'll wait."

"But, you're going out." She waved at his elegant evening clothes. "You must be."

He shrugged. "There's a ball later. It won't signify if I'm late."

She forced back the whirling panic. There had to be a way out of this, if she could only think of it. Somehow she had miscalculated. He was angry. Angry with Lionel for supposedly leaving her here alone too much…. She let out a breath.

"Very well. I'll…I'll need to leave a note so he doesn't worry."

Evelyn bit back the obvious retort; that if Lionel was worried about her he wouldn't have rented rooms in this area, let alone left her unguarded in them. God! If he had ignored Lionel's request for the commission… His gut churned.

"Good idea," he said.

It had to be safer to take her out. If they remained here alone… His body hardened. Six years had not quenched his desire for Loveday Trehearne. Once, he had taken advantage of her innocence. She should hate him for that, yet it appeared she was still vulnerable to him.

He watched as she hurried around, found a scrap of drawing paper and wrote a brief note. Despite her assurances, he couldn't rid himself of the idea that there was something wrong between Loveday and Lionel. Something was eating at her. In the growing gloom she looked pale, hesitating over the note, as though choosing her words carefully. Her gaze skittered to his face, then she wrote hastily and propped the paper against a candle near the tinder box.

"It's easy to see there," she said, her gaze not quite meeting his.

"Very easy. Are you ready?"

She bit her lip. "Is there time for me to change?"

He swallowed. "Of course." There was probably time for him to go insane, too. He repressed the instinct to follow as she vanished behind a curtain into the other room.

He tried to ignore the soft, intimate sounds that spoke of a woman undressing, the trickle of water, the faint splashing that told him she was washing. His imagination painted the images for him: Loveday in her chemise, naked; the washcloth caressing her pale, delicate curves, stroking over her breasts; cool water peaking the dusky pink nipples. He remembered their satin softness, remembered their taste... the sweet scent of apple and cinnamon that had always been a part of her...

The memories flooded him, dissolving the years...Loveday, shy before him in her stays and shift. Her skin like peach silk under his touch, flushed to rose in the lamplight. Loveday, naked in his arms, so sweet and generous. And his. All his, yielded beneath him. A madness he regretted more than he could say. All very well to assure himself that he would have stopped if she had asked. She shouldn't have needed to ask; he should have damn well stopped, anyway. Better, he should never have let it start. Instead, selfishness had won. Even now he remembered her soft cry spilling into his mouth, her body stiffening in shock....

His foot caught against a painting, sending it clattering to the floor. Shaken, he realized that he had taken several steps toward the curtain dividing them.

"Evelyn? Is something wrong?"

Blood pounding, he forced himself to stop. "It's nothing. Caught my foot."

No matter how much he wanted to, he wasn't going to seduce Loveday again. He breathed deeply, trying to steady his hammering pulse and shaking hands. He turned his back on the useless blasted curtain and let out a pent-up breath. His gaze fell on the note against the candlestick.

He strode over and picked it up:

*Evelyn came by to collect the paintings. I have gone out for a meal with him. I won't be late. L.*

Brief. To the point. And so unlike the way she would have once written to Lionel. Lionel, who had once savagely demanded to know what Evelyn's intentions were toward Loveday. He remembered with shame his wordless reaction, his shock at the thought of marrying so far beneath him, his horror at the thought of his family's likely response.... Lionel had read his answer in his face, dropped him with one swift blow and left.

Evelyn picked up the pencil and scribbled a note at the bottom.

He was waiting by the outer door when she emerged, and his breath hitched. It wasn't the gown. That was gray, ill-fitting and buttoned to the throat.

It was her hair. Released from the imprisoning knot, it was pinned up more loosely, curling around her face as it always had, so that his fingers itched to slide in and tumble the fiery mass around her shoulders, spread it over crisp white linen as he—

He clamped down on his unruly thoughts, glancing at the note to remind himself of the promise he had written there. To himself as much as Lionel. His word, irrevocably given.

"You'll need a cloak," he said, picking up his own evening cloak and moving to the door to open it for her.

She shook her head. "No need."

"Don't be an idiot. It's cold out. Fetch your cloak," he said, swinging his to his shoulders and feeling for the clasp.

She swallowed. "I don't have one."

His fingers stilled on the fastening. Her cheeks were fiery.

"Why not?"

Her jaw tightened. "Because I sold it, if you must know!"

His stomach clenched. Things had been that bad? He held back the words that leaped to his tongue. He had bought the paintings. The money was in the bank, albeit Lionel's account. They would be all right now.

"No matter," he said. "Use mine." Swinging the cloak from his shoulders again, he went to her and settled it around her, drawing it close. A mistake. The fragrance of cinnamon and apple curled through him again. Sweet. Spicy. Intoxicating.

With a mental curse he stepped back from her quickened breathing and the temptation of the drifting curls.

"Come. You must be hungry." God knew *he* was. He held the door for her and tried not to breathe as she passed.

Halfway down the creaky stairs she stopped.

"Oh!" Her hand went to her mouth. "I might have left a candle burning. In…in the back room. Wait here. I'd better check." And she hurried back up the stairs.

He waited at the bottom. Moments later she reappeared.

"Had you?" he asked.

She looked blank. "Had I what?"

"Left a candle burning."

In the gloom of the yard he could have sworn she was blushing.

"No, I hadn't." Then, her voice a little high, she said, "We will not be very late, will we?"

"No. Not late," he replied. And wished it were otherwise—that he could keep her out shockingly late, scandalously late. That he could take her home to his bed and spend the whole night ravishing her and being ravished in return….

She forgot all her worries. Forgot everything except that she was with him again, and that they were Loveday and Evelyn, not the aristocrat and the painter's sister. She remembered things, too. Such as his undignified enjoyment of hot, roasted nuts bought straight from the vendor's brazier.

And if her heart skipped a beat to find that he remembered things, what did it matter? Did it matter that he bought her eels down by Westminster Bridge, and stole several bites as he had always done? Or that he wiped her fingers afterward with his handkerchief, as he had done long ago, laughing at her protests?

She floated through the evening enfolded in his cloak and scent, a fragile bubble of joy surrounding her. She knew it could not last, that when he took her home she must let the evening's delight pass from her, and not try to cling. That would extinguish even the memory of joy. But she would not think of it now.

She had relaxed. And he had never enjoyed an evening more. The ball he had planned to attend later was far from his mind. And as for the dinner he was supposed to be enjoying right now at his aunt's house, while meeting the lovely and wealthy Miss Angaston…well, Aunt Caroline was going to tear strips off him, but the bites of jellied eel Evelyn stole from Loveday were far more to his taste. He shared the roasted nuts with her, too, popping them into her mouth one by one, holding back the rising tide of desire when her lips closed on his fingers.

The evening wore on. Nine o'clock came. And went. Ten o'clock. He should be at the Hardress ball by now. Aunt Caroline, already furious at his non-attendance at her dinner, would be fuming. Every polite smile and charming excuse she made for him would only add to the reckoning. But what if he took Loveday home and Lionel wasn't there?

Even here, out in the street, he was aware of her every breath, the fragrance of her hair, every eyelash. In the confines of her lodgings his control would be stretched to breaking point.

He shouldn't have brought her out like this, though. She was far from the only woman being escorted by a man. He knew what many of them were. Once, he would have been looking at them. As the other men looked at Loveday. Even men with other women. Snared by the flaming hair and pausing to look further, hot speculation in their eyes.

Evelyn thanked God for the enveloping cloak, but nothing could veil the sparkle in her eyes or hide the sweet fullness of her mouth. Fortunately, a threatening glare from him was enough to keep the others at bay.

Until they ran into Huntercombe.

"Hi—St. Austell!"

He would have kept going except that Loveday, hearing him hailed, had stopped.

"Evening, St. Austell." Huntercombe's gaze flickered to Loveday, slid over her in speculation.

A slow burn ignited in Evelyn's gut. Huntercombe was the sort of pond scum that gave ponds a bad name.

"Huntercombe. You'll excuse us."

Lord Huntercombe grinned. "Oh, of course." He cast another appraising look at Loveday and Evelyn felt her shrink closer, felt as though a bucket of slops had been tipped over them both.

"Huntercombe at your service, my dear," the man murmured.

Loveday said nothing, but Huntercombe didn't seem to care. He addressed Evelyn again. "Very nice, St. Austell." He leered at Loveday. "As tasty a morsel as ever I saw. Let me know when you're done plowing her, and I'll—"

Huntercombe crashed into the gutter, doubled over, clutching at his midriff, blood pouring from his nose. And Evelyn found himself standing over him with clenched fists, his knuckles bruised, rage burning unfettered, and Loveday clinging to his arm.

Slowly her voice penetrated the red mist. "…No, Evelyn, please. You mustn't. Please, come away."

Huntercombe sat up, wiping away blood. "Good God, St. Austell!" He staggered to his feet with the help of one of his friends. "Are you mad? What's the—"

"Apologize." It was all Evelyn could get out from between gritted teeth.

*"What?"* Huntercombe's eyes goggled. "Damned if I will! Apologize? To some doxy you're— All right! All right!" He backed away, stumbling over the gutter.

"Beg pardon, ma'am. Didn't see how it was." He shot Evelyn a confused glance that suggested he still didn't see how it was. Shaking off his friends' hands, he pushed his way through the gathering crowd, a handkerchief held to his nose, and was gone.

"Evelyn!" Loveday was tugging at his arm. "You shouldn't have done that. Please—can we go?"

He looked down at the huge golden eyes raised to his face. Her distress scored to the bone. What had he been thinking, to bring her out like this and expose her to—

To what? Insult? Men who would look on her as a tasty dish to be sampled and shared with a friend? Men who would look at her as selfishly as he had once done? With shaking hands he drew her closer, tucking her against him with an arm over her shoulders.

"I'm sorry," he said. "Come. I'll take you home."

They walked. He suggested a hackney, but she refused. Part of him exulted secretly, because she would be with him that little bit longer. Nor had she pulled away, but stayed close, nestled against him. And part of him burned with shame that she considered *him*, of all men, a refuge, when all he wanted was to take her back to his own lodgings and make love to her. While he was supposed to be courting Miss Angaston.

What was he to do if Lionel had not returned? Was she safer with him or without him?

Joy had drained from the evening, leaving a sour taste, and when they reached Little Frenchman's Yard mist slithered from the dark passage to coil about their feet. Involuntarily, Evelyn's arm tightened around her.

"Is something wrong?" she asked.

"No." But he held her closer, as if the pale streamers could slide between them and steal her away. He stepped into the shadows with her, savagely aware of the softness of her body against his, the weight of her head on his shoulder, her sweet fragrance all about him. His body had hardened, blood beating in a heavy, urgent rhythm.

She stopped. Turned to him, her face a pale blur in the enveloping darkness…

*She deserves better. You hurt her once. You swore you wouldn't do it again!*

"We shouldn't stop here," Evelyn said. Not just because he didn't think he could withstand much more, but because the darkness was alive, might swallow her…take her away again.

She might be safer if it did…

Her hands were spread against his chest and, helplessly, one of his came up to cover them, press them against his heart. And she leaned into him, stretching up, and her mouth was close. Too close, so that her soft breath sighed over his lips. With a groan of despair he bent his head and surrendered.

She kissed him. All soft, warm lips. Hesitant. Shy, yet eager as he returned her kisses, fighting for control of the storm surge that rode him. He fought to feather gentle kisses over her mouth, fought the urge to ravish as her lips parted and she invited him in. He gave her what she asked for, feeling her tremble as he licked into the honeyed warmth. Her tongue met his in a wondering, perilous dance as he gathered her against him, brutally aware of his aching length pressed into her belly…of her sweet, spicy fragrance, warm with her arousal. His mind reeled as her hips moved against him. Tempting. Inviting.

He broke the kiss and drew back from her, feeling as though he had been ripped apart. Breathing hard, he shook his head to clear it.

"I'll—" His voice was hoarse. Dragging in a breath, he tried again. "I'll see you to the door."

God help him if Lionel hadn't returned. Evelyn wasn't sure he'd have the strength to stop if she kissed him again.

Trembling fingers traced his lips. He jerked away and her hand fell.

"No more," he said, more harshly than he intended. "I swore this would not happen." He dragged in a breath to strike the blow that would cut them apart. "I'm leaving town tomorrow. The likelihood is that I'll be betrothed by the time I return."

Loveday became very still.

"It's better if we don't see each other again," he said

quietly. "Tell Lionel I was sorry to miss him. My people will let me know when the paintings are complete."

Not daring to meet her gaze, Evelyn turned away. Without another word he crossed the yard, aware of her behind him as they trod up the steps. Once on the landing, she slipped around him and unlocked the door.

Lamplight spilled out and a queer stab of emotion went through him. Relief? Disappointment? A shabby old cloak was cast over a chair by the table, the note they had left lying beside the lamp, rather than under the candlestick. Lionel was home. She was safe.

"Wait, you mustn't forget your cloak," said Loveday. Her voice sounded constricted, and her fingers fumbled with the clasp. She was shivering, and his gut clenched.

He reached out and stilled her hands. They were cold. "Keep it." He couldn't bear to think of the cold eating at her. If he couldn't remain to keep her warm, then his cloak could do it.

"Keep it?" She stared at him. "I can't do that. It's far too expensive!"

"The money doesn't matter," he said. He just wanted to know that she was warm. One way or another.

"But—"

"Keep it. For me. Please." He managed a smile, gathering every remaining vestige of willpower. "Good night."

Loveday stood, bereft, huddled in the warmth and musky male scent of Evelyn's cloak. It was just a cloak. An elegantly cut piece of cloth that didn't fit her. She had no business feeling cherished in it.

Any more than she ought to feel cherished in Evelyn's arms. She didn't fit there, either. Not really. The leering gentleman he had knocked down, and the news that he was intending to marry, had only reminded her of what she already knew—that if she had any part in Evelyn's life it could only be as his mistress. She couldn't find it in her to condemn him for that. It was the way of the world.

He was a viscount. Marriage for him was a matter of wealth and lineage. It wasn't his fault she wanted more than he would ever be able to offer. He was wiser than she. Kind, too, because instead of staying and taking his pleasure, he had left.

She belonged in one frame, he in another. And although he might briefly step beyond his boundaries to enter her world, she could never follow him back to his. She could have asked him to stay, but if she had she would have had to confess the truth. All of it. That he had been deceived in every possible way.

Blinking hard, she stepped over to the table and picked up Lionel's shabby old cloak. Her gaze fell on the note she had left. Something extra was written at the bottom. She picked it up.

*Lionel—don't worry. I swear she will be safe with me this time.*

*Evelyn.*

A tear splashed onto the paper. And another. Angrily, she dashed them away, hanging Lionel's old cloak behind the door. Tears wouldn't help. Anyway, things were better now. The money Evelyn had paid for the paintings was a godsend. It meant safer lodgings, fuel for a fire, painting supplies, food. Another week or so and it would have been the streets.

She looked at the shabby old cloak and trailed her fingers down Evelyn's fine garment, which she was still wearing. It should be hung up, too….

Half an hour later she was curled in its warmth on her narrow cot in the empty lodgings. Evelyn's male scent wrapped around her. If she closed her eyes she could pretend in her dreams that he was there, that his arms held her safely. That they fitted, belonged together.

He moaned as she kissed her way down his body until she knelt before him. Dazed, he stared down at her, read her intent. Tried to summon the strength to refuse, to say she didn't need to do that…but his voice was as much a prisoner of her sweet sensuality as his body….

The caress of her soft breath was both promise of heaven and torture…. *Please, have mercy*…. He could only submit as a silken cheek stroked over his aching, heated length. He shuddered, consumed with need, as her warm breath bathed him…and she took him into her mouth. He groaned, head flung back as pleasure raked him, and slid a shaking hand through tangled fire to caress her throat. He needed to speak her name to know her, to truly possess her…. It was in his heart, on his lips, but even as he drew a shuddering breath to speak it, and turn dream to reality, the mist swirled, taking everything….

Evelyn cried out in protest, but his voice was swallowed in the mist. He tried to hold her, but she faded all the faster through his fingers into memory and then beyond memory…and there was nothing but aching need and searing loss….

He sat up, sweaty and shaken, his heart pounding as he grasped at the fading fragments of his dream. At least he supposed it had been a dream. It had felt so real…. An erotic dream? He was hard and aching, but he didn't remember anything…not really. Just that he had wanted… wanted who?

A face slid into focus, all golden eyes and unruly curls… and his body hardened to the point of pain. He jerked upright. No! He'd sworn he wouldn't seduce her again.

He wasn't even sure that he *had* been dreaming about Loveday.

Evelyn forced himself to think rationally. It had been months since he had been with a woman. No surprise that he was having erotic dreams.

It would be easy enough to find a mistress. The only problem was he didn't want any of the available women. He wanted only one, a woman honor forbade him to take.

He left town at first light, grim-faced.

As house parties went it was not too bad. He knew most of the people present, and if his aunt's machinations to match him up with Miss Phoebe Angaston—accredited Beauty and Heiress—were annoying, at least the lady herself was pleasant enough. Although holding herself aloof at first, she apparently had forgiven him for not attending the dinner and ball. Pleasant, kind, beautiful, and she was almost his own age rather than an eighteen-year-old innocent—the perfect bride, in fact.

And Evelyn couldn't for the life of him stir up a scrap of interest in her. He liked her. She was a nice person, even delightful. It would be no hardship to marry her.

Only he couldn't bring himself to make the offer she clearly expected. It wouldn't be fair, because every time he tried to bring himself to the point of doing his duty to his lineage and title, he thought of having to paint over Lionel's murals, and found something else to talk about.

Eventually, Miss Angaston brought matters to a head.

"Who is she?"

He stared. They were seated slightly apart, courtesy of Aunt Drummoyne, at a picnic.

"Who's who?"

"The woman you're in love with."

His throat closed and his cravat seemed likely to choke

him. Kind, beautiful, charming—add second-sight to her qualifications.

"What makes you think I'm in love with someone?" Was he in love?

She smiled. "You've been trying to bring yourself to propose to me for the past week. Something is stopping you, and I doubt it's fear of my reply. You stare into space constantly and you frequently look sad. As if you've lost something."

"I see." He wasn't going to confirm or deny. *Love*.

"May I make a suggestion?"

He could only nod.

"If she isn't married, or something utterly impossible like that, then marry her. I fell in love when I was nineteen, and my father insisted that it would be better to wait for what he considered a more *suitable* husband." Gray eyes met his. "Being young and dutiful, I obeyed. My suitor was dismissed, and now he is about to marry someone else." Something glittered in the corner of her eye. Something that she blinked away. "I've lost him. My advice is that you don't make the same mistake." She reached out and patted Evelyn's hand. "This is where you tell me to mind my own business."

He shook his head. "Instead, tell me. Had I offered, would you have married me?"

She frowned. "Probably. We would get on well enough" Her smile returned. "But I think you need more than that, St. Austell."

She came to him in the darkness of his bed. All spicy fragrance and slender limbs that wound about him. Mysterious and yet familiar, her body sliding against his, her mouth a dream of tender, teasing seduction. There were no words. Words had no place here. Only her trembling sighs and his own harsher breathing as he loved her. Slowly. Tenderly. As she yielded to him and he discovered her secrets one by one with hands that shook with restraint.

Softer, sweeter than his memories, she burned in his arms, all silken seduction. One hand fisted in her hair, holding her for his kiss. Her mouth was his, surrendered utterly to his demands as he pressed between her thighs, parted slick, swollen folds with gentle fingers, and felt at last the hot, liquid welcome of her body. He knew her now. His. All his. Only his. And at last, at last he knew his own heart.

His mouth took the soft cry as her body surrendered its innocence, and he felt deep within himself an answering pang. They were joined, fully, sweetly, and he made love to her with an aching tenderness…. Only the mist was now swirling between them, and she was fading, fading into it. Or the mist was fading into her.

He woke, her name on his lips tearing the darkness as he spilled himself in his empty bed. And he remembered his dream. Loveday. The murals. He fell back against the pillows with a groan and covered his face with his hands. It was Loveday who had been haunting his dreams. And Loveday who had modelled for those curst murals. Loveday. The woman he wanted above all others.

Unable to sleep again, in the end Evelyn rose, found a robe, and went down to the library. To his surprise, a lamp was burning in there.

A familiar voice spoke from near the fireplace. "Up rather late, aren't you, Eve? Can't you sleep, either?"

David Winslow, one of his guests, sat there in the dancing shadows, nursing a large brandy. At least Evelyn assumed it was brandy, since the brandy decanter was on a wine table beside him.

"No. What are you doing in here?" He hadn't seen much of David since his friend's recent return from Italy, and there was rarely time at a house party to really talk to anyone. Unless you were meant to be courting them.

David shrugged. "I had plans for the evening. They involved spending the night in Lady Beaumont's chamber, but her husband showing up just before dinner put paid to that. Apparently he had the same idea."

"Ah. How tactless of him."

"Quite. Heard you were having some murals painted."

Evelyn froze. "Yes. That's right." David had known Lionel, as well.

"By Lionel," said David. He picked up the decanter and poured another glass of brandy, took a swallow. "Hmm. Excellent. Are you having one?"

"No." Evelyn needed to think. He walked over to his desk and sat down. He wondered how his family was going to react when he announced that he was going to wed the penniless sister of an indigent artist. He didn't care, any more than he should have cared six years ago. More to the point, was the indigent artist himself going to permit it?

"Just one problem," continued David. He rose, picked up the decanter and strolled across to the table where it usually sat.

Evelyn shot him a glance. "What? With my brandy?"

David shook his head, pouring an extra glass and swirling the amber fluid around, squinting at it in the lamplight. "No. Brandy's excellent. Problem's with Lionel."

His casual tone chilled Evelyn. "What's amiss? Have you seen him?"

"You haven't, obviously."

*Obviously?* "No. We arranged it by letter. Why?"

David regarded him thoughtfully. Without answering, he walked over to offer him the brandy.

Evelyn looked at it. "I told you I didn't want one."

Raising an eyebrow, David set the glass down beside him, anyway. "Lionel died in Italy six months ago. I helped Loveday bury him."

Very carefully, Evelyn picked up the brandy glass and drained it.

He was on the way back to London before the sun rose, leaving a brief note for his aunt that explained only that he was gone, another for Phoebe Angaston thanking her for excellent advice, and a very confused and sleepy groom who had come down to find out exactly *why* a horse was being saddled at dawn.

*He got into a fight, Loveday said. At the local tavern. Some bruiser didn't like Lionel painting his girl. Beat him up. A few days later, apparently his sight failed. Gone. Just like that in both eyes. I'd been visiting them and Loveday wrote to beg me to come back and help. She said he was in despair.*

Winslow's mouth had been grim.

*By the time the letter reached me Lionel was dead.*

David hadn't been able to tell him very much more. Only that he had arranged safe passage back to England for Loveday with a lady wanting a companion. That she had brought most of Lionel's remaining work with her... and her own.

The difference Evelyn had seen in Lionel's style had been because it hadn't been her brother's work at all. It was Loveday's. She had painted the seascape—he would swear it. Loveday had always painted; he'd known that. But she'd never permitted anyone but Lionel to view her work.

Evelyn reached London in the evening, to discover Loveday had abandoned the rooms in Little Frenchman's Yard.

"Not here," a blowsy woman told him. "Gone, she is. Got herself a man, they say. There were one sniffin' round a while back and she moved out right after. So I moved in." The woman jiggled her breasts at him. "I'll do yeh, if yeh like."

A chill slid through him as he declined politely. *Gone.* He'd wanted her out of here, but how the devil was he supposed to find her now? With nowhere else to go, he hurried back to the Strand, hailed a hackney and gave the town house address.

He stared up at his darkened house. At this hour Loveday would be long gone, but there might be some sort of clue to where she was living. She might even have left an address with Hurley, the caretaker, or his wife.

Hurley took his time answering the banging on the area door. He glared out at Evelyn in the light of a flickering candle. "Who the he—" He broke off. "'Tis you, m'lord!"

Grumbling under his breath, Hurley found a lamp for Evelyn. "Be you stayin' here, master?"

Evelyn realized he would have to; he'd given up the lease on his lodgings. Leaving Steynings in such a rush, he hadn't thought about such things as a bed for the night.

Upon hearing this, Hurley grumbled even more. "Need to make up a bed in one of the spare chambers, then," he said. "Your room's still a main mess. Paint pots everywhere, and—" he fixed Evelyn with a disapproving eye "—Mrs. Hurley says you'll need to cover up them paintings before any respectable maid'll go in there! Like to have a fit, she did, when she saw them!"

His dreams and fantasies rioted on the wall. The god Apollo, with the nymph in his arms stretching up on tiptoe to kiss him, caught at that single instant just before their lips met… All longing, yearning and surrender. The god, who bore *his* face, braced, head flung back in ecstasy as she knelt, veiled only in tumbling red-gold curls, to enslave him…and the sweet moment of possession; Loveday—for it was she, and always had been—cradled in his arms, their bodies joined, two halves of a puzzle. And finally, she lay asleep in his arms, her face hidden against his shoulder, his body cradling hers. Forever.

She had painted his dreams. Even the last one, which he had not had the sense or courage to dream until now.

A soft, shocked gasp brought him around.

She was there. Sitting up, tousled and blinking in sleepy dismay in the shadows of his bed. Stunned golden eyes flickered from him to the paintings.

"I…I fell asleep." Her husky voice stroked his senses, left him breathless, wondering what it would be like waking up to all that sleepy softness every morning. For the rest of his life. "Why are you here?"

"Partly because David Winslow told me that Lionel is dead." Evelyn didn't know what else to say. Hell, he didn't even know what he felt. Only that it was going to tear him apart. "When were you going to tell me, Loveday?"

Something glimmered in her eyes. "I couldn't," she whispered. "It was my fault—"

Evelyn was across the room and had her in his arms before she could go on.

"Dammit! How was it your fault?" He held her against his heart, her head tucked under his chin. He knew what had happened; Winslow had told him. But Loveday needed to say it. Exorcize it before it could fester.

Her breath came raggedly. "Because I left him alone. He wanted to get outside. To the shore. So…I took him. Led him down there, and when he asked me if we'd brought anything to eat—"

"You left him sitting safely on the sand and went back to your lodgings for it." Evelyn pressed a kiss to her hair. "It wasn't your fault."

"I shouldn't have left him!" she cried, pulling free of his arms. "I knew how he felt about being blinded! And when I came back—" Her voice broke and the tears spilled over.

Evelyn drew her back into his arms. David had told him what she'd found. Her brother gone, his clothes left in a neat pile weighed down with his shoes, and a wavering line of footprints leading down to the water.

"You painted the seascape."

Pain twisted inside her. "Yes." Even now she didn't understand why she had taken her paints to the shore the following evening, after some fishermen had brought home the body. Why it had spilled onto the canvas, all the loneliness of the dreaming, empty water. Then, all she had wanted was someone to hold her and tell her it was all a bad dream. Now she wanted something just as impossible.

She pulled free of Evelyn's arms and felt a pang of hurt that he didn't attempt to hold her this time. "I'd better leave. I only meant to rest for a moment."

She picked up Lionel's shabby old cloak from the end of the bed and stood up.

"Is that what you want, Loveday?"

Dark eyes watched her and his hands were balled to fists at his sides.

"What I want has nothing to do with it," she said quietly. "It's always been about what you want."

He flinched. "Dammit, Loveday! I was a young fool!"

She nodded. "Yes. And I was younger. Sixteen, and even more foolish." She swallowed. "I thought it was forever. I know better now. Lionel explained, and when you stayed away I understood." She lifted her chin. "You'd tired of me."

Evelyn let out a breath. "No. No, I didn't. But I was wrong. Wrong to touch you. That night—" His hand raked through his hair. "Lionel was coming home as I left. And he knew when he saw me where I'd been. He came to me the next day and told me exactly what he thought of me. I stayed away because I knew he was right—that I was a selfish, aristocratic bastard who'd seen something I wanted and taken it without a thought for who might be hurt." His mouth twisted. "So I tried not to be an even more selfish bastard than I'd already been. Or so I told myself."

"It wasn't only your fault," she said. "I wanted you. If I hadn't—"

"No!" His eyes blazed. "Don't you dare blame yourself! You were an innocent. It was my fault—I was older and I knew damn well what was happening. I should have left before—" He broke off, took a shuddering breath, and asked calmly, "So, how did you hear about the murals?"

"I saw Colby."

"Ah."

"He was fuming because you'd rejected his sketches." She swallowed. "I had all Lionel's sketches. There were plenty of myself, and some of you, nudes, that he'd never let me even see…. I used those and my memory and, well, I thought if only you didn't know it was me—"

"Why?"

"I didn't want charity!" she snapped. "I wanted my work accepted on its merit."

"But surely, once I'd done that—!" His anger flared again. "Good God, Loveday! Why not tell me then? You can't have thought I'd take further advantage of your situation! Put conditions on the commission…" He was white, dark eyes blazing into her. "You did, didn't you?"

In that searing look she saw the self-loathing for what he had done, his vulnerability, and a terrible fear.

"Loveday—you were alone, desperate—" Evelyn's voice cracked. "How desperate?"

"No!" Words tumbled out as she understood his fear that she had been reduced to selling herself. "It didn't come to that, and I never thought that you would take advantage of my situation!"

His taut expression eased. "Thank God. But why not tell me the truth, then?"

"I didn't want the commission to be because I was Lionel's sister," she said. "Or even because I was me. That was never what I wanted from you!" She pressed a shaking hand to her mouth. Better not to say more. She turned to leave.

"What did you want, Loveday?"

She stopped and drew a ragged breath. The very gentleness in his voice cut to the core, demanding truth.

She didn't dare turn back, but she looked over her shoulder, summoning a smile, praying her tears wouldn't fall.

"You, Evelyn. Just you. There's only ever been you."

She saw her words hit him. For a moment he said nothing, just stared at her.

"I don't deserve that," he said. He shook his head as though awakening from a dream, and held out his hand, saying quietly, "Then come and take me."

"Are you betrothed?" That would be one sin Loveday could not reconcile with her conscience.

"No. Nor will I be." He hesitated. "We agreed we should not suit."

Loveday still hesitated, all the other reasons she should deny him clamoring in her brain. She scarcely heard them over the call in those dark blue eyes and the answering leap of her own heart as she turned back and went to him.

He frowned.

"Evelyn?" Her heart faltered.

He looked confused. "I've...I've dreamed of this."

Oh, so had she. So many times over the lost years, trying to hold the memory of how it had felt to be in his arms—

They closed around her, and she remembered...their warmth, their strength. She raised her head, expecting his kiss, but gentle hands framed her cheeks and he stared down at her. She stared back, drinking in his face, etched in shadows, a blaze that threatened to consume her lit in the dark eyes. Slow, shaking fingers traced the line of her jaw, lingered over her skittering pulse, found the trembling curve of her lower lip, so that her breath shuddered unevenly at his burning touch, as it had once before.

Yet it was different. More. Now there was tenderness. Oh, he'd been gentle with her all those years ago. Careful, caring. But now it was as though he scarcely dared to touch her, and couldn't bear not to.

Every nerve alight, she stretched up to kiss him. All the unspoken longing, all the love—it no longer mattered if he knew how much she cared.

He took her kisses, returning them fiercely, all hot demand, his tongue teasing, probing at the corners of her lips so that she opened to him. He ravished her mouth in slow, deep surges that echoed the beat of desire in her body.

He released her mouth. "Loveday..." His voice shook. "If you don't want this, for God's sake tell me now."

Her breathing hitched. She didn't know what *this* was. Not for him. A brief affair, or a longer liaison? But she knew what it was for her, and now was not the time to ask that question.

She raised trembling fingers to graze his cheek, felt the prickle sear her fingertips, and saw his eyes flare.

"I want you," she whispered, and gasped as he turned his head to nip her fingers, and dark heat erupted inside her.

"And I want you," he said. His hands were at the top button of her bodice and her whole body stilled, caught in the moment as he released that first button. "I want you," he repeated. His lips brushed hers, as achingly tender as his voice. More buttons surrendered. "All of you," he murmured against her lips. His hand slipped inside the gown. "All of you. Always." And she gasped as his roving fingers found the sensitive upper curves of her breasts, trailed fire in their wake.

"It can't be just for tonight, Loveday. Do you understand?" He lowered his mouth to the wildly beating pulse in her throat, and licked. Sucked gently. "I won't be able to let you go again," he whispered. "This time I'll be keeping you."

"Then take me," she murmured, echoing his invitation, pressing against him.

Evelyn's heart shook. "You'll trust me, again?" he said. "God knows, you shouldn't! I swore that I wouldn't seduce you." And still his fingers traced the satin curve of her breast, sliding beneath stays and chemise.

Her hand traveled down his body, found the buttons on his breeches. There were other things he'd meant to say, but he couldn't form the words.

"You aren't." Her voice caressed him and one of those buttons slipped open. "It's my turn." Two more buttons abandoned their posts, as he fought for control, not to tumble her to the floor and take her right there…and to make sense of her words…

"Your turn?"

"Umm. *I'm* seducing *you*." A small hand slid into the open placket of his breeches and closed over his shaft, which agreed wholeheartedly with her assessment of the situation. He groaned as she squeezed gently.

That small, wicked hand explored its captive, crept lower and cupped him so that another strangled groan escaped. "Loveday—" He reached down and pressed her hand against him, took her mouth hungrily. Shuddering in pleasure at her gentle touch, he ravished her lips.

Garment after garment fell to the floor unregarded as they kissed. His coat and waistcoat, her gown sliding off her shoulders and past her waist to fall at her feet, leaving her in stays and shift. Lamplight shimmered over her, gleaming in her hair, gilding her slender arms in gold and shadow as she reached for the lacings of his shirt. Two gentle tugs and it hung open. Her stays took a little longer to unlace, but at last she wriggled free, and he took them off over her head. She stood before him wearing only her chemise and a rosy blush. His throat tightened, words banking up behind the lump.

He reached for her, but her hands lifted. He stilled. Was he going too fast? Frightening her?

"Wait," she whispered, and his gut clenched. It had been only that one time six years ago, and while he might have behaved like a fool since, from what she had said, Loveday had never given herself again. If she needed time, reassurance… He prepared to step back.

Still blushing, she raised her arms, crossing them over her head, and her chemise came off.

His lungs seized, every nerve igniting, every muscle hardening. He could only stare as shock slammed through him. She stood, biting her lower lip, with the chemise clutched in front of her, as though afraid she had gone too far…. If he had needed assurance that she had only ever been his, this shyness was it.

His gaze never leaving her face, he slowly removed his

shirt and dropped it on the floor. Her fingers clenched. Opened. And dropped the chemise.

Shadows and candlelight played on every dip and curve of breast and waist and hip, shadow sliding over the lissom form, candlelight dancing in her eyes, glinting in the curls at the base of her belly.

One small hand reached out, careful fingers tracing the lightest of paths on his chest. Exploring. His breath shortened; control quaked. He hardly dared breathe lest her fragrance snap the fragile chain holding him in check. Curiosity found one nipple. Circled so that it hardened, and he gritted his teeth against the urge to sweep her up and onto the bed, ending the sweet torment.

"You're killing me," he ground out

Her slow smile told him she knew.

She leaned closer and kissed him. Warm, wet kisses, and gentle nips that spun his senses close to insanity as he fought to let her have her way with him. Her mouth found the nipple her fingers were teasing. He tensed, ready, but she kissed around it, just one brief swipe of her tongue over the aching centre. He groaned, ready to beg…and she pressed her open mouth over it, sucking lightly. He couldn't take much more of this…but he held still as she slid lower, kissing and nibbling her way down his body until she knelt before him and drew his trousers down….

No. Surely not…

He stared down at her, eyes dazed.

"Loveday—sweetheart, you don't have to—" A gentle sweep of her tongue silenced him, except for a helpless moan as his hands fisted in her hair.

His taste was hot on her tongue as she cupped him, leaning forward to take him into her mouth.

She should have felt subservient, kneeling there before him, but she did not. She felt powerful, feminine. She licked delicately, and gloried in the harsh groan, the jerk of his body. *She* had done that to him. And felt the answering surge of desire in her own body as his hand slid over her throat, tender, possessive.

His taste, hot and potent on her tongue, the satin-steel shape of him, the shuddering restraint of his powerful body as she pleasured him…

It was his dream. His dream made flesh, his dream awoken to exquisite, shocking life. He could barely breathe, let alone think as the lush heat of her mouth caressed him. A groan ripped from his belly as she sucked gently, and pleasure stabbed deep. *The Nymph, Worshipping at the Feet of the God…*

God? He was her slave. He could only stand, burning, as she took him to the quaking edge of madness. At last, with a shuddering groan, he reached down and freed himself gently.

"Enough."

He hardly knew his own voice, harsh with restraint as he drew her to her feet, yet he caught the flare of uncertainty in her eyes. "My turn," he whispered against her lips, and tasted himself. "Consider me seduced." Enslaved was more like it.

He swung her up into his arms and headed for the bed. He tumbled her onto it and followed her down, rolling with her so that she was half beneath him, one of his thighs between hers, opening her to his possession. His, all his. Soft, yielding. Wide golden eyes in her flushed face. All delicate pale curves wreathed in shadows, she reached up, brushing a caress against his jaw, sliding her fingers into his hair, drawing him down. He went, a willing captive, taking the sweetness of her mouth, groaning as she wriggled against him. Not to escape, but to get closer to him, her hands a tender fire on his body as she followed the hollow of his spine with curious fingers, slid lower to curve her hands over his buttocks, lifting to him at the same time.

He fought to hold back. So easy to accept and take all of her now, but he wanted more. He wanted to give, not just take. He needed her to know the truth: that it could never be just for one night. Releasing her mouth, he looked down at her. Desire bucked. Her lips parted slightly, moist and pink, and trembling.

"Evelyn?"

"Soon," he promised.

He touched a gentle finger to her lips, tracing the lush curves, hot need spiking low as she gasped, her arms tightening around him. So sweetly sensitive. And she had other sensitive places. Propped on one elbow, he traced the line of jaw and throat with his fingertips, lingering over the dancing pulse, adoring the tender swell of her breast. Lower to circle a nipple, loving the swift response as it sprang to urgent life and her breath came in soft gasps.

"Evelyn, please…"

Her plea nearly undid him, but he bent and kissed it from her lips, as he cupped her breast and rubbed his thumb over the taut nipple. "Not yet, sweetheart. It's my turn." His turn to reduce her to desperate need. His turn to worship. To give. To love.

She could only cry out in pleasure as he slid hot, open-mouthed kisses along her jaw and over her throat. As she burned and hungered in his arms. And oh, the glory of his mouth on her breasts, all heat and demand. Fire leaped in every vein as his hand drifted lower, over her belly, where the wicked probe of his finger in her navel found an answering echo and ache in the emptiness between her thighs, so that she arched, sobbing in need.

And at last, at last he cupped her there. There where

she so needed to be touched and ravished. There, where she was so hot and wet. And still he teased, tracing her quivering inner thighs, skirting her need, brushing lightly over her core so that she lifted against his hand in frantic want.

Hot kisses trailed over her belly; his tongue, all silk and sin, circled her navel, seduced in the same languid rhythm as his long fingers in the damp heat between her legs. Pressing a last kiss to her belly, he sat up, his hand still stroking in tender intimacy, and knelt between her thighs, pushing them wider.

Wanton heat poured through her as he gazed, as he traced the hot, exposed wetness at her core, his fingers sliding easily. Slowly, so slowly those two fingers eased into the tight, slippery ache. Lightning laced her, streaking down every vein, every nerve as he stroked, as he found a place inside her that wept for his touch, and pressed up. Hard. A frantic cry tore from her throat as pleasure burst into desperation and the fire burned hotter.

He slid lower and, sprawled at his mercy, she didn't have to ask what he intended. It was there in his dark, hungry gaze, in the slow pressure of his fingers in her slick, aching need. *His turn*. Slowly, so slowly those fingers withdrew, and her world nearly cracked apart as he replaced them with mouth and tongue. All hot, wicked seduction as her body arched wildly at the lancing pleasure, and her hips bucked. One powerful arm over her waist held her safe, captive to his mouth. Broad shoulders held her thighs spread and a hand under her buttocks tilted her for his pleasure. And hers.

She sobbed, twisting and shimmering in his arms, her taste and fragrance bathing him. His body pounded with the need to have her, and she was ready, so ready….

He surged over her, guiding himself to her entrance,

sliding just within, with a shuddering groan at the tight, wet heat that welcomed him. Shaking with need, he reimposed control. *Slow. Tender.* But her body danced beneath him, lifting to take more of him, his name sobbed in desperate plea...*possession.* Lost, he thrust into her, driving himself to the hilt in her sweetness. She cried out, fingers sinking into his arms, and, every muscle rebelling, he stilled, deep, so deep inside, her yielded body all his. Her eyes were closed, her breath coming in uneven gasps.

"Loveday?" He hardly recognized his voice. Her eyes opened, clouded, stabbing into him, even as the need to move raked him. She was so tight.... If he'd hurt her... "Sweetheart?" *Oh, God. Loveday...*

"Please...Evelyn—"

She was stretched tight, full to bursting, but he had stopped and she was dying, burning, wild for the continued rhythm of his body within her. But he held still. His eyes on hers, his hoarse voice told her why he'd stopped, but even to reassure him, words jammed in her throat. Instead, she lifted against him, begging with her body for his possession, moaning at the fierce pressure within her. His groan answered her wordless assurance, and he began to move in deep, long strokes that found every hidden need of body and soul, and assuaged them with fire. And she responded, finding and matching his rhythm so that he became hers, just as she was his. So that the fire leaped and redoubled between them.

He held her spread beneath him and loved her deeply, fiercely, every stroke of his body into hers a claiming and a surrender. She no longer knew which was which. He lowered his mouth to hers and took her cries, absorbing them into his own deeper groans, filling her mouth to the same ancient rhythm that rocked them until she flamed, and whirled to the edge of the abyss to hover there, crying out for release.

And he gave it to her. One strong hand slid under her bottom, lifting her into his thrusts so that she broke and fell, shattering, dissolved in ecstasy.

Evelyn felt it, let it take him, sheathing himself deep in her convulsing body. Every muscle hardened to steel, and his world shook, splintered as his own consummation flared white-hot, spilling into her in fierce joy.

They had forgotten to draw the curtains, and the pale dawn crept in, gilding the soft, fragrant curls that flamed across his chest. Every silken curve snuggled against him, her hand resting over his heart. He lifted it to his lips, kissed the slender fingers and replaced them. Nothing had ever been so right.

"We have a problem," he murmured, nibbling at her ear.

She wriggled, squirming against him so that he hardened. "Hmm?"

"Your paintings. I'll have to commission some nice sedate tapestries to cover them."

*"What?"* She sat up, realized she was naked, and clutched at the sheet to cover her breasts. "The devil you will!"

He grinned and twitched the sheet away from her. "You haven't considered the scandal, sweetheart."

"Having paintings of your mistress seducing you all over the walls will upset society?" All vestige of sleep had vanished from her eyes, which had narrowed to golden shards. "You should have thought of that before you commissioned them!" She tried to grab the sheet back, but he hung on, and she glared at him.

He glared right back. "Mistress be damned! It's the

scandal of having erotic murals of my *wife* seducing me that will rock society!"

There was a moment's silence. Then she whispered, "Wife?"

"Wife," he said firmly. "I may be a selfish aristocratic bastard—Lionel had that right—but I'm not stupid. I don't make the same mistake twice. I told you I was keeping you this time, and you agreed."

Heart pounding, she said, "I know you said you were going to keep me, but you don't actually have to marry me to do that, you know." It would be easier to remind him if her foolish heart could forget the tender words he'd whispered during the night. Words of love. Words she had given back to him. In his world love didn't necessarily include marriage…. "I mean, I'm here now. In your bed. I thought you were asking me to be your mistress. Just because I'm Lionel's sister—"

"No." Evelyn drew her into his arms and pushed a tumbled curl out of her eyes. "You're Loveday. Not Lionel's sister. And I have to marry you because I love you."

Her heart shook, more at the tenderness in his voice and hands than the words themselves. She couldn't doubt that he loved her, but she was still a nobody. He was a viscount. "But—your family won't like it now any more than they would have six years ago. And I…I won't know anyone. No one will want to know the sister of an artist! And what about my painting? I *can't* give it up!"

He actually laughed. "Is someone asking you to give up your painting?"

"Wouldn't you?" She couldn't quite believe that he wanted to marry her, let alone permit her to continue painting.

"No."

She still wasn't convinced. If he thought she'd paint as a ladylike hobby…

"Professionally?"

He grinned. "It will make up for your lack of dowry. Just don't sell any nudes of yourself to anyone but me. That's my only condition."

He viewed her outraged expression with satisfaction. "And my family can mind their own business," he went on. "They'll come around." They would have no choice.

He thought of Phoebe Angaston. "Also, I can guarantee you at least one female friend in society." One who would use her considerable influence to help Loveday. A portrait of the lovely and wealthy Miss Angaston, for example… Besides…" he gestured to the paintings "…you haven't considered. This is my town house! I can't marry anyone else *but* you with those on the walls!"

\* \* \* \* \*

# PLEASURED BY
# THE VIKING

Michelle Willingham

**Author Note**

The Vikings have always had a strong presence in Ireland, all around the coastal areas. By the medieval era, they had blended in with the Irish tribes, intermarrying with them.

*Pleasured by the Viking* is the story of Gunnar Dalrata, a Viking warrior who falls for an Irishwoman, Auder Ó Reilly, whom he knew years before. The awkward, adolescent girl has transformed into a stunningly beautiful woman, but Auder is promised to another man. Gunnar's protective instincts are on edge, for he has no intention of letting her go.

This story is connected to Harlequin Historical *Surrender to an Irish Warrior*. Gunnar Dalrata plays an integral role, and I hope you'll enjoy learning his connection to the MacEgan Brothers.

I always enjoy hearing from readers. You may email me at michelle@michellewillingham.com or by mail at P.O. Box 2242, Poquoson, VA 23662 USA. Visit my website at www.michellewillingham.com or on Facebook at www.facebook.com/michellewillinghamfans.

**Look for Michelle Willingham's**

*Claimed by the Highlander*

**The first of a Scottish family miniseries coming soon from Harlequin® Historical**

# Chapter One

Glen Ocham, Ireland
1181

Twilight descended, casting shadows upon the *cashel* in a fading veil of gray. It was a spring night of celebration, a time when the Irish gave thanks for their prosperity. But for Auder Ó Reilly, it was the beginning of the end.

Her skin was frigid, for the life she'd known was slipping away, like water from between her fingertips. In two days, she would travel north to the Norman settlement governed by Lord Miles de Corlaine, Baron of Maraloch, to be his bride.

The very idea of surrendering herself to the Norman made her shudder. Aye, she would protect the lives of her kinsmen, by forging this alliance. They would be safe from invasion, their lands joined together. And Lord Maraloch was a wealthy man who could give her everything she would ever need.

But that wasn't the reason she'd agreed to marry him.

Auder's gaze settled upon her mother, who was sitting

apart from the other women. Halma Ó Reilly's thin face held a serene expression, but there was pain and loneliness beneath it. The shadow of humiliation from her husband's misdeeds surrounded her still.

*It's not your fault,* Auder wanted to tell her mother. *You don't deserve to suffer for what Father did.*

She wanted to see her mother laughing again with friends. She wanted her to have a reason to lift her head up, knowing that her daughter had created peace where there had been a threat. And for that reason, she'd agreed to the marriage.

Halma had protected her in so many ways. Could she do less for her mother?

Auder crossed the *cashel* until she sat beside Halma. The matron's green eyes stared at the others who were feasting and gossiping. "You haven't touched your food."

"I'm not hungry." Halma patted her hand. Concern lined her face, and she added, "Auder, I'm not so sure you should marry this baron. We don't really know the man."

"It was my choice, Mother," Auder pronounced. "I've agreed to accept the honor." Though she tried to summon a smile, she couldn't. Right now, she felt as though she were disappearing from her own body.

"You're a beautiful woman," her mother said, touching Auder's cheek. "You could have your choice of any man here. Why would you give that up?"

*For you,* she wanted to say. *To take away the shame you're feeling right now. To give you a reason to be proud again.*

"None of the men here interest me," she lied. "And don't you believe the lives of our clan members are more impor- tant than my personal feelings?"

"You have the choice to say no," Halma said. "No one

will force you into this marriage." Her face grew tight with worry. "Or his bed."

A shiver crossed over Auder at the thought of submitting to the Norman. She was not a virgin, but the one time in her life she'd taken a lover, it had not been pleasant. Something to be endured rather than enjoyed. Afterwards, the man had left her without speaking, and she was left to wonder what she'd done wrong.

Since that time, she'd held herself apart from all men. Though she was never impolite, she'd made it clear that she had no interest in any of them. But instead of making them keep their distance, it only made matters worse. The men tried to compete for her affections, each believing that he was man enough to wear her resistance down.

"I'm feeling tired," her mother said, rising from the bench. "I think I'll go and rest for a while." Her face was bright with embarrassment, as though she didn't want to discuss Auder's impending marriage any further.

When Halma had gone, Auder's mood dimmed further. She didn't feel like celebrating, not when she had only two days left. In dismay, she stared down at her hands. They were stained from madder root, not at all a lady's hands. The markings were a part of her, a visible sign of her love of dyeing cloth. Women from all over the region traveled to bring her their lengths of wool and linen. It filled her with pride to see women and men wearing the rich crimsons, emeralds and saffrons.

If she wed the Norman, she suspected she would have to give it up. Ladies of noble birth did not soil their hands with common labor. Auder closed her eyes, wondering if she could convince her husband to let her continue her craft.

In the distance, she saw the chieftain's wife Morren struggling with a basket. Auder pushed her way past the others, making her way toward the pregnant woman. Morren adored plants nearly as much as she did, and although she'd known the woman all her life, they had become closer friends over the past few months.

Auder took the basket from Morren and walked alongside her. "Tired?"

"A little," Morren admitted. "I'll be glad when this child is born, near the end of summer." She risked a glance at her husband, who was standing on the opposite side of the *cashel* with several of their clansmen. "Trahern is more afraid of the birth than I am."

Morren settled to rest upon a bench and motioned Auder to sit with her, her gaze turning serious. "Auder, you should know…the Norman soldiers are patrolling our lands again. Trahern has posted sentries, but I don't know their intent."

A coldness settled within her stomach, and Auder veiled her fear. "Perhaps they've come to escort me to my marriage." Looking into the other woman's eyes, Auder tried to show a courage she didn't feel. "I'll go with them if I must."

Morren didn't smile. "Until we know why they're here, I don't want you to be alone at any moment." She looked around and caught sight of Gunnar Dalrata, beckoning him to join them.

Tall, with sun-darkened blond hair and cloudy gray eyes, Gunnar was one of the few men Auder felt comfortable around—namely because they'd been friends since four summers ago, when she'd visited her mother's Norse family. Although he'd been handsome even then, not once had he shown her any interest. It was no wonder, since she'd been inches shorter and hadn't developed as a woman.

But even after she'd arrived home, he'd kept his distance, not speaking to her at all. She'd caught him watching her from time to time, but it was as if their friendship had disappeared. Though it bothered her, she supposed his actions were out of respect for Clár Ó Reilly, whom he'd been courting.

"Gunnar, will you stay with Auder and guard her?" Morren asked, glancing back at her husband. "The Normans—"

"I've seen them." His expression tightened with anger, but he gave Morren a nod. "And you're right. Auder shouldn't be alone while they are about."

His tone made her feel like a child not old enough to be left by herself. He hardly looked at her, and the easy friendliness he'd always shown was gone. She couldn't understand why.

"Good." Morren rested one hand upon her spine as she stood and started walking away. "I'm going to speak to Trahern about the celebration tonight, and if you'd stay with Auder, I'd be grateful."

Unrelenting and fierce, Gunnar stared at Auder in silent disapproval. "So. You're still planning to go through with this?"

"That's all you can say to me, after I've returned from traveling?" She crossed her own arms, sending him a dark look. "Not even a greeting?" It annoyed her for it seemed that she'd imagined their friendship.

Gunnar's eyes turned to steel, and she was startled by the restless anger brewing within him. "I can't believe Trahern would let you do this. He's lost his wits if he thinks you should wed the baron."

Auder straightened her shoulders, using her height to meet his gaze directly. "It's the right thing to do, if it protects us from an invasion." *And if it protects my mother.*

"We can defend ourselves, Auder," Gunnar argued. "Just

because there are more of them doesn't mean we cannot fight."

"But if I do this, there is no need for fighting." The Ó Reillys couldn't withstand another attack—not after the devastating massacre they'd suffered a year ago. The survivors were gradually returning, but the damage was done. Fewer than twenty remained.

Gunnar studied her as though he were trying to find a way to talk her out of the marriage. His gray eyes bored into hers, moving past her face and down her body. "And you don't mind being used in that way? You're just a girl."

A flustered air enveloped her as his words conjured up the vision of her marriage bed. She imagined the Norman's heavy weight bearing down upon her, while she had to endure his touch. Auder knew she wasn't capable of feeling passion; her last lover had taught her that lesson well enough. There would be no pleasure; it was a matter of distracting herself with other thoughts while he satisfied himself.

"I'm not a girl anymore, Gunnar," she made herself say calmly. "Not that you've noticed."

He stared at her, his eyes meeting hers. "I noticed." His mouth drew into a line, and he took a step closer. She could almost feel the palpable change between them, and she couldn't have moved if she wanted to.

"I suspected you'd grow up into a beautiful woman," he said, touching her cheek with his palm. "But I never thought you'd give yourself up to a Norman."

A hard pressure built up within her throat, but Auder forced herself to look at him. "If this will protect my mother and the others, then it's worth it." The whispers about her father would eventually stop. And maybe she could bring something good out of Lúcás's mistakes.

"There are other ways, Auder."

She fell silent. The gentle touch warmed her skin, and her cheeks flushed. Though it was nothing more than the touch of friendship, she'd never expected to feel this uneasy around him.

*This is Gunnar,* Auder reminded herself. *There's no reason to be nervous. His interest lies in Clár, not you.*

She tried to take a breath, but it was as if the air around her had grown thicker. She saw his mouth tighten in a thin line, and his grip upon her hands grew protective. An invisible cord drew her to him, and she noticed things she hadn't seen before. There was a darker gray ring around his eyes, and he'd taken a blade to his cheeks, shaving them clean. She wondered what his skin would feel like against her fingertips. Or his mouth, heated and demanding upon hers.

Her embarrassment deepened when she saw his expression transform. He was looking at her as though he wanted to act upon her desires. Like he wanted to take her face between his hands and kiss her senseless.

"Auder," he murmured, his tone darkening. She could almost hear his unspoken warning that she'd come too close.

To distract herself, she brought her attention to his worn hands, which were callused and scraped. "You've been working on the new wall, haven't you?" Turning his palms toward the light, she saw several splinters. She edged one of them out, and he pulled his hands back as if he didn't want her touching him.

"It's nearly completed."

The shielded distance was back, and with it, the awkward silence. Since she'd met him, she'd rarely seen him unoccupied. Gunnar enjoyed building, creating structures with his hands. His home was one of the nicest she'd ever seen, with tight walls and a strong foundation.

Auder frowned at his skinned flesh. "Clár won't like

what you've done to yourself." She deliberately mentioned the widow, to remind herself that Gunnar was involved with someone else.

"Clár is used to my rough hands."

With that remark, Auder had the sudden vision of Gunnar's calloused fingertips moving over her own body. Her skin flushed, and an ache formed within her breasts. What was the matter with her? She knew better than to entertain such foolish thoughts. Immediately, she shut the thought away, refusing to think of it.

"I imagine she is." Auder glanced outside the *cashel,* feeling the sudden need to escape the boundaries. She wanted a walk to clear her head. "I'm going outside for a few moments."

"Not with them out there." He blocked her path, resting his hand upon the battleaxe hanging from his waist. "You're safer inside."

"They're camped a few miles away, and I won't go far. I just need…to get out for a few moments." The very walls of the *cashel* felt like a prison, closing in on her. If she could gather even a few moments of freedom, she could endure what lay ahead. She gripped her hands into fists so tight, the knuckles whitened. "You can come along and guard me if you want."

Discontent lined his face, and she suspected he wouldn't allow it. If it weren't for his promise to Morren, no doubt he'd be enjoying the feast with Clár at his side.

But when she repeated her plea, at last he shrugged. "For a short time. And not any further than the river bend."

She let out a slow breath of air. "Thank you."

Gunnar walked with her along the edge of the river. The waters were higher than usual, from all the rain. Most of the homes were elevated, to protect them from flooding, but nevertheless, she didn't like the look of the swollen water or the brooding clouds.

Auder sat down in the grass, letting her ankles dangle over the water, the scent of fresh greenery surrounding her. In a few more months, the hills would blossom with gorse and heather, exuding rich colors. But she wouldn't be here to see them.

Gunnar remained standing beside her, his hand resting upon the battleaxe at his waist. He stared out at their land boundaries, searching for any threat. There was a different edge to him, and she found herself watching him. Her awareness deepened, even as she warned herself not to fall into that snare.

He held a warrior's stance, and it seemed that every sense was attuned to danger. His eyes never left the perimeter, constantly searching.

Gunnar kept his grip upon his battleaxe, his mood growing as dark as the fading landscape. Although a marriage alliance was a civilized method of bringing the Normans and Irish together, he didn't trust the invaders. And the idea of handing Auder Ó Reilly over to their leader infuriated him.

She was far too good for the Normans. She was beautiful and shy, and nearly every man among his tribe and the Ó Reillys was infatuated with her. Her height rose well above most women, and when she stood, her mouth rested at his chin. She kept her hair tightly braided against her scalp, but below her nape, it hung free, down to her waist. It was a mixture of brown and red, almost like autumn leaves. Her eyes were blue and green, ever-changing in color.

"Tell me why, Auder," he demanded. "And don't give me reasons about protecting your clan. You hardly lived among them."

She wouldn't look at him, letting her wrists rest upon her knees. "You saw the soldiers. They want control of our *cashel,* and we can't withstand another attack. If my marriage will bring us together without fighting, it's for the best."

"That's not your reason. I know you better than that." He sat down beside her, reaching for her hand. It was stained red, and it evoked memories of when she'd been a girl, and he'd met her four summers ago. Each time he'd seen her, she'd had a different color of hands. One day blue, another day green. She'd been awkward then, with no curves to speak of, and a rounder face. More than once, he'd defended her against the taunts of foolish young boys.

He'd seen the promise of beauty in Auder the girl. But even then, he'd never suspected how beautiful she would be as a woman.

"My reasons shouldn't matter. It's the right thing to do, even if I am afraid." She straightened her shoulders, and it drew his attention to her lean body and generous breasts. Her skin was smooth, her lips the soft rose color of a seashell.

He found himself studying her in the torch light. A curl broke free from her braid, falling against the line of her jaw. The strands caught the light, a fiery red shining beneath the brown. He wondered what she would look like with that hair falling around her shoulders, down to her hips.

*Not yours,* he warned himself. Best to turn his attention back to Clár Ó Reilly, the widow whom he was courting. Clár had a young son, Nial, who would be sent for fostering soon. Gunnar had an affection for the five-year-old boy, and he planned to teach Nial how to fish for his supper this summer. He'd show the boy how to guide a boat out on the waves, and it warmed him to think of becoming a father.

In his mind, he imagined his future children running up to him, laughing when he swung them in the air.

It was a dream so nearly within his grasp. Clár would give her vow, if he asked it of her. But something had kept him from asking her to wed, and he suspected it had everything to do with Auder.

She cleared her throat, suddenly looking embarrassed. "Gunnar…there's something I want to ask you. About men."

He waited, unsure of what she expected from him.

There was sadness in her eyes, as if she'd experienced failure. "It's about my wedding night." She gripped her knees with her hands, her face pale. "I didn't enjoy lovemaking the last time. There's something wrong with me, and I want to know what I should do to please my husband."

It took a great deal of effort not to choke over her words. "The last time?" He'd always believed Auder was a virgin, untouched by all men. "When did you ever take a lover?"

"A year ago." She shrugged. "I thought I'd see what it was like. I don't suppose he enjoyed it either. He left me as soon as it was over."

Gunnar wanted to ask who the man was, but didn't. The idea of breaking every bone in the man's body had a certain appeal. "If you didn't enjoy it, then it was his fault. There's nothing wrong with you."

She shrugged. "I think it's something only men like. Women merely put up with it, because they want children."

He bit his tongue so hard, it was a wonder it wasn't bleeding. "Auder, you're wrong. Most women do enjoy lovemaking quite a bit. Why do you think they still hold festivals to celebrate the old ways?"

"Because it's tradition?" she offered. Within her eyes, he saw the innocence. Whoever had claimed her virginity had obviously taught her nothing. It made him wonder what she had endured the time before.

"Because they want an excuse to join with a man of their choosing," he said.

She didn't return his smile, and her eyes held only suspicion, as though she didn't believe him. With a grimace, she added, "Perhaps the baron won't want to join with me after that first time. He already has a son, so I've heard."

Gunnar's jaw tightened at the thought of her enduring the Norman's bed. But even so, he wanted her to understand what she was agreeing to.

"If you wed him, he's going to want you each night." He stared into her eyes, willing her to understand what would happen. "Your body will belong to him. And he'll not hesitate to claim you."

She shivered, her lower lip dropping slightly. "Will I learn to like it?"

He edged in closer, until his forehead nearly touched hers. The urge to kiss her, to tempt her into experiencing her first taste of pleasure, was undeniable. If she belonged to him, he'd coax her until her body arched with need, trembling on the brink of release. He'd use his mouth to tease her flesh, until she was wet with wanting him.

"You might," he murmured.

A slight smile tipped at her mouth and a shaky breath escaped her. "Good. Then there's hope."

And she stood, walking away from him, back to the *cashel*.

"The contests are beginning," Morren said, and eased herself beside Auder, wincing as she sat. "I suppose we should enjoy the view."

Auder frowned, not understanding what she meant. But a moment later, she saw the men stripping down to their trews. Some had smeared animal fat onto their bodies, to make the wrestling more challenging.

She stared at the oiled skin, and something within her stirred. Although she'd seen the men bared before, there was something different in the atmosphere tonight. Now that the sun had set, torches flared all throughout the *cashel*. There was a primeval sense of barbarism, as though the men had become warriors of old. Some of the visiting Norsemen had dark runes tattooed into their skin, while others wore a gold arm band that gleamed in the torchlight.

But it was Gunnar Dalrata who made her breath catch. When he pulled off his tunic, baring himself from the waist up, Auder shut her mouth to keep from gaping. His wide shoulders were firm, his ridged muscles tight. The physical strength of his body was nothing she'd ever imagined, almost as if it had been carved from a piece of granite. She wondered what it would be like to touch his skin. Would it be warm and firm?

Even more, what would it be like to feel his body moving upon hers? Without warning, she thought of his promise, that a woman truly could enjoy joining with a man. Her imagination conjured up the vision of Gunnar lying with her, his hands sliding over her skin. A chill rose up, and she shifted her legs together.

*Stop this. He's a friend, nothing more. He doesn't think of you in that way.*

As if in answer to her self-chastisement, Gunnar approached Clár Ó Reilly, who sent the man a vivid smile. Petite and fair-haired, Clár was pretty enough that she could have nearly any man she wanted. An unexpected jealousy lashed out from within her, and it startled Auder, though she knew there was no reason for it.

Gunnar was free to choose any woman, whereas she

would be married to the Lord of Maraloch within two days.

She reached for a cup of mead and swallowed quickly, while the men faced one another in the contests. One by one, they wrestled each other, their muscles flexing as they drove their opponents' faces into the dirt.

Match after match Gunnar won, until at last, he was offered the chance to kiss a woman of his choice. His gaze searched the crowd, many of the women calling out to him and preening. But then, his gray eyes settled upon her. Auder lost her breath, half-afraid Gunnar would approach. Her pulse quickened, and several of the others let out whistles of approval. She clenched her fingers together as the crowd parted, and he walked toward her.

*Oh Danu, he was going to do this.* Auder knew she should protest, say something to remind him of her betrothal. But her body was frozen in place, and she couldn't have moved if she wanted to.

He walked right past her, until he reached Clár, who was standing just behind her. Gunnar caught the widow's nape and kissed her hard, as though he wanted to drag Clár off to his bed.

Auder wanted to hide beneath the table. How could she have thought he'd meant to kiss her? Clár was the woman he wanted. Not her. Embarrassment flooded her cheeks, and she prayed Gunnar hadn't noticed her mistake.

A shiver trembled through her as she imagined Gunnar's mouth trailing down the curve of her neck. She crossed her arms, and the pressure against her breasts evoked another unintentional response. Between her legs, she felt an unusual ache and the moisture of arousal.

*Even if you weren't betrothed, Gunnar never wanted you,* she reminded herself. And…she didn't want to share any man's bed.

A loud cheering noise caught her attention, and she found herself rising from the bench, crossing through the men and women to see what was going on.

The chieftain Trahern motioned for her to come forward. "We have our first! Who will join her?"

"First what?" she asked, uncertain of what he was asking her to do.

"The first in the women's contests," he said, grinning. "I'd say you have a definite advantage, Auder."

No. She was *not* going to be the center of everyone's attention, making a fool of herself. "That isn't why I—"

But her words were cut off by the men cheering. She thought she saw a few men exchanging money, placing bets.

"What sort of contest is this?" she demanded, fully intending to leave.

"A race," the chieftain answered. "If you win, you may claim a favor from any of these men." Trahern sent her a teasing smile. "You might as well torment them in the last two days before you leave."

"No, thank you," she said, and turned to leave. At that same moment, Gunnar stepped into her path. The faint stirring rose up again, at the sight of his sleek muscles and handsome face.

She glared at him. "Gunnar, let me pass."

"I thought you wanted to learn how to please your husband." He took her by the shoulders and turned her back to face the gathering women. "This is your chance to practice on the other men. If you're fast enough to claim a kiss, that is."

Though he spoke with the casual air of a friend, the weight of his hands pervaded the wool of her gown, the heat of his touch distracting her.

"There is no man here whose favor I want." She was

about to push her way free of him, when she suddenly spied Clár Ó Reilly joining the women, her laughter mingling with the others. The widow winked at Gunnar as she prepared for the race. Seeing the woman's happiness provoked even more jealousy.

Right now, Auder craved release from the physical frustration and anger that filled her up. A hard run was exactly what she needed. Though she loathed being at the center of anyone's attention, she lined up beside the other women.

After a deep breath, she raised her shoulders back, trying not to think of how much she towered over the others. As the chieftain prepared to start the race, her attention stole back to Gunnar. She found herself studying his mouth, wondering what it would be like to kiss a man like him. Would his lips be soft and yielding? Or would they take command, forcing her to surrender?

*Enough,* she warned herself.

When the chieftain brought his hands down, signaling the start of the race, Auder picked up her skirts and ran hard. Her long strides cut across the *cashel* while the other women lagged behind.

No longer did she care that everyone was watching. Nor that she would have to wed the Norman baron in only two days more. She ran as though she could flee from the unwanted marriage, tearing herself free of the obligation. And when she crossed the line in the dirt, she heard the roar of approval from the crowd.

Everyone around her applauded, and Trahern took Auder's hand, raising it high. "The winner!" Laughing, he led her forward, adding, "Choose the man who will grant your favor. Your last favor, perhaps, before your marriage to Miles de Corlaine." He smiled. "And we are all grateful that you've agreed to this alliance."

The praise sobered her mood, for she'd wanted to forget

all about the Norman. Several of the wrestlers lined up, each smiling as if he wanted to claim her kiss. The devastating shyness took hold, and more than anything, Auder wanted to flee again.

Gunnar stood on the outskirts of the men, in a clear message that he was not among those who wanted her favor. There was amusement in his face, along with a look of admiration at her win.

"Well?" the chieftain demanded. "Who is it you will claim?"

Her heart was pounding within her chest, and though she knew any of the men would accept her kiss, the fear seemed to solidify and freeze within her veins. This wasn't the sort of woman she was. If she offered a kiss to any of them, they might believe it was an invitation for more. And she wasn't prepared to take another lover.

This dilemma was Gunnar's fault. Were it not for him, she wouldn't have run this race. Suddenly the solution was easy, for there was only one man it was safe to kiss— someone who didn't want her.

She strode toward Gunnar and saw his amusement transform into apprehension.

"I'm sorry," she apologized to Clár, who had come to stand beside Gunnar. "But since this was his idea, this will be his punishment."

Lifting her head to meet his, Auder dropped a light kiss upon Gunnar's mouth. Then with a friendly smile, she turned away, leaving him to stare at her.

# Chapter Two

Gunnar had known she was going to kiss him. And though he'd wanted to tell Auder no, the words remained caught in his throat. It was a kiss, nothing more. A brush of her lips against his own, in a light gesture that a friend would give another. Easy enough to forget.

Only it wasn't.

Auder didn't know how to kiss a man—there was an innocence beneath her lips, of someone unawakened to the ways between a man and a woman. Like a spring bud, tightly wrapped, she kept herself hidden, not letting anyone know her.

She'd openly admitted that she didn't know how to please a man or how to gain his affections. Her shyness had held her back on more than one occasion. With such a powerful lord as her husband, Gunnar suspected Auder would fade into the shadows. The man would use her and discard her. There was no guarantee that the baron would keep the peace, either.

He still couldn't believe she'd volunteered for this. Were Auder as strong-willed as his sister-in-law Katla, she might have stood a chance. But she was softhearted and timid, too afraid to make trouble.

Clár reached out and took his hand as he walked her back to her house. "Why did Auder kiss you?" she asked. Though the widow's tone was friendly, he recognized the suspicion beneath it.

"I don't know. It was nothing." He pulled Clár into an embrace, dropping a kiss upon her cheek to reassure her.

Clár's arms slid around his waist, and there was no doubt of the invitation she offered when she pressed her body closer. But the widow's kiss did nothing to him. It didn't warm his skin the way Auder's had. It was pleasant enough, but it conjured up no desire or need.

The truth was, a simple press of Auder's lips had made a far greater impact.

Gunnar broke away, unsure of the troubling thoughts brewing inside. Clár seemed to sense his unease, and in her face, he saw disappointment. "It's late," she murmured. "I would invite you to stay, but I can see that your thoughts are elsewhere. Good night, Gunnar."

He couldn't bring himself to deny it before the door closed behind Clár. Honor demanded that he forget about Auder. She wasn't the right woman for him, nor could she belong to him even if he wanted her to.

But the memory of her kiss haunted him, making him wonder why she had provoked him in such a way. And what on earth he was supposed to do about it.

In the morning, Auder blinked at the harsh sunlight. She'd hardly slept at all last night, for today was her last day among the Ó Reillys. It also marked the feast of *Bealtaine,* a time when prayers were spoken to bless the land and the animals. A time honoring the fertility of women, when the old ways were remembered.

Men and women would lie together this night, and many children would be born the following spring. More of the Dalrata tribe members would join them, and several men and women would handfast, marrying for a year and a day, if not longer.

A sense of isolation shadowed her, for she would not participate in the celebrations. In the morning, she would travel to the Norman settlement, and this night would be her last among friends and family.

Near the outer gate, she saw the glint of chain mail armor. Two of the Norman soldiers were speaking to Trahern. One stared at her, and her lungs seized with fear. Though she knew it was irrational to be so afraid when she would be living among them soon enough, she couldn't cage her feelings. Trahern's hand rested upon the sword at his waist, while Gunnar was nowhere to be seen. Several of the other men were approaching the soldiers, their hands gripping weapons in a silent threat.

"Auder, go back and remain hidden," came a female voice. She saw Morren standing behind her, and the woman's face was pale. "Let Trahern handle this."

"Why are they here?"

Morren shook her head. "Just go. Quickly."

Her heart was racing, but Auder turned her back and obeyed. She didn't want to leave yet—it was too soon. But if the Norman baron commanded it, she doubted if she could refuse.

With the uneasiness weighing down upon her, Auder entered the storage hut that led to the hidden *souterrain* passage beneath the *cashel*. Though it was likely unnecessary to hide there, it was the safest place she could think of.

She climbed down the ladder until she reached the stone-lined chamber below the earth.

The air was cooler, and she sat down against the frigid wall, flinching as she wondered how long she should remain here. With her knees drawn up, she exhaled, shivering as a cloud formed from her breath.

"Auder, what are you doing here?" came a voice. Gunnar returned from the opposite side of the *souterrain* passage, his face shadowed in darkness.

"The Norman soldiers are here." She gripped her arms, steeling herself against the cold. "Morren ordered me to remain hidden. What about you?"

"Trahern asked me to guard this exit, in case anyone tried to invade the passage."

She glanced back at the ladder leading to the storage hut. "Should I go back?"

"No. I'd rather be the one to guard you." He set down his shield and leaned against the wall beside her. She couldn't read his expression, since the only light came from the overhead entrance by the ladder, but she could hear the tension in his voice. Whether he was angry at the soldiers or at her, she didn't know.

Several minutes passed before he demanded, "Last night…why did you do it, Auder?"

"I didn't want to kiss any of the others," she admitted. "I thought you wouldn't mind. Besides, it was your idea for me to enter the race." She turned her gaze away, not wanting to hear any reasons why he hadn't wanted her kiss.

Gunnar shifted his weight against the wall, and she heard him expel a sigh. "Auder, I don't know. As friends, we—"

"I know what you're going to say." She hugged her knees tighter, cutting off his excuses. "Gunnar, you don't need to explain why I don't interest you as a woman. I know it already, and it doesn't bother me. Your interest is in Clár."

"I'm glad you understand that." But there was something else in his tone, almost as if he wanted to say more.

"Good." She waited for him to go, or to make some sort of pitying remark. Instead, he reached down and helped her to stand up. He took both of her hands in his, as though he were trying to make a decision. "Is something wrong?"

Gunnar didn't answer. The heat of his skin warmed her, and she had the sense that he was choosing his words carefully. Long moments passed before he finally asked, "Did you believe that was a real kiss?"

"Of course." She frowned. Was he criticizing her lack of experience? She'd been nervous enough, and she'd gotten it over with as quickly as possible. "It won't happen again," she promised. "You can go back to Clár with a clear conscience." She tried to pull her hands back, but he refused to allow it.

"The problem is," he said slowly, "I've been thinking about it ever since yesterday. And I don't know why."

Against her better judgment, her heartbeat quickened. She tried to keep her tone unassuming. "Gunnar, I meant nothing by it. Truly."

Never in a thousand years would she admit to him that she had imagined him kissing her back, the way he'd kissed Clár. There was no reason to humiliate herself, not when it would never happen. Best to pretend it was of no importance.

Gunnar released her hands, but she didn't move. He leaned in so that his mouth rested against her ear. "I don't believe you."

A chill rose upon her flesh, a tightness at the lie. His fingers moved lightly up her back, and an almost violent tremble poured through her. He was so close, she could smell the light scent of oak and wood ashes upon his skin.

She didn't dare move, terrified he would stop. Within his

posture, she sensed a mixture of interest and shielded anger at himself. It took everything she had to take a step away from him. "I'm going back now. And I think you should return to Clár."

But he took her hands and trapped them against her own waist. She could feel his warm breath against her mouth.

"What are you doing, Gunnar?" she breathed.

"Damned if I know."

There was hesitation in Auder's eyes and a shocked awareness. Though there were a hundred thousand reasons why Gunnar shouldn't kiss her, the doubts about Clár were growing darker. He liked the widow, but before he made any commitment to her, he needed to know if he was making a mistake. If perhaps, there should have been something more.

Auder's gentle brush of lips lingered with him still. It had haunted him last night, and perhaps kissing her again would end all of the forbidden thoughts. It might solidify his decision to choose Clár and settle for a quiet, pleasant handfasting.

He slid his palms upon her nape. Strands of her hair had fallen about her face, despite the braids pulling it away from her cheeks. When he bent his mouth to hers, she caught her breath, their lips merging in softness. He nipped at her upper lip, coaxing her to open more.

She faltered at first, as though uncertain of what he wanted. But then, when he kissed her harder, she melted into him, her hips seeking his. Her arms wrapped around his neck, as though she needed him to keep her balance. The softness of her breasts pressed into his tunic, and he couldn't stop the roar of desire that awakened.

She had an instinct of what to do, and as he deepened

the kiss, her tongue slipped against his. "That's right," he encouraged her, threading his own tongue with hers.

Sleek and wet, she let him invade her mouth, kissing him back as though he were the only man left in the world. There was an eagerness, a willingness to please, that made him forget all the reasons he was courting Clár. His hands moved down Auder's back, over her taut bottom. He kissed her until his mouth grew numb, until he caught himself rubbing his shaft against her, needing to satiate the rigid lust.

Gunnar let go, jerking away as though she'd caught fire. Auder's breathing was unsteady, her shoulders trembling. Her hair hung over one shoulder, against the breasts he wanted to touch. He wanted to peel off her gown, to expose her skin and watch the nipples pebble in the wind. To take the tight buds into his mouth, making her moan with the same lust he was feeling right now.

God help him, he needed to cease this madness.

"Was that…a real kiss?" she ventured. She clenched her waist as though trying to hold herself together.

"I'm sorry." He strode past her, to the exit of the *souterrain,* furious at himself for starting this. He'd been caught up by her innocence and the way she'd responded to him. If he hadn't stopped himself, he'd have taken her right here, claiming her with his body.

Gunnar didn't look back, for his thoughts were in complete disarray. He wished he'd never kissed Auder, for it had only driven home what he'd already suspected.

It couldn't be Clár. Not anymore.

The light at the edge of the *souterrain* was shielded by the underbrush. The sound of voices outside caught his attention, and Gunnar's hand went to the battleaxe at his waist.

Without warning, the branches moved, and men charged inside the *souterrain*.

"Auder, get out!" he roared, as he unsheathed the axe and swung hard.

They were going to kill him. She was sure of it. Auder didn't know what power moved through her, but instead of obeying Gunnar, she ran for one of the torches near the ladder that led above to the *cashel*. If he couldn't see, he couldn't fight.

A scream tore from her throat as she raced with the torch, using it to illuminate the narrow passage. She saw the Norman soldiers, their swords drawn, as Gunnar defended the *souterrain* with his battleaxe and the shield he'd dropped earlier.

One of the soldiers tried to move past him, but Auder swung her torch, the fire nearly singeing the man's beard. "Is this how you honor your lord's alliance?" she demanded. "By sneaking into our *cashel* like thieving animals?"

The leader of the men met her gaze, his expression furious. "We could take this *cashel* by force within a few hours. Then there would be no need for an alliance."

Gunnar shoved the point of his sword at the man's throat. "Try it, and you'd be dead."

Auder's voice froze within her throat as the soldier dove away from the blade, slicing his sword at Gunnar's stomach. At the last second, the man's weapon bit into the wooden shield, and Gunnar slashed the battleaxe at the man's face.

Auder watched in startled fascination as Gunnar unleashed the force of his rage, like one of the legendary berserkers. One of the Norman soldiers fell to the ground, and whether he was dead or alive, she didn't know.

When she saw another soldier coming up from behind,

she cried out a warning. Gunnar spun, and caught a shield against the side of his head. Blood poured from his temple, and God help her, she couldn't let the soldiers harm him. Not when she held the power to stop it.

"Don't," she pleaded. "I am the woman betrothed to Lord Maraloch. Release Gunnar, and I will go with you back to your camp."

She lifted the torch, meeting the leader's gaze. "We will keep the alliance and avoid further bloodshed." Swallowing hard, she stared at Gunnar. His expression was like stone, impenetrable and furious.

A movement from the *souterrain* exit caught their attention, and she saw Trahern arriving with half a dozen men. More of the Ó Reillys came from the ladder above, surrounding the Normans on both sides.

"Go back to Lord Maraloch," Trahern ordered the soldiers. "And tell him that he will only have his bride if he honors our agreement for peace." In the torchlight, the chieftain's face was rigid with anger. "I will have words with him about this treachery."

The Norman took a step backward, never taking his eyes off Auder. As they departed, they took the wounded soldier with them, and then they were gone.

Auder rushed to Gunnar's side, touching the blood at his temple. "Are you all right? Can you stand?"

Gunnar caught her wrist, his eyes burning into hers. "You're not going to go through with this marriage, Auder."

She didn't answer him, for though it terrified her to be living among these men, worse was the thought of war between them and her clan. His blood stained her fingertips, and everything inside her clenched at the thought of Gunnar coming to harm.

"I don't have a choice."

*Later that evening*

The Bel fires blazed upon the hillsides, and the clouded sky held off its rain. As the night of *Bealtaine* began, the Dalrata tribe members mingled with the Ó Reilly clan. Trahern sat in the midst of everyone, preparing to entertain them all with his stories. After the attempted invasion earlier, the atmosphere among the people was strung tight. Both the Irish and the Norsemen took turns guarding the *cashel,* though it seemed the Normans had indeed gone.

Her mother Halma sat with Maeve Ó Reilly, a matron who loved to gossip. Maeve sent Auder a nod of approval and continued speaking with Halma. It was the first time in many weeks that she'd seen her mother smiling.

When she went to join them, Maeve reached out to take her hand. "You've done the right thing, Auder Ó Reilly. I've been telling Halma that I can think of no one more courageous to marry the Norman."

"I'm still not so sure," Halma began.

"Nonsense." A mischievous smile perked at the matron's mouth. "With her looks, she'll have that Norman eating out of her hand after one wedding night."

Auder didn't believe that at all, but she wasn't about to ruin Halma's evening. For now, her mother looked content. Not nearly as alone as she'd been. And for that, she was grateful to Maeve.

"When I was married," Maeve continued, "I kept my husband well satisfied. If I asked him to bring me the stars from the sky, he'd have tried his best to get them." To Halma, she added, "Stop your worrying. She's a brave girl, and you should be proud of her."

"I am," Halma said. And with the soft words of praise, tears brimmed in Auder's eyes.

"It's going to be all right, Mother," she said. "Enjoy yourself tonight."

When she left the two women alone, she blinked until the tears faded away. Maeve's prediction couldn't be further from the truth. Auder knew she thoroughly lacked the ability to please a husband.

Her doubts multiplied until she found herself walking toward the storytelling. She saw Morren moving among the people, seeing that everyone had enough food and drink while Trahern settled back to begin his tales.

The chieftain's voice took on a mystical quality as he transformed the mood of the clan, capturing them in the spell of his words. As the evening drifted into night, children began falling asleep in their mothers' arms. Trahern took his wife's hand, and pulled her to his side. It was as if he drew strength and comfort from Morren, and Auder envied the love between them.

Would any man ever look at her in that way, as though she meant the world to him? The weight of her betrothal vow grew more difficult to bear, for she suspected the marriage was of little importance to the baron. He'd never even seen her face, though he'd agreed to wed her.

She forced her thoughts back to Trahern's story, wishing she could lose herself within it. She needed to hear the tales, to drown out her fears of tomorrow.

Trahern spoke of a young woman named Sinead who was taken by the faeries when she neglected to give them an offering on the night of *Bealtaine*. "Her lover Kel went in search of her for a hundred nights," he continued, his voice weaving its spell. "No matter how long it took or how many miles he had to go, he swore to find her. For she belonged to him in this world and the next."

A strange prickle formed upon her neck while Auder listened to the story. Across the *cashel*, she saw Gunnar standing with Clár. The widow was speaking to him, and seeing them together broke something inside Auder. Though it shouldn't have made any difference, she couldn't stop the suffocating disappointment. It seemed that the kiss Gunnar had given her meant nothing, despite the feelings it had aroused.

*She* meant nothing to him.

Auder retreated from the crowd, needing to be alone with her bruised feelings. In the distance, she saw Gunnar watching her, an unreadable expression on his face. Nothing about her feelings was rational or reasonable. Her mind was in disarray, and her anger with Gunnar kept growing higher.

She wished he'd never kissed her a second time. Torches flared in the darkness, and for a long time, she stared at the rippling flames, trying to calm her wayward heart. Within the shadows, she found her refuge, turning her face away from everyone.

She returned to the gates, watching the darkness that lay beyond the torches. Were the soldiers still there? Or had they gone back to Maraloch?

She started walking over to the sentries, when a low voice resonated from behind her. "Don't move another step."

Gunnar had never felt so blindingly angry as right now. "Where are you going, Auder?"

"I don't even know anymore." There was a wrenching pain in her eyes, as though she were about to shatter. "It's hard for me to watch the men and women going off alone together. My fate isn't the same as theirs."

"Then tell Trahern you won't marry Maraloch. You have that choice."

A single tear rolled down her cheek. Then another. "I'm

not trying to martyr myself, Gunnar… But I don't believe I can say no. Not after what happened earlier." She tried to venture a smile and took his hand.

"You can't trust them, Auder." He needed her to understand it, to refuse the alliance. This was no longer about his friend endangering herself—it was his own unexpected jealousy. He didn't want any man touching Auder. Not anymore.

He ignored the warnings that resounded through his brain, and claimed her mouth once again. Within her innocence, he tasted something else. A yearning, as though she needed him tonight. He kissed her back, letting the thunderous desire claim him, and she responded in a way that tore his control apart.

The pale silver moonlight illuminated the *cashel* and the surrounding land. Upon the hillside, the bonfires blazed, while in the distance lay the threat of the Normans. Gunnar didn't care about them or anyone else. Right now, he needed to convince Auder that she could never consider giving herself up. He wanted her in a way he hardly understood. It went beyond the casual friendship they'd shared or his desire to keep her safe.

Breaking free of the kiss, he held her closely. She trembled within his embrace. "Gunnar," she whispered. "This isn't right."

He drew her to face him, locking his hands around her face. Her blue-green eyes were fringed with tears, her lips swollen from where he'd kissed her.

"I'm not letting you go." He spoke the command while keeping her imprisoned in his arms. "You're staying with me."

"What about Clár?" she asked. Within her question, he sensed her unrest and belief that he didn't truly want her.

"I told her that we wouldn't suit any longer," he said,

running his mouth against her throat. "It's why I spoke with her earlier, though she already suspected it."

With his hands, Gunnar loosened the tie that bound her braid, bringing her hair to spill over her shoulders. "I want to know what sort of spell you've cast over me. Why my blood rises at the sight of you." He leaned in, his mouth grazing hers in another kiss. "I want to know the woman who was standing in front of me all these months, the woman I was too blind to see. I'm not going to let anyone take you away."

The need to claim her, to mark her as his, was rising hard within him. He invaded her mouth with his tongue, leaving her with no doubt of how much he wanted her.

Something about Auder had captivated him. When he'd seen her starting to surrender herself to the Normans, a primitive urge had taken him with no warning. He didn't understand what it was, but this night, he intended to use every means to change her mind. Even seduction.

Breaking free of her kiss, he demanded, "If you tell me no, I'll take you back to the others this very moment." His hands rested at her waist, waiting for some sign. When she didn't move, his hands moved up to cradle her face. "Or I'm going to touch you the way I've wanted to since the day you returned to Glen Ocham."

Her lips were wet, her eyes wild as she stared at him. It had happened so fast, she could hardly breathe. Gunnar's gray eyes were the color of smoke, his shadowed face fierce with sexual need. Tonight, there would be far more than a single kiss, if she allowed it.

Did she dare? Though her feelings ran deep, she knew what had to happen in the morning. She couldn't abandon this alliance, despite her personal misgivings. She stared back at the torches outlining the *cashel*. Tomorrow, she would offer herself to protect her friends and family.

But tonight belonged to her.

She could stay with Gunnar, letting him do as he wished. Already she sensed that it would be different with him, that she would not disappoint him as she had her previous lover. The aching need and desire ran deep. She admitted to herself that Gunnar was the man she wanted more than any other, the man she'd dreamed of. She might never again have this chance.

She'd always felt so awkward and clumsy around men, never knowing how to behave. Reaching up to his face, she ran her fingers from his temple down his jaw. "I should say no to you."

"But you're not going to. You know this was meant to happen between us."

Beneath her fingertips, she felt his pulse flaring. And when she leaned in to kiss him, it was as if she'd unleashed a storm. He devoured her mouth, cupping her bottom and nestling her hips close to his. The length of his desire rested between them, and she shivered at the thought of joining with him.

"I want to stay with you," she whispered. "Even though I know it's wrong."

The air was growing cooler, and Gunnar held her close, warming her with the heat of his skin. "Come with me while I get a horse."

"Why? Where are you taking me?"

"Far away from everyone else," he swore. "Tonight, I want no one to interrupt us."

The long ride was dangerous in the darkness, but Gunnar used the moonlit river to guide them. He brought her to a grove of trees, several miles south of the *cashel,* and far from the place where the Norman soldiers had made camp. "I'm going to build a fire," he told her.

He removed his cloak and spread it on the ground. Auder helped him gather branches and within another half hour, he had a warm fire licking at the wood.

Against the flames, his silhouette reminded her of a conqueror, bold and demanding. She understood that the time for changing her mind was long past. This was a man who intended to claim her, and a surge of desire held her unable to grasp the threads of reason.

Gunnar knelt before her, guiding her to sit with him. Auder brought her hands to rest upon his chest, and the old fears brimmed up inside her, though she tried to push them away.

Was it so wrong to want a memory for herself? She deserved at least that much, didn't she? And though it might break her heart to leave him in the morning, she would have this night as her own.

Gunnar moved his hands to the brooches at her shoulders and unpinned them. Auder reached up to help remove the apron that covered her dark green gown.

As he took away each layer, baring her skin, he kissed her, sending ripples of intense pleasure rising up. His mouth moved to the softness of her throat, while his hands reached to fill up with her breasts.

"You weaken me, Auder," he said, and with his thumbs, he caressed her erect nipples.

The pleasure rocked through her, and she touched the scar that ran down his neck, needing to reach his skin. Gunnar removed his tunic, baring his warrior's body. A strange shell hung from a leather cord, and he set it aside. "It belonged to my mother," was all he would say.

He wove his hands into her hair, sliding it down her breasts to cover the nipples. He used the glossy strands to arouse her, and she shuddered as her body grew warm with desire. "Ever since I kissed you yesterday, I've been wanting to do this." He bent down to kiss each nipple lightly, his tongue sliding across the hard nubs.

He drew her mouth to his, and Auder clung to him while he struggled to remove the rest of their clothing. The heat of his skin seemed to brand hers, and she welcomed his weight atop her, even though she shouldn't.

"Gunnar," she said softly, her voice breaking slightly. "I'm not good at this. I'm sorry if I displease you."

"You couldn't displease me if you wanted to." He claimed her mouth in a rough kiss while he rolled onto his back, bringing her atop him. The motion brought her into full contact with his shaft, and she couldn't stop the shudder of need that pulsed inside. She was wet, ready for him to claim her. Parting her legs, she straddled his waist, kissing him deeply. In response, Gunnar moved his hips, lifting her body against his erection to caress her.

"This is your last chance, Auder," he breathed against her throat. "If you want me to leave you untouched, I will. Or…" He ran his hand down her throat to the generous curve of her breast. The nipple tightened instantly, and she felt his thick length nudging at her opening.

"Or what?" she whispered.

"You're going to be my captive. And I'm going to touch you until you scream with pleasure."

## Chapter Three

Her heart was beating so fast, she could hardly speak. It was both terrifying and exhilarating, watching Gunnar's face transform with harsh need. "I don't want you to stop," she admitted.

"You told me that you'd taken a lover before. And that you didn't enjoy it."

She shook her head slowly. "I thought I'd done what I was supposed to do. I lay beneath him and let him join with me." Her face was burning with shame. "Afterward, he left without saying a word. What else was I to think?"

"He was a selfish bastard," Gunnar said. He laid her down gently upon his cloak and reached for her shift. Made of the softest linen, she wondered if he meant to put it back on her. Perhaps he'd changed his mind after all.

Instead, he took her wrists and bound her hands together. "Tonight, I promise you'll enjoy every moment."

The wool of his cloak was rough against her bare back, and the sensation of being bound was unexpectedly arousing. Though she wanted to touch him, he lifted her wrists above her head, trapping her in place.

"You're a beautiful woman, Auder. And tonight, you're mine to claim."

With that, he took her nipple into his mouth, his tongue moving over the hardened tip. She was helpless to stop him, and he sucked gently, tantalizing her. Between her thighs, she could feel his length, and she grew wet simply imagining him inside. His mouth caressed and nibbled at her skin, and she couldn't stop herself from arching against him, wishing he would release her hands.

"I'm going to take your body and sheathe myself inside you," he said against her navel, and his tongue swirled against it, make her shiver. He let go of her bound hands and spread her legs apart, forcing her to bend her knees. His mouth was dangerously close, and she didn't think—

Sweet God above. His tongue slid over her woman's flesh, and she couldn't stop the cry that broke free. Her nipples were tight, and she couldn't stop the trembling when he licked her intimately. He used his tongue to massage the hooded flesh above her opening, and the sensations brought even more wetness surging.

"Let go," he demanded. "Give yourself to me." He sucked against her, his tongue caressing her, while his hands filled up with her swollen breasts. Her hips arched, the rigid need rising higher, achingly close.

When he pulled back, she nearly sobbed with frustration, until he started again with the torment. His mouth devoured her secret flesh, and he used one thumb to enter her body. Perspiration broke over her skin as he stimulated her with his thumb, entering her in a gentle rhythm while his tongue lapped at her most sensitive place.

"Gunnar," she cried out, trying to reach for him.

In answer, he used his strength to keep her bound hands trapped while he raked his teeth and tongue over her. When he entered her again with his fingers, his stroking rhythm finally pushed her over the edge. A sudden release broke over her, and Auder pulsed against his hand, shattering with the melting pleasure.

When she met his eyes, no longer was he the kind man she'd fallen for. He'd become a ruthless invader, intent upon taking her. She bit her lip, waiting for the moment when he would press himself inside.

Instead, he sat, guiding her bound hands around his neck. It forced her breasts against his hardened chest, and her wet folds came into contact with his manhood. He teased her, lifting her hips to graze his length. "Did you like that?" he murmured, taking her breast into his mouth once more.

Her breath caught at the savage pleasure of him suckling at her breast. It was as if she felt an echo within her womb, and she rose up, trying to slide his length within her opening.

"I want you inside me," she pleaded.

"Not yet." He lifted her until his erection was positioned against her entrance. He lavished attention upon her breasts, caressing the hard nub of one, while he took the other in his mouth. His arm gripped her tight, keeping only the head of his manhood inside.

She was shaking hard as he moved her against him, using his erection to tease and torment her. "Please," she begged him. "Finish this."

"I want to watch you come apart again," he murmured. And then he pushed himself all the way inside. She could feel him filling her, stretching her, until he was buried inside her. The sensation of fullness was so much better than she'd expected, and she rose up a little, adjusting to his size. Her body was so wet, she shuddered when he filled her again.

"Your turn," he said. "You're going to ride me."

Auder shivered, but understood that he was giving her

the power to do what she wanted. She rose up on her knees, sliding up until only the tip of him remained inside, before she lowered herself down again. The deep pressure of his flesh within hers was shocking, and she struggled to find a rhythm.

It was unbearable, feeling how hard he was inside, and her body gripped him tightly, wet against his length.

"Faster," he commanded, taking her hips and surging against her. Her breath came out in quick gasps, but she obeyed. Moving wildly against him, she felt the tremors once again. His length became more aroused, like an iron rod inside her.

Gunnar's eyes burned into hers as he met her thrusts, driving her past the point of reason. She surged against him, another release breaking over her, and he forced her onto her back once more, never breaking contact.

In that moment, she did scream, as he filled her. Gunnar never stopped his rhythm, thrusting inside her over and over again. She was shaking so hard, she wrapped her legs around him, shattering once more as he joined his body with hers. The madness swirled inside as he penetrated, until at last Gunnar let out his own groan of pleasure, filling her up with his seed.

Auder trembled beneath him, her arms still trapped around his neck. Gunnar used his tongue to tease her nipples, gently biting the tips and causing her to shudder.

"You belong to me, Auder," he murmured against her skin.

She didn't speak, hardly able to find the words. He had shown her the immense power that could happen between a man and a woman. And in this moment, it was as if he'd reached inside and captured her heart.

Right now, she wanted to weep. She clung tightly to him, wishing to God she didn't have to leave him. But somehow there had to be peace between the Normans and her clan. How could she refuse the marriage when it might save their lives?

Beside them, the fire had begun to die down. Gunnar extricated himself from her body and untied her before he stoked the fire up again. In the light, his body gleamed golden. He was staring at the flames, as if he didn't know what to say. Neither did she.

Though she wanted to know what was bothering him, Auder didn't ask. She'd wanted a night like this with Gunnar, more than anything. But instead of being able to confess how much she cared for him, she held back the words. It didn't matter what she felt inside, for her fate was unavoidable. All she had was this last night.

She saw the nick upon his temple where the soldiers had barely missed his head. He could have been killed this morning. Without a word, she pulled him close, resting her head beneath his chin. Against her cheek, she heard his heartbeat, and she vowed that no matter what lay ahead, she would do whatever was necessary to keep safe those she loved.

Gunnar reached out for Auder before the sun had risen. He'd made love to her twice more that night. She'd climaxed with his shaft buried deep, and the feeling of her body squeezing him, wet with her arousal, had sent him into his own shuddering release. He'd experienced an undeniable physical pleasure, but somehow he'd sensed her holding back from him.

Now that he'd taken her for his own, he would stop at nothing to keep her at his side. His hand touched the empty cloak and he sat up, a cold fear suddenly dawning. The horse was gone, along with her clothing, making it clear that she'd left long ago.

Damn her for this. She'd gone, no doubt intending to give herself over to the Norman baron. Gunnar threw on his clothing, taking off in a fast run. Even so, it wouldn't be enough to overtake her on horseback.

His legs burned as he tore across the fields, his mind raging. Just imagining the baron touching her, much less claiming Auder with his body, made him want to hack the man to pieces with his battleaxe. He wasn't about to let Auder—shy, beautiful, and with a heart too big for her own good—make the worst mistake of her life.

He ran until his chest was about to crack open, sweat pouring over his skin. The physical exhaustion didn't matter—only reaching her in time. The morning sun beat down on him, burning his eyes as he kept up the punishing pace.

When he reached the *cashel,* he stumbled inside, praying he wasn't too late. When he saw Morren speaking with Auder's mother, he knew the worst had already happened. She was gone.

"You let her go, didn't you?" he demanded.

Morren's face revealed her worry. "Trahern took her to meet with Lord Maraloch early this morning."

Gunnar let out a foul curse and barked out an order for a horse to be readied. "How long ago?"

Morren shook her head. "More than an hour, at least." She rubbed at her stomach, as if to soothe the unborn child. "Gunnar, she seemed determined to make this marriage. It was her choice."

Her choice to leave him, to run away. He couldn't accept that, not after the night they'd shared together. Had he frightened her? From the way she'd fallen asleep in his arms, he couldn't believe it was true. Whatever had happened between them, he needed to confront her.

"I'm going after her." He started to approach the stables when Halma Ó Reilly moved to stop him.

"Wait," she said quietly. "There's something you should know first."

The matron looked first at Morren, then at him. "Auder is trying to protect all of us," she whispered. "Especially after what her father did, when he was chieftain. And though I've tried to tell her that she does not have to wed the baron, she won't listen."

He didn't speak, but a hardness gathered inside. "What did her father do?"

Halma's face saddened. "My husband…had a weakness for young girls. He was not well liked among our people." A shiver crossed over her, and she clutched her hands together. "Then I saw him looking at our daughter one day."

A sickening feeling sent Gunnar's stomach falling. He exchanged a look with Morren who paled, closing her eyes. "He didn't try to—"

"No. I kept her away from him." Shame darkened the matron's cheeks, and she let out a sigh. "It's why I sent her away, year after year. But Auder knew why I wouldn't let her return home. And ever since her father died, she's tried to take care of me."

Halma took a breath, adding, "If you can stop her from marrying Lord Maraloch, I would be grateful. Perhaps she'll listen to you."

"I'll do everything I can," Gunnar swore. His mind began to center upon the true problem—the alliance between the Ó Reilly clan and the Normans. There had to be another alternative, something they hadn't considered before. Auder would never abandon the marriage unless she believed her family and friends would be safe.

"I need to speak with Clár," he said suddenly. His idea was a rough one, at best, but it was all he had.

Morren frowned. "She's with her son at home. But why—?"

Gunnar ignored the question and began to run toward the widow's hut. If the baron wanted an alliance, there were other ways to achieve it. He only hoped Clár would agree.

In the late afternoon, a maid helped Auder dress in the gown given to her by Lord Miles de Corlaine of Maraloch. A wedding gift, he'd said. The cloth was a stunning blue color, and she found herself examining the silk closer, trying to determine whether or not woad had been used for the dye.

As she ran her fingers over the finery, her eyes welled up. Though she'd tried to push away the memories, it was as if Gunnar had branded himself upon her skin. She could remember every last touch of his hands and the way he'd made her feel. And though it broke her heart to leave him, she knew there was no other choice.

The safety of her clan—and Gunnar—was more important than her personal feelings. Now that she'd met the baron, he didn't frighten her as much as she'd thought he would. He was an older man with gray hair and vivid blue eyes. The lines upon his face revealed a person of strength and power.

Lord Maraloch had apologized for the soldiers' invasion, explaining that they had acted against his authority and had been punished. He'd also granted Trahern the gift of several horses as restitution.

Though his actions should have made her feel better, Auder couldn't abandon her disappointment. She'd been hoping Lord Maraloch would be cruel, thus giving her a reason to back out of the agreement. But Miles de Corlaine had been kind, even introducing her to his seven-year-old son. The lad was bright with a cheerful smile, a boy easy to love.

There was no reason not to go through with this marriage. She might have given her heart to Gunnar, but she'd given her betrothal vow to the baron. And…Gunnar had not once spoken of his own feelings. He didn't want her to wed the Norman, but neither had he offered for her himself.

She didn't want to be cast aside, or worse, pitied. She couldn't bear to see that upon his face.

Her heart was frozen inside, as if she could close off the feelings she didn't want to feel. Auder reached around her neck for the leather cord she'd taken from Gunnar early this morn. The seashell rested against her heart, as though she could claim this small part of him. Something to keep.

A knock resounded at the door and a maidservant went to answer it. When she saw Trahern standing on the other side, Auder knew the time had come. As she followed him down the winding stairs, she closed off her grief and prepared herself to face what lay ahead.

Gunnar rode hard, racing across the Norman lands. He ignored the sentries standing guard outside Maraloch, only slowing his pace slightly to lift both hands in surrender. They saw the offering he'd brought and lowered their spears.

Within the inner bailey, he spied Trahern, the man's height towering above everyone. A priest stood nearby, about to offer a blessing, while Auder's hand rested within the Norman's grasp.

Rigid fear tore through Gunnar, that he was too late to stop the marriage. He brought his horse through the people and dismounted, lifting down the young boy he'd brought with him. Clár's son Nial was wide-eyed as he stared at the

soldiers surrounding them. Behind him, Clár followed on
her own horse, her tension evident.

The Norman baron lifted his hand in a silent signal, and
within moments, Gunnar was surrounded by guards. He
ignored the spears aimed at him, shielding the boy from
their weapons.

"You're interrupting my wedding, Irishman," the Norman
said coolly. Auder had gone pale, her face stricken with
fear.

Gunnar ignored the weapons and the people around him.
Staring into her eyes, he demanded, "Is this what you want,
Auder? Would you rather have him at your side?"

Tears glimmered upon her lashes, and within her eyes,
he saw her pain. It was as if she didn't believe he could love
her.

"My own wishes don't matter," she whispered. "It's for
the good of my people."

He didn't believe her words. "I spoke to your mother,
Auder. But there are other ways to protect her. Other ways
to change what your father did."

A tear streamed down her face, and he saw that she was
listening to him, at last. Gunnar drew as close as he dared.
"I won't let you go. Not after last night."

She lowered her eyes, as if she couldn't bear to look
at him. And it was as if she'd driven a blade through his
ribs.

To the Norman, he said, "I have a different alliance to
suggest. Clár Ó Reilly has agreed to let her son be fostered
here, if she can remain with him. In return, we will care
for your son as though he were our own blood."

At his vow, the widow stepped forward. Lord Maraloch's
gaze met Clár's, and she sent him a tentative smile. There
was courage beneath it, and a note of interest in the widow's
face.

"If this is an acceptable alternative to the marriage,"

Trahern began, "then we can proceed with fostering arrangements."

The Norman released Auder's hand, not hiding his annoyance. "Either is acceptable to me. Though I suspect this lady would prefer that I release her from this betrothal agreement."

Auder stared at Gunnar, her blue-green eyes hesitant. Almost as if she weren't certain he would want her anymore.

He started to meet her halfway, but then Auder started to run. He caught her in his arms, and she clung tightly, her face wet with tears. Although the baron looked irritated, he turned his attention back to Clár and her son.

"I'm sorry," Auder whispered, as Gunnar lifted her onto his horse and swung up behind. "I never wanted to leave you. But I couldn't have lived with myself if they attacked our *cashel* and you were killed."

"You should have trusted me instead of running away." He framed her face with his hands. "I want to take care of you. And I'll make certain that no one ever speaks a word against your mother. What happened wasn't her fault or yours."

"I wanted to do something to make up for what he did."

"It's not your blame to shoulder. Nor your mother's." He bent closer, resting his cheek against hers. "Make the choice of what you want. Not of what you think others want from you."

She leaned back against him, lifting her face to his. "I won't run from you again, Gunnar." With a faint smile, she offered, "I'll run to you. If you'll have me."

*Two nights later*

Auder kept her eyes closed, upon Gunnar's command. Her new husband had brought her to the house he'd built, and as she lay upon his bed, the cool night air blew over her naked skin.

"Don't open your eyes," he ordered.

Though she obeyed, she felt his weight sinking down beside her on the mattress. A light floral scent made her wrinkle her nose. Had he brought her flowers?

The fragrance grew stronger, and she felt the softness of petals against her cheeks, across her breasts, and more flowers upon her stomach.

"Can I open them now?" she said, laughing at the ticklish sensation. A soft silken texture brushed against her nipple, and she shuddered, her breasts straining toward her husband's touch. His mouth replaced the flower, and she caught her breath at the heated texture of his tongue. He tasted and teased her, applying the slightest suction until she grew moist within her womanhood.

"Open your eyes," he murmured. Auder obeyed and saw that he'd selected woad, madder and saffron, among other herbs. Rather than selecting flowers, he'd brought her the plants she used for dyeing cloth. "Morren helped me choose them," he admitted. "I thought they might be useful to you in your work."

She reached up and pulled him down on top of her, the herbs scattering everywhere. "They're wonderful, Gunnar." Her mouth met his in a deep kiss, and she tried to show him all the feelings she couldn't put into words.

His hands moved over her skin, and the rough skin provoked a desperate need to take him inside her, to claim him as her own.

She pulled at his clothing, and as the layers fell away, she lifted her leg over his hip, granting him access to her body.

"Do you still believe this is something only men enjoy?" he teased, as his hand moved down to caress her.

When his thumb brushed against her hooded center, she smiled against his mouth. "Not anymore."

He stroked her, and she reached between them to take his manhood into her palm. With her hand wrapped around his length, she fisted him until his face tightened. The moisture of his arousal coated her fingers, and she tried to guide him inside.

"No other man will ever touch you this way," he swore, sheathing his shaft within her. He brought her hips to the edge of the bed, still keeping them joined together while he stood. "You're mine, Auder."

He angled her body to meet him as he withdrew and thrust inside. Slowly, he joined with her, as though trying to reach the deepest place within her heart. She shivered as his gentle penetrations conjured up a swollen desire. When his length grew even harder within her, she pushed against him with a counter pressure. Eager to please him, she arched her back, moaning when he quickened his rhythm.

Gunnar showed no mercy as he filled her, like a conqueror bent upon ravaging her. Auder's fingers dug into the flowers, and she was unable to stop her cry of ecstasy when the tremors took her apart, shattering her body. Her husband pushed her back again, wrapping her legs around his waist as he stole her breath away.

And when at last he'd finished, he rested his head against hers, holding her close. Lifting one of the flowers to her cheek, he brushed it down her skin, making her smile.

As he held her tightly, their bodies fused together, she murmured against his skin, "I love you, Gunnar."

He kissed her softly, tucking a strand of hair behind her ear. "As I love you, my wife." His hands moved over her skin in a gentle caress. "And my friend."

* * * * *

# THE CAPTAIN'S
# WICKED WAGER

Marguerite Kaye

## Author Note

Gambling has long been the vice of choice for the rich and famous, from horseracing, the traditional sport of kings, to today's televised celebrity poker tournaments. It is easy to see the attraction. The heady mix of glamour, money and drama is both alluring and seductive. This was certainly true in Regency London when the *Ton* and the *demi-monde* flocked to Hells of St. James's and Piccadilly in search of illicit thrills and excitement.

But what if more was at stake than money? What if someone was driven to gamble with their body, their feelings, even their virtue? What if losing became more appealing than winning? Freed from society's conventions and constraints— for how can there be guilt when one has placed one's fate in the hands of the Gods—what might the gambler learn about his or her secret self?

This is what I wanted to explore through Isabella and Ewan's story, where a turn of a card, a throw of the dice, decides how shockingly they must behave, what sensual acts they must indulge in. And at stake, love, the ultimate prize, can be either won or lost.

I hope you enjoy reading this, my first ever Undone, as much as I enjoyed writing it. I'd love to hear what you think. You can email me at marguerite_kaye@hotmail.co.uk.

If ever any beauty I did see,
Which I desired, and got, 'twas but a dream of thee.
—John Donne, The Good Morrow

*For J, who makes any room our everywhere. Just love.*

**Look for Marguerite Kaye's duet**
*Innocent in the Sheikh's Harem*
*The Governess and the Sheikh*
**Coming soon from Harlequin® Historical**

# Chapter One

⤳⧼⧽⤳

London, 1785

The gaming saloon was packed, the clientele mostly male but with a fair sprinkling of women present, too. Thanks to the notorious Duchess of Devonshire, playing deep was very much *à la mode* for the fairer sex. The air was stifling, the atmosphere redolent of hair powder and scent, brandy and wine, mingled with the musky smell of too many bodies crowded into too small a space. Candles sputtered and flared, casting distorted shadows on the walls.

"Eight wins." The large woman in charge of the faro bank glowered as she pushed a pile of counters across the table.

Isabella Mansfield, her attention focused on trying to calculate the value of her winnings, ignored the woman's growing animosity. Faith, but it was hot! The fan she wore tied round her wrist provided her with precious little relief. The unaccustomed hair powder irritated her scalp. The rouge she had so carefully applied to her cheeks and lips prickled her delicate skin. The folds of her dark blue polonaise dress and the ridiculous layers of undergarments required to hold the shape in place at the back all contrived to make her distinctly uncomfortable.

Though they also, she reminded herself, served to ensure that she blended in, looked just like every other woman present. Aside from her complete lack of jewellery, that is. Her great-grandmother's pearls, the only thing of value she owned, had been discreetly sold to provide her stake for this evening. Two more wins, if her luck continued to hold, and she would have enough.

Captain Ewan Dalgleish watched with interest as Isabella pushed her entire stack of counters onto the two, causing a crackle of excitement to fizz round the throng of eager onlookers. There was something driven about her demeanour, quite different from the recklessness of a genuine gambler. She was clearly nervous: long fingers plucking at the sticks of her fan, her eyes fixed on the dealer's card box as if it contained the key to her very destiny. Which, he thought, raising his eyebrows as he calculated her stake, it most probably did. He was intrigued.

On the anniversary of the day he had resigned his commission following his father's death, and on his thirtieth birthday to boot, he had come to this newest hell made popular by Fox and his cronies in search of diversion. In the past year he had sampled every pleasure, licit or otherwise, the town had to offer, kicking over the traces and flaunting his newly-inherited respectability in the faces of his critics with gusto. Sport, women, sprees like this latest outing—they all provided temporary excitement, but nothing matched the visceral thrill of battle, the gut-clenching intensity of combat. He was coming to believe that the army had leeched all feeling out of him. An intense *ennui* threatened to overwhelm him.

He'd had the devil's own luck with the cards tonight, but it meant little. The fortune his father had left him was immense. And as for the brandy he had imbibed—his mind might be somewhat befuddled, but the abrasive edges of his poisonous mood had been in no way smoothed. To hell with all of it! Even his burning desire to try to right the wrongs of the world offered little solace. What he needed was something more exotic by way of an antidote.

The beauty at the faro table was most definitely that. Despite the regulation paint and powder, there was something distinctive about her. Winged black brows sat above cobalt-blue eyes fringed with long black lashes. There was a spark of intelligence there. A mouth wider than the fashionable rosebud, the bottom lip full. The long line of white throat swooping down to a luscious swell of bosom. The same flawless white skin on her arms, delicate wrists and long fingers. Slumbering sensuality combined with a haughty touch-me-not air. A challenging and enticing combination.

At the faro table Mrs Bradley, the banker, was declining the beauty's bet, clearly afraid it would break the bank. Her many chins wobbled as she shook her head. "I'm sorry, madam, that is twice the maximum stake permitted."

"But…" Isabella looked up, embarrassed to find all eyes upon her. Impatient. Speculative. Inquisitive. Leering. Under her rouge, she blushed. Not all the women here were ladies of the *ton*. Not all the gamblers were gentlemen. With a heavy heart she took back half her counters. At this rate, she would never win as much as she needed. She must have the full funds by the end of the week or all would be lost. She simply had to win enough tonight.

"With the bank's permission I will cover the bet, and any others the young lady cares to make." The deep voice had just the trace of a Scottish lilt.

Startled, Isabella looked up into the most striking pair of eyes she had ever seen. Amber tinged with liquid brown, the colour of autumn leaves. For a moment they clashed with her own, causing a flicker of excitement to shiver down her spine. A sculpted mouth curled in a half smile.

"Captain Dalgleish," the banker exclaimed in surprise. "This is most unusual."

He flashed her a smouldering, flirtatious smile. "Unusual, Mrs Bradley, but I'm sure you can find a way to accommodate me."

The banker smiled coquettishly. "Captain Dalgleish, I'd wager there's scarcely a woman in London who wouldn't be willing to accommodate you in any way you saw fit. If I was twenty years younger I might even be tempted myself."

A ripple of laughter spread through the onlookers.

Ewan's eyes twinkled mischievously. "Madam, that is a regret we will both have to live with." The crowd roared its approval. "Perhaps this will ease the pain somewhat," Ewan said, passing her a sweetener which she quickly palmed, indicating her acceptance with a coy fluttering of her lashes.

An air of heightened excitement eddied round the room at this new, unexpected development. Jaded gamesters tilted back their straw hats to stare. High-class birds of paradise and raddled society *grandes dames* alike peered curiously from behind their painted and lace-trimmed fans. Into the brief silence blew a flurry of whispered asides.

*"Rescued the climbing boy himself. They say he whipped the master." "Apparently, he's no stranger to the Round-house at St Giles. Locked up overnight with common thieves more than once." "They say he found an escaped slave begging on the streets, set him up as an apothecary, no less."*

Captain Dalgleish drew the attention of the whole room inexorably towards him with all the natural and unconscious ease of a magnet pointing a compass northward.

In common with everyone else, Isabella stared. When she had first heard tell of him he had been new to town, as famed for his daring exploits on the battlefield as he was infamous for his public condemnation of the American war in which he had fought. Now he was just as notorious, but for his hell raising. Ewan Dalgleish was not a man who lived by society's rules. A rebel in every sense, she thought enviously. Why on earth would he want to cover her bet? But unless he did—no, she would not allow herself to think of the consequences of failure.

She watched him covertly as he placed a roll of notes onto the table. He was tall, with his coat cut in the new fashion buttoned tight across his chest, showing off the breadth of his shoulders, the severity of the rich black velvet cloth lightened only by the glimpse of a dove-grey waistcoat, the fall of white linen with just a hint of lace at his throat. The deep copper of his hair glinted bright as a new-minted penny in the candlelight. It was a memorable face. High cheekbones with a small scar visible on the left one, a sabre cut no doubt. A strong, determined jaw. His colouring gave him an untamed look. The perfection of his tailoring somehow served to draw attention to the muscles hidden underneath. A mountain lion, Isabella thought with a shiver. Strength and power barely concealed under a veneer of sophistication. A fierce Highland warrior in the sober garb of a gentleman.

She smiled at herself for being so fanciful and then flushed as she caught the echo of her smile returned from across the table. For a second she met his glance haughtily, amber clashing with cobalt-blue. An almost tangible current of awareness crackled between them. She dropped her eyes.

"Madam?"

Mrs Bradley's voice recalled her to her purpose. Isabella pushed all of her counters onto the table. The watching crowd craned ever closer for a better view.

The banker's card was a six of diamonds. The *carte anglaise,* the winning card, was hers.

"The lady wins," Ewan Dalgleish said softly in his husky Scottish burr, pushing her counters back towards her and adding the same amount again from his own supply. He had just lost a fabulous amount, yet it seemed he was content to do so. A quirk of his mouth, a quizzical eyebrow formed the unspoken question.

Isabella took a deep breath and returned the entire total to the table, raising an audible gasp from the audience. It took all her courage, such a fortune as she had before her, but it would not yet suffice. Coming up short was not an option. A life depended upon it. Heedless now of everything but the game Isabella clenched her hands together. *One more turn of the cards. Just this one.*

Ewan did not take his eyes from her. Her face was a mask of concentration, her eyes focused on Mrs Bradley's hand, which rested on the dealing box. Whatever she was playing for, it was not the thrill of it. He was conscious that a part of him wanted her luck to hold, no matter that he would be the poorer by thousands.

The cards were dealt and the colour drained from Isabella's face as they landed face up on the baize. A small sound, like steam escaping from a pot, hissed round the table.

She had not even a stake left with which to continue. Blindly, Isabella got to her feet. The gilded chair on which she had been seated fell backwards. The lace at her elbow had become entangled with her fan. *Her gloves...where were her gloves?*

Suddenly, he was there in front of her, handing her the gloves and her wrap. He took her arm firmly. "Come with me."

"No, no, I…"

But it was to no avail. A strong hand guided her away

from the curious faces of the onlookers. She was propelled out of the crowded room and into an unoccupied one across the passageway.

Ewan closed the door behind him and pressed her onto a chair by the fire. A glass of fiery spirit the same colour as his eyes was handed to her. "Drink this," he said firmly.

Isabella drank. The brandy made her gasp, but it also revived her spirits. She took another gulp.

"Slowly, take your time."

The amusement in his voice served to rile her. Defiantly, she drained the glass. "What does it matter if I'm drunk? You've already made me penniless."

"It was your choice to play so high, not mine," he said pointedly. "If you are now penniless, you have no-one but yourself to blame."

The truth of the remark hit her like a deluge of ice-cold water. Isabella slumped back in the chair. What had seemed, when she started out tonight, like an inspired solution to her problems, had left her worse off than before, for now she did not even have her pearls.

"You are right. I beg your pardon," she said, shakily placing the empty glass down on a side table. "You are the winner, and I the loser." She rose to leave.

"You don't have to be." It was a crazy notion, but he felt fate had sent her to him. He could see his own concealed desperation reflected in her beautiful eyes. And something else. Defiance in the face of defeat. He recognised that, too, from the battlefield. Unusual in a woman. Admirable. And very, very desirable. Like a call to arms.

Isabella eyed him uncertainly. "I've already given you all my winnings. I have nothing else to offer."

He towered over her. There was an animal grace in the way he moved. She was conscious of the palpable maleness of him. His laugh was like a low growl of pleasure. It made the hairs on the back of her neck stand up. "The sum you've lost means nothing to me. In any event, I'll wager you have much more need of it than I."

Her smile was twisted. "You can have no idea."

A long finger under her chin. Amber eyes looked deep into her own. "You can have it back if you agree to my terms."

She held his gaze proudly, her heart thumping. "I am not a courtesan. I won't be bought."

Ewan placed the money casually in front of her. "I don't want to buy you. All I ask is that you agree to take part in another, different sort of wager."

Isabella tore her eyes from the money to his face. "What kind?"

Aware he was behaving outlandishly, conscious that his mind was excited from brandy, Ewan eyed her speculatively. Her lovely countenance was flushed. Excitement there was in her striking eyes, in the rapid rise and fall of her breasts. Defiance and daring, too. Beautiful. And highly alluring.

It was an impulse, nothing more. He wanted to see how far she could be pushed. Had no real intention of seeing it through, though he knew deep down even then, that whatever it took he could not let her go. "You spend three nights with me. The outcome each night will be dependant upon the fall of the dice. The winner to decide what happens between us. Anything…" he heard himself say, unable quite to believe he was uttering the words "…or nothing at all, if your luck holds. What do you say?"

Ewan's smile entreated trust, but Isabella was not fooled. He had the look of a lion confronted with a wary prey. She swallowed her instinctive flat refusal and forced herself to think rationally. The money would allow her to fulfil the plan which brought her here in the first place. This was her last chance, and she knew it. In the past three months she had exhausted all other avenues. But what price might she pay in the three nights which lay between now and then?

The man in front of her was a complete stranger, known to her only by reputation, and a disreputable one at that. If he won, and the odds were that he would on at least one occasion, she would have to give herself to him. Shocking to even consider it. Scandalous. No lady in her right mind would. And yet were not the circumstances so extreme as to justify the gamble? Would it not be more scandalous still to let this unexpected final opportunity to provide desperately needed salvation slip through her fingers?

In any event, the fates might favour her and allow her to win all three throws of the dice. She had been lucky tonight, until the last. She might be again. And if she was not? She probed deep, but could find only a strange quiver of excitement at the prospect. What was convention after all, when the stakes were so high?

"Why not, Captain Dalgleish?" she finally said, with a shaky laugh. "I agree to your wager."

He took her hand and raised it to his lips, soft against her skin. "Ewan," he said, "my name is Ewan. And what might yours be, my fair opponent?"

"Belle," she replied instinctively.

"Belle," he whispered. "I would not have had you for a Belle, but it describes you well enough." Now was the time to laugh, to pass it off as a jest. Now was the time to step back. Instead, he kissed her, and in doing so hurtled both of them irretrievably beyond the point of no return.

Gently, he kissed her, his lips cool against her own, his fingers tangling in her elaborate coiffure to tilt her head up. Isabella stood compliant, her mind numbed, conscious only of his mouth, his fingertips, the nearness and heat of his body. She was alarmed by the power she sensed there, yet reassured by the gentleness of his touch. Strangely, detachedly, exhilarated by the sensations he was arousing in her. A craving for more awoke in her but he stepped abruptly back.

"One thing you must know," he said, taking her hand, "I will neither harm you nor hurt you. I have already seen enough cruelty to last me a lifetime. Come then, I'll have them call my carriage."

*What had she done? What on earth had she let herself in for?*

# *Chapter Two*

Sitting beside Ewan in the carriage as they rattled their way along the cobblestones towards the imposing, recently-built mansions of Cavendish Square, Isabella tried to quell her jangling nerves. Whatever happened now, she reminded herself, she had secured the funds she needed. But it was not this, the much longed for achievement, which caused the fluttering in her stomach.

The carriage lurched over a hole in the road surface, throwing her against Ewan. A strong arm righted her. She could see his eyes glowing in the soft light. Nervousness turned to anticipation. Guiltily, she realised that the prospect of winning was not the only option which held allure. She had the sense to realise she had best keep such thoughts to herself.

An impassive servant opened the door to them. Handing over his hat and sword stick, Ewan gave him his instructions in a soft undertone before leading the way to a small saloon upstairs. Long curtains of heavy green damask were drawn against the night. A fire crackled in the grate, the light from the many candles reflected in the two long mirrors hung on the walls between the windows.

The reality of her situation struck Isabella with the force of a hammer. Whatever happened now, it was irrevocable. She was not sure she could go through with it. She knew she *should* not.

Something of her panic showed in her face. "You do not have to do this," Ewan said abruptly. "I will understand if you want to reconsider now, before it is too late."

"No," she said with a defiant tilt of her chin, throwing the last seeds of caution to the wind. "I will not renege on our terms—you need have no fear of that."

"I don't," Ewan replied, confident now that the rules of engagement were understood between them.

His touch sent a shiver up her arm. His extraordinary amber eyes glinted down at her. Desire. Confidence. Knowledge. As his gaze flickered over her face down to the neckline of her dress, Isabella flushed. Her breathing quickened.

"Shall we," he said seductively. "You may have the honour."

Isabella picked up the dice, running her tongue over her full bottom lip, where traces of rouge lingered. "Five," she called, throwing a six and a three. Ewan was watching her, catlike. Devoured. She would be devoured, she thought with shocking relish.

"Six," Ewan called with assurance before he threw. A five and one rolled obligingly onto the table.

Expressing neither surprise nor disappointment Isabella turned towards him, her eyes almost navy blue, dark with the rush of anticipation. "You win."

Without a word he led her from the room, along the corridor and through a doorway at the end into another room. Candles were lit on the mantel, another branch on the large inlaid chest which stood in the corner. A bottle of champagne and two glasses sat waiting atop a small table as Ewan had requested, so confident had he been of victory. A chair and a chaise-longue sat at right angles to each other in front of the grate. Crimson hangings covered the windows. The polished floor was strewn with rugs, soft silk and rich wool. The room was dominated by a large four-poster bed, the hangings of silk damask the same colour as the curtains, the counterpane of velvet strewn with tasselled cushions.

Isabella sat on the chaise and took the glass of champagne he poured, her hands trembling.

"Wait here," Ewan said, opening a door in the panelled wall which presumably led to his dressing room.

She sipped on the ice-cold drink, feeling the bubbles sparkle and burst in her mouth. The unaccustomed alcohol relaxed her. She felt as if she was in a dream, observing herself from a distance. Disconnected. Isabella waiting in the background to see what Belle would do in the fore. She poured herself another glass of champagne, drinking it quickly down.

Ewan returned clad in an exotic banyan of Chinese silk tied loosely around the waist. As he sat down on the chair beside her, she eyed him cautiously. A long muscular leg emerged from the folds. A well-shaped calf. A glimpse of thigh. He was clearly quite naked underneath his robe. Isabella dragged her eyes upwards. A sprinkling of hair at his throat, a darker copper than that on his head. A strong neck. His hair, unfashionably untied, reached his shoulders. It suited him. Like a mane. She tilted back her glass, surprised to find it empty.

Long fingers relieved her of it. "You have a debt of honour to pay. I would have you sober enough to deliver it properly."

Beneath the cool tones his rich Scottish timbre served to threaten and entice at the same time. She glared defiantly at him. She was his prey, but she would not be his victim. "I am perfectly aware of my obligations sir. You have me at your disposal."

Ewan reached out to clasp her hand. Long fingers. Pink nails. Pulse fluttering visibly on her wrist. He kissed it, his tongue touching her flesh. Inhaled the light flowery scent there, feeling his own pulse pick up a beat in response. "Not at my disposal, Belle. At my command."

For a fleeting moment he thought he detected fear in her expression, then it was gone. "And what would you command me do?" she asked somewhat breathlessly, rising to the challenge as he had known she would.

"Undress for me. But do it slowly, I want to enjoy the spectacle."

Isabella stared in consternation.

"You cannot deny me. I won, remember."

That mocking smile of his riled her. So confident he was. Toying with her, she could see that now. It was a game. She could not allow herself to be defeated by her inhibitions. *She would not allow it!*

Ewan sprawled back on the chair. The sash on his banyan had loosened. Isabella's eyes widened as she took in the rapidly hardening length of him nudging against the embroidered silk. He saw her looking. She must not turn away. She tried instead to imagine how it would feel inside her, but could not. A frisson of almost-fear surged through her.

Slowly, she started to disrobe, embarrassed and self-conscious as she tugged at the lacing behind her dress. The silk gown spilled at her feet, leaving her in her shoes and underclothes. Blushing, she snatched a look at him. Broad shoulders, a muscled torso tapering down to where the belt tied, then up to his unblinking gaze. She heard his breathing, quicker surely than before?

Relief washed over her. He liked what he saw—was anxious to see more. *Slow, she should slow down.* Postpone his pleasure. Delay her own unveiling. Turn it into a performance, a contest.

Belle untied her petticoats and bustle, trying to make a

drama of each button and string, stretching and bending to conceal and reveal. Embarrassment dissolved as she gave rein to her instincts, her confidence growing as she watched the effect on her audience through her lashes. Shocking. Her behaviour was outrageous, yet gratifyingly effective.

She stood before him in her stays and chemise, the ribbons of her stockings fluttering against her knees. When he reached for her she stepped back, and knew it for a turning point. She had learned how to tease. Pain and pleasure intermingled. She saw it in his eyes. Felt it take a tentative hold on herself. Ewan was not the only one enjoying her show.

Slowly, she twirled for him, like a dancer on the stage. Posing now as if for a portrait to show off the line of her throat, the curve of her spine, conscious of her breasts rising and falling in the confines of her stays. Discarding her inhibitions with her clothing. A transforming. She was not Isabella stripped. She was Belle revealed.

In front of her Ewan no longer smiled. His face was a mask, eyes golden slits of light, lids heavy. Belle's glance flickered down to his manhood. She had never seen a man naked before. It was strangely beautiful, smooth and curving, like a separate being. She wanted to touch it. To run her fingers along its length. To caress it.

Her muscles clenched in anticipation. Her breath came faster. Ewan's gaze locked onto hers. Watching her watching him. A reflection of desire. And in the reflection a multiplying. Sure of her instincts now, she stepped out of the garments at her feet. Deliberately turning her back to him, she rested her foot on the chaise-longue, provocatively stretching over so that her chemise was pulled tight against her bottom. A shoe removed. Her stocking followed. She could hear Ewan breathing. She could smell her own scent. Salt and spice. Her other foot on the chair. Shoe. Stocking. She turned and walked towards him, the urge to touch was almost irresistible but she managed to restrain herself, presenting her back to him.

His hands on the laces of her stays. His fingers running down her spine, setting every nerve end on fire. She stepped away again. Slowly, she pulled her chemise down. The soft material felt strangely coarse on her nipples. Distracted, she touched one curiously with her finger. It was pebble hard. Amazingly sensitive. She closed her eyes at the spark of feeling. Opened them again as she heard Ewan's intake of breath.

"Sit down and do that again," he said, his voice ragged.

Embarrassment briefly flared. Mortification threatened. Then she remembered; *perform.*

Belle sat naked on the chaise-longue. Tentatively touched her nipple. That strange feeling again. Abrasive. Pleasure and pain. Like the teasing. She closed her eyes as her untutored touch sparked a connection, from her fingertips to her nipples to the knot in her belly and the heat between her legs. The damask covering of the seat had a deliciously abrasive quality. She writhed against it.

"Lower," Ewan rasped.

Her eyes flew open, startled. She must be mistaken. *Surely, she was mistaken?*

He raised his eyebrows, patiently waiting. The tussle for supremacy was almost tangible between them. She would not surrender so easily. He would not be the only one to exercise control.

She knew with shocking clarity what he wanted of her. *She could not!* But to deny him would be to admit defeat. She would not be defeated. In his eyes she was already a wanton, after all. Why not complete the illusion?

Closing her eyes, Belle sprawled back on the sofa. Released from shame by his command, she touched herself. She was in uncharted waters, navigating by intuition, steered by Ewan's visceral reaction. Tentatively, she allowed her finger to slide over the most sensitised part of her, dipping down, inside, then back. Slippery. Swollen. A feeling like waves rolling into the shore, like breakers ready to foam. Astonishing and yet somehow completely natural.

Then, a hand on her wrist. Her eyes flew open. Ewan was standing over her, his face hard planes and rigid control. "Not yet," he said harshly, placing her hand onto his erection.

Belle sat up. Giddy. Disoriented. Edgy. She touched him. Skin like velvet. A pulsing vein running up to a hot tip. She ran her fingers over it, felt him shudder and ran her fingers back down, mimicking the way she had touched herself. Trailing and fluttering. Now cupping. Feeling him contracting against her, feeling the roughness of hair on her palm, enjoying the contrast of his satin smoothness in her other hand.

"Like this," he said, wrapping her fingers around him.

She watched, fascinated by his response to her touch, and smiled with satisfaction at the pleasure she was giving, for in his pleasure lay her victory. She looked down, lest she give herself away, moving her hand more purposefully. Feeling a shifting response in herself she moved closer, grazing her breasts against him.

Ewan pushed her back onto the chaise-longue. Unresisting, Belle lay waiting for his next move. She did not know, but she knew. He had won the throw, and in the end she must capitulate. She did not care, as long as there was an end, and soon.

He pushed her legs apart to kneel between them. He touched her. A whisper of sensation in the delicate crease at the top of her thigh. The heel of his hand between her legs, cupping her as she had him. She pushed against him. Harder, she wanted to say, but didn't. His finger eased her open, as if separating the petals of a flower.

His touch sliding over her, she felt gripped as in a vice. She struggled to breathe. Clenched to resist him. Hold on, she thought desperately, but she wasn't sure she could. Sparks of heat flickered out from where he touched her. She no longer cared what he did, so long as he did. It was profoundly different from her own caress. A change of tone and note.

Ewan plunged his finger deep into the honeyed flesh spread out in front of him, relishing the way she bucked up against him. Relishing the pleasure he could see etched on her face. Exulting in the knowledge that he caused it, controlled it.

Belle moaned, pushed, writhed. With every stroke she curled tighter into herself. She wanted only to complete this journey, to release the clutching, pleasurable tension between her legs.

Ewan rubbed and dipped and stroked. Faster. Then slower. She could not bear to wait. She reached down to grab a fistful of his hair.

He shook her away with a strange smile on his face. Vaguely, she recognised it as victorious. A sweeping, stroking, pressing movement, and she held it, clutched at it like something which would fall—and then she did, holding tighter, taut, resistant, until she could hold it no more and set it free like a bird soaring from her, flying high with a shattering pleasure, moaning, mindless.

Ewan pulled her onto the floor beneath him and entered her with one hard thrust, pushing into the hot, wet centre of her. So tight. So ready. He paused, his breathing ragged.

Beneath him, Belle said something inarticulate, her muscles gripping, holding, urging. Moving again, he was pushing hard into her, thrusting, a welcome sensation high inside her. So hard, questing, pushing in until she was sure he could not go further, but still he did. Her legs lifted over his shoulders. Pulled tight against him. Thrusting, all of him now, all of him, and she could feel every inch. She tried to hold him, feeling her own excitement build again as he moved. Harder. Higher, until she felt she would die of the tension. She wanted to scream from it, and just as she thought she would, it snapped, different from before, a sheer exhilarating drop.

Ewan could not think, his mind filled with the image of her spread out for him, creamy white thighs, full breasts, the nipples hard and dark, black curls hiding the hot pink centre into which he thrust again, oblivious now of everything save his own pleasure, holding her by the waist to pull her into him. Sharp nails dug into his buttocks, long legs curled round him. His eyes were screwed tight shut as he climaxed, pulsing into her, relishing the feeling of power and pleasure and release all rolled into one. He lay spent, breathing hard against the soft white flesh of her body.

Belle felt as if she were floating on a cloud somewhere. Sated. Now she understood the word. She could feel Ewan's breathing slowly return to normal. She had done something irrevocable, but she had enjoyed it. Relished it even.

Ewan raised his head to look at her and smiled. "Come to bed," he said, sweeping her up effortlessly in his arms. "To sleep," he added in answer to her questioning look. "Tonight's wager has been settled in full."

# Chapter Three

He was awoken by the grey light of dawn creeping in through the gaps in the curtains. Sitting up groggily, he was startled to find an extremely beautiful naked woman lying asleep next to him. Then he remembered. Belle. Ewan groaned. He must have had far more brandy than he'd realised. He searched his mind for regret, but could find none.

She lay on her back before him, a picture to drive any man wild with desire. Lips swollen from kissing. Lids heavy and slumberous. Full ripe breasts. Hair strewn out on the pillow behind her. "Perfect antidote, I knew you would be," he muttered to himself.

Slipping out of bed, Ewan threw on his robe and padded silently from the room, closing the door quietly behind him.

Isabella awoke to the appetising smell of fresh chocolate and warm bread. She rolled over in bed, wondering what on earth she had done to merit such an unaccustomed treat. Sitting up, she rubbed her eyes and shivered with the cold, realising with astonishment that she was naked and not in her own bed.

"Charming," a deep voice said.

Ewan was standing by the bed, holding a tray and smiling appreciatively at the vision of her black hair glinting through her powder and tumbling down over her back, her shoulders and her breasts.

Isabella grabbed the sheet, blushing furiously, images of the night before whirling through her mind like leaves in a gale. She had behaved shamelessly. She risked a glance at Ewan, busying himself with the chocolate pot. He looked tired, but showed no other outward signs of last night's events. It occurred to her that *she* must look different, changed somehow. Of a certainty she felt it.

Ewan handed her a delicate china cup patterned with dragons. Isabella took it gratefully, mumbling her thanks without meeting his eyes. She had no idea how to behave.

"I am no more familiar with the situation than you," Ewan said, echoing her thoughts. "I don't make a habit of letting women into my home. In fact, you are the first."

He stood by the bed in a heavy brocade dressing gown, smiling mischievously down at her. In the light of day she could see streaks of gold glint through his copper mane of hair. The stubble on his chin was the same dark shade of copper as the hair on his chest. The animal magnetism which had drawn her last night seemed enhanced by his dishevelled state. Really, he was quite unfairly attractive.

"Belle?"

His voice interrupted her reverie. There was an edge of amusement in it which made her certain she had been staring. She met his gaze. "I beg your pardon."

"I was asking if you regretted our wager."

Isabella eyed him speculatively. "And if I said I did?"

He laughed, sure now that she did not, for there was

no indication of either tears or recriminations. "And do you?"

She shook her head. "I had no choice."

"You prefer the illusion that you are acting under duress. You will not admit you are enjoying yourself."

"The only thing I am interested in is my money," she said firmly.

"You are being less than honest, Belle."

Her winged brows rose. Her mouth quirked. It was as if they were redrawing the battle lines for later, and she knew she had to muster every advantage. "I was your prize. I did as you asked, nothing more."

Ewan remembered now what it was about her which had drawn him to her in the first place. Defiance in the face of adversity. A determination to win against the odds. He liked it. And in the luminous daylight, she was quite simply breathtaking. He was intrigued as well as aroused. "Let us call a truce for now. Have your breakfast, and then join me in the garden. You will find clothes in the chamber next to this one. My sister's. She is recently married, and left them behind when she bought her trousseau." He noted her sceptical expression. "I may have a reputation but I don't lie, Belle, you may count on that."

He disappeared into his dressing room. Isabella took her time, enjoying the rich hot chocolate, nibbling hungrily on the bread and butter as she pondered her own feelings. Had it not been for the extremity of her circumstances she would not have dreamt of entering into such an outrageous bet, but having done so she could not regret it one little bit.

She had secured the funds—that was surely all that mattered. Even as she thought it, she knew it was a lie. Last night she had discovered something shocking about herself. She had relished every minute of what had taken place. The memory of it aroused her now. More shocking still was the admission that she wanted more, and with it the understanding that it wasn't just the physical act she had enjoyed. She had pleasured herself before, but it had never felt like that. So intense. So gratifying. So primeval. Ewan's touch was part of it. Having Ewan inside her was another part—and a very large one, she remembered with a saucy smile.

But it was more than that. It was seeing him wanting her. It was about teasing him and taunting him and flaunting herself in front of him. It was knowing she was desirable and desiring to be more so. A heady mix, made all the more complex by their sparring.

Power was at the root of it all. And confidence. She trusted him enough to expose her secret self to him, though she could not have said why. She knew he had done the same. He was a stranger, yet he was familiar. As if she had always known him and somehow forgotten.

It was with a renewed sense of anticipation that Isabella dressed in a robe *à l'anglaise* of pale blue muslin. With her coal-black hair free from powder, she looked much more like her true self. Last night she had crossed over into a new world. Or so it felt to her. She was surprised to see no evidence of the journey reflected back at her from the mirror.

Tripping lightly down the stairs, she let herself out of a side door and into the walled garden at the back of the house. It was clement for the time of year, with the sun shining high in a pale blue sky scattered with puffy white clouds. A paved path meandered through formal beds, the edges bordered with lavender and thyme which brushed against her skirts as she made her way towards an arbour at the centre of a rose garden where she could see Ewan waiting.

He was looking serious, but rose to greet her with a warm smile she could not but return with one of her own. He was so handsome, and the day was so perfect, and Isabella was so glad to have escaped the worries and sadness of the last few months. She felt released. Free.

"I'm sorry, Belle, but there is something I must ask you," Ewan said as they wandered arm in arm towards a small fountain playing in the middle of a lawn at the bottom of the garden. "What need have you for such a large sum of money?"

Isabella hesitated. "To pay off a debt," she replied cautiously.

He raised his brows. "That is a lot of debt. May I ask how you incurred it? Surely, not through gambling. Despite your best efforts you had not the look of a seasoned gamester."

"And yet, in a sense it is a gambling debt none the less," she said sadly. "My father's, originally. And now my brother's."

"Tell me," Ewan said gently.

They had reached the fountain, a frothy confection of nymphs and seahorses disporting themselves playfully. Isabella sat on the stone basin, trailing her hand in the icy cold of the water. The urge to confide in him was strong.

"My father was always a bit of a dreamer. Always full of hare-brained schemes to make our fortune. When my mother was alive she kept his reckless impulses in check, but she died five years ago and since then—well, suffice it to say he was not inclined to listen to my advice."

"You mentioned a brother. Surely, he had some influence?" Ewan sat down beside her on the stone basin.

Isabella smiled. "Robin is my twin. I love him dearly. We are very alike to look at though not at all similar in character, I'm afraid," she said with a rueful smile. "Robin had rheumatic fever as a child, which left him with a weakened heart. His delicate constitution combined with his natural inclinations make him even more unworldly than our father."

"Leaving you to look after them both?"

"Not any more. Robin is married now. To Pamela, last year. She is a good wife, she nurses him devotedly. They moved to the country when Papa settled an annuity on them, his wedding gift. They are very happy."

"So happy that they did not enquire how your father funded his gift, I gather," Ewan said dryly.

Isabella looked at him in surprise. "You're quite right, they didn't. It was another of Papa's schemes of course. His grand design, he called it. Said it would shape our future. He was certainly right about that." She was silent for a moment, staring off into the distance. Continued in a curiously flat tone, as if reciting something by rote. "The scheme involved buying ships and speculating on the value of the cargo of precious spices and the like they could pick up in the West Indies. I tried, but nothing I said could dissuade him. In fact, the more I begged him to back out, the more determined he became to prove me wrong. He borrowed an enormous sum—privately, of course No bank would have given him the money. He sailed with the ships. They were attacked by pirates. The ships and cargo were taken and Papa killed in the melee." Isabella's eyes filled with pain. "Poor Papa. He may have been foolish but he only wanted the best for us."

She straightened her back and shrugged her head as if to cast off unwelcome thoughts. "That was some months ago. As his heir, poor Robin inherited the debt, which is far beyond what could be recovered by the sale of his property. He has tried, God knows, to find some means of generating sufficient funds, but without success. Now we have run out of time. We have until the end of the week, or Robin will go to prison." She swallowed, brushed impatiently at a tear. "The doctor has made it clear my brother would not survive the harsh conditions of prison. It is as good as a death sentence. So you see, I had to do something."

"Does your brother know of your actions?" Ewan asked harshly.

"No, no, of course not. I will think of some tale to satisfy him, you needn't worry."

"He does not deserve you," Ewan said, anger on her behalf warring with a kernel of guilt. With her hair unpowdered and her face free of rouge Belle looked younger and far more innocent than he had taken her for last night.

"I won't have you judge my brother," Isabella said vehemently. "You know nothing of him. And I won't have you judge me, either."

Ewan disarmed her by kissing her hand. "I would not dream of judging you. You have my deepest admiration, Belle. It is myself I would judge."

"I don't regret last night if that is worrying you. I have already told you that." Unwilling to have him question her motives further, for she was not ready to examine them herself, she gave him a challenging look. "Do you?"

Here at least he was on firmer ground. Ewan smiled. "Not if you don't. I knew the moment I saw you that we would give each other pleasure."

She blushed. "Don't be ridiculous."

"Come on, Belle, you felt it, too, admit it."

She shook her head, turning aside to hide her smile. "That is the second time today you have tried to make me do so, but I won't. I needed your money. That is what I found attractive."

He touched her, a finger on the shell of her ear. His voice became low and husky. "You wanted me as much as I wanted you. I felt it in your kisses," he whispered, his mouth on hers. "And in your touch," he said.

She brushed his hand away. "You are quite right, I did," she said, looking at him with the determined tilt of her chin he already knew well. "It was not just your money I wanted, it was you. But not for the reason you think."

"My instincts tell me you are about to launch an attack. Yet still I would know. Tell me," he said with a sardonic smile.

She crossed her arms defiantly. "It's simple. I was curious. I am four and twenty, with no prospects. I do not want to die a virgin. I wanted the experience without creating an obligation. The terms of our bet made that possible."

He had known, of course he had known, that he was her first. It was inappropriate, but he could not help it. He was gratified as well as confused. "You should have told me. I would not have…"

"What," she interrupted, anxious to stall the guilt she saw looming in his eyes, "what would you have done differently? I knew the risks. I accepted the odds. I put up a creditable performance—at any rate, you seemed to enjoy it. That is what it was, though, a performance." She shrugged with what she hoped was nonchalance and turned to go, but a strong hand on her arm wiped the triumphant smile from her face.

"I wonder, though, my lovely Belle, why you waited so long? Had you made your need for a candidate to deflower you known, any man on earth would have been willing. Yet you chose me. Why?"

She licked her lips nervously.

Ewan laughed. "Take some advice from an experienced campaigner and retreat while you're ahead, Belle."

Isabella glared at him furiously, but could think of no retort.

Ewan took her arm. "It's gone one o'clock," he said, his tone more conciliatory now. "I find a night such as the last makes me uncommonly hungry. Let us go in search of sustenance."

With her nose studiously in the air and her temper simmering, Isabella walked with him back to the house.

But it was not in her nature to sulk, and over a repast of

cold cuts and hothouse fruits, Ewan set out to charm her. Since he touched not on the personal, and his opinions happily coincided with her own on an astonishing number of topics, this he did very well. He had a dry humour and pithy wit which Isabella found most invigorating. He made her laugh. She realised it had been many months since she had done so. His tales of his army days were fascinating, recounted with a modesty and humour which made her warm to him all the more.

"You're very self-effacing about your exploits," she said teasingly. "I had heard you were quite the dashing hero."

"I prefer to let my actions speak for me, rather than words," he replied with a shrug.

"Tell me," she asked, "what turned you into such an avid supporter of Mr Fox and the Colonists—Americans, as I believe they like to be called? Having fought so loyally for the King, it seems a rather paradoxical stance to take."

"Some would even say traitorous," Ewan said bitterly.

"Not I," Isabella said firmly.

He looked at her searchingly. "Thank you for that."

Silence reigned for a few moments and Isabella held her breath, aware that the matter was important to him and deeply personal.

"I suppose it started at Bunker Hill," Ewan said in a low voice. "I was just twenty, too young to question why I was there, nor to doubt that I was fighting on the right side. We won, but it was a pyrrhic victory, the casualties were severe. You can have no idea how…"

His grim expression bore testimony to the dark memories crowding his mind. Isabella took his hand.

"Anyway," Ewan continued, "it was horrible for both sides. And that's when I began to realise it was wrong, too. We British were the trespassers, the usurpers. I realised that, but I could not do anything about it. Soldiering was my life. Loyalty to my colonel unquestioning, even if I did question the cause. Then our old enemies the French joined the Americans, and confused the issue. It was only years later, after Washington took our surrender in Yorktown, that I had time to sort out my feelings. And only when I left the army could I speak my mind without being disloyal."

"You certainly did speak your mind," Isabella said, remembering that even her father had called Ewan a turncoat.

Ewan shrugged. "Much good it did. I was cut by a number of my comrades. I featured in one of Mr Gillray's caricatures as a wild Scotsman in a kilt, and now Fox looks like he'll be stuck in opposition to Mr Pitt for the rest of his life."

"Have you no desire to take a more active part in politics?" she asked curiously.

Ewan shook his head. "Words and posturing are not for me."

The ormolu clock interrupted their conversation by striking five, taking them both by surprise.

"We should take the opportunity to rest before dinner," Ewan said with a wicked glint in his eye. "With any luck it's going to be an eventful night."

A frisson of pure anticipation coursed through Isabella's veins. What would the fates have in store for her this time?

# Chapter Four

Belle dressed simply for dinner in a gown of pale green muslin worn open over a white slip, the sleeves tight to her elbows, below which the ruffles of her chemise billowed. Green ribbon formed a sash around her waist, and was also tied artfully into her hair, one long ebony curl allowed to trail over her shoulder. She studied her reflection in the long mirror with satisfaction. *Au natural,* a veritable milk-maid in the style made popular by Queen Marie-Antoinette. With a frisson of excitement she headed downstairs to the dining room. Whether she won or lost, she was determined to have Ewan in a fever of wanting.

He was different in the candlelight. Less approachable in his dark evening clothes. More self-contained. She felt a quiver of apprehension. Or was it some less admissible emotion?

They sat adjacent to each other at the oval table. Ewan dispensed with the servants and served her himself. She took claret, he burgundy. Roast woodcock met with her approval. Expertly, he carved the game bird and placed a portion on Isabella's plate.

White teeth nibbling on the tender meat. Fingers first

licked, then sucked clean, one by one. A luscious mouth dabbed delicately with the table linen. A glimpse of pink tongue. Ewan shifted uncomfortably against the high back of his chair, feeling himself stiffen against his breeches. He could not but help imagining her mouth on him. Licking. Sucking.

"What have you in mind for me if you win again tonight?" she asked, fixing him with her gaze.

He grinned. "It does not do to depend upon winning, for that way disappointment lies."

"So you would be disappointed if I win," she teased.

"I would not be the only one."

"Sir, you flatter yourself."

A hand grasped her firmly by the chin. "At least I am honest with myself, Belle. I want you. If I win the throw I will have you, and you will be willing. But if you win, what then? 'Twill be a frustrating night, for you will spite us both."

She pulled back, anger sparking in her eyes, not wanting to hear the uncomfortable truth. "For you perhaps. I told you earlier, you have already served your purpose for me." She pushed back her chair impatiently. "Come, let us settle it at once then, since you are so clearly unable to wait."

Ewan laughed softly and followed her wordlessly upstairs to the small saloon where the dice box lay waiting on the table.

Isabella looked blankly at the dice when they stopped rolling. "It seems you have won, Captain Dalgleish. Once again, I am at your disposal. What would you have me do this time?"

"Come here, Belle." He could see her breathing through the thin muslin of her dress. A long curl, glossy black, trailed down over the white skin of her neck. So lovely.

She stepped closer. He smelled of clean linen and soap,

a hint of wine on his breath. She looked up, found his lips close, felt his breath warm on her cheek, an arm snaking round the ribbon at her waist. She could feel her nipples harden against the cotton of her chemise. Wanting flared in her, a need she had not known until yesterday and which since then had stubbornly refused to subside.

Her wrists were captured, tugged tight behind her back. She was pressed close to him, chest to chest, so close she could feel the buttons of his coat digging into her. His smile was cruel but she was not frightened.

"So I have served my purpose have I? You do not dispense with me so easily, Belle. I will make you ache for me."

His words served to boost her determination to deny him. "You may try, but you will not succeed," she said with a taunting smile. "There is nothing singular about you, Captain Dalgleish. What you can give me, I don't doubt I could have from any other man of my acquaintance. You said as much yourself."

"As I also pointed out, you chose to wait for me," he reminded her. Her wrists were released abruptly. Ewan strode over to the door of the saloon. The lock clicked home.

He moved purposefully towards her. "Turn around."

The ribbon from her waist was untied and placed around her eyes as a blindfold. "What are you doing?" Belle asked, a tremor in her voice.

"Proving a point. Since you cannot see me you are free to imagine me whichever man of your acquaintance you choose. But you will not be able to, Belle. No matter what you may say, I know you want only me. And you will admit it."

"I am at your command. I will say anything you would have me say."

"No, Belle, you will say it because it is true."

Strong hands on her. Her dress untied. Her petticoats, her stays, her chemise, all expertly removed. The pins taken from her hair. She could feel it cascading down her back. She stood, vulnerable in her stockings and slippers, unable to see, afraid to move, yet unafraid.

"I won't say it because it isn't true," she said, knowing she was lying, knowing he knew it, too, knowing that the battle of wills enhanced the wild excitement of the battle of the flesh.

Nothing happened for a few agonising seconds. Time seemed to stand still, the sense of anticipation almost unbearable. Suddenly, she felt a hand touch her head, long fingers combing through her hair, fanning it out over her shoulders. He was standing behind her. She could feel the cloth of his coat. His mouth on the nape of her neck. Cool lips on hot skin, on the lobe of her ear, trailing kisses down to her shoulder. Fingers kneading her flesh. Hands reaching round to cup her breasts, trailing down to the curve of her waist, a tantalising flicker on the soft skin at the top her thighs. Belle stood motionless, her mind floating, empty of thoughts, allowing sensation to take over. Cloth on skin. Cool on heat. Dry on wet.

Ewan guided her towards a sofa and arranged her there on her stomach, running his hand along the perfect contour of her spine, curling into her waist, curving out to her bottom. Such skin, such softness. Curves and flesh, all so different from his own. She smelled of flowers and spice. As she shifted restlessly under his caress, he caught a glimpse of black curls curtaining flesh darkened by arousal. Desire twisted like a knife in his gut.

Quickly, Ewan divested himself of his clothing. To take her, possess her utterly was what he most desired. But first he needed her, more than he cared to admit, to put the evidence of her own desire into words.

The delightfully ticklish sensation of something

unbearably light being trailed over her back raised goose bumps on already over-sensitised skin. Belle shifted on the sofa. Between her thighs now, whispering down, on the backs of her knees, her ankles. Back again. She arched her bottom up, pressing her knees into the sofa to give her purchase, inviting the soft caress back, down, between.

A quite different sensation now. A tongue, licking down the curve of her bottom, velvet soft, dipping into the curve of her thighs, away again. She tried to imagine another man as he had commanded, but it was impossible. She did not need to see him. Her body knew it was Ewan. Could only be Ewan.

Something else now, playing on her skin. Silken, hard, nudging against her thighs. "Ewan," she said, arching against him.

Cold space. "Say you want me, Belle," Ewan whispered.

Silence.

His erection was nudging against her, sliding against her. She felt the tip of him part her. Feelings almost painful in their intensity. Deprived of her sight it was as if all her other senses were enhanced.

"Belle?"

Silence.

Cold again. She was turned over. Sprawled on the settee, one leg trailing on the ground. She wanted to touch him, reached out blindly for him, found her hands pushed away.

Her legs parted. That tantalisingly ticklish sensation again. A feather…that was it. On her thighs. Between her thighs. Brushing her heat. Tickling her curls. Now fingers doing the same. Now a gentle breath. His tongue. *Oh,, his tongue.* Licking her thighs. Closer. Flickering round the edges of desire. Then not round the edges. A gentle touch… too gentle. A sweeping movement now, hot on hot, wet on wet. Such sweet pleasure, she was melting. Belle pressed herself against his mouth. More.

Instead, his voice, insistent now. "Who is it you want, Belle?"

Edgy, he sounded edgy. Passion, but it could be anger. She could not tell. She bit back the urge to plead with him.

Tongue and mouth again. Sucking and licking. Twisting and clenching. Throbbing. She was so close. He stopped. "Ewan." Her voice was husky with passion and need. Her fingernails dug cruelly into his shoulders. "Ewan, for heavens' sake, I want you. Now." Co-operation, not defeat. There was a limited pleasure in resistance and she had expended it.

For what seemed like eons nothing happened. Belle waited impatiently in the enforced darkness. Then suddenly he was kissing her—a hard, insistent kiss. She could feel tension in his shoulders but it was not anger. He was as desperate as she was. All of a sudden, she wanted to give him what he needed. "I chose you. I wanted you last night. I did not care about the bet. I want you now."

The blindfold was torn from her, and she saw amber eyes gazing at her, dark with passion. A mouth sculpted into a victorious smile. She cared not, secure in the knowledge that she possessed him as much as he did her. Her nails dug harder into his flesh.

Ewan knelt between her legs. No teasing now, he licked her roughly, unerringly, tugging and sucking with just enough friction to drive her into a frenzy, pulling her hard against his mouth as she climaxed, pulsing into him, onto him. Waves turned to ripples and he licked again, turning the tide back from ebb to flow, pulling her to her feet, bending her over the sofa. She could feel him behind her, the hard length of him nudging against her.

Ewan rubbed himself against the perfect white cheeks

of her bottom, his hand cupping her, feeling her rippling, so achingly arousing on his palm. He could see her, dark pink and wet as he entered, slowly, pushing in between layers of heat and damp, her muscles pulling him in, feeling her parting, gripping, holding him as he pushed in and in and in, all the while watching himself as he thrust into her, feeling as if every fibre of his body was being set ablaze.

Belle clung to the back of the sofa. Her knees were pressed against its edge. Ewan's legs pressed into the backs of hers. Rough hair. His breathing heavy. His hands clutching. Higher than before he was going, more and more until there was no more and he paused tantalisingly. She pushed back against him, gripped him, experimentally rocked back and forth, loving the way even such a tiny movement rippled inside her. He felt thick and hard and high.

Ewan withdrew then plunged in again with that same deliberate, excruciatingly exciting slowness. It became another battle; the need to keep him inside her, to stop him withdrawing, to hold him. And she was winning. He was thrusting harder now, faster. She could feel the delightful slap of him against her bottom as he bucked. She could tell from the way he seemed to expand inside her that he was close. She felt her own muscles contract in response. An echo of her climax or a continuation or something new, she didn't care, except it whirled her away unexpectedly, and immediately she felt him shuddering in response, a thrusting becoming a pounding becoming a release, and she felt him spilling into her and she moaned his name without realising, holding him vicelike to feel and feel and feel as he spent himself.

Afterwards, he was tender, sitting her down beside him on the sofa, holding her close, stroking her hair as she nestled into the hollow of his shoulder. They sat thus for a long time, neither willing to break the spell. Later still he took her by the hand and led her to the bed chamber. They lay in the dark together under soft cotton sheets gazing without seeing.

"Is Belle your real name?" Ewan asked unexpectedly.

"Why do you ask?"

"A feeling. At times—these times—you seem to be Belle. But in the day when I speak your name, you look at me as if I am talking of a stranger."

"You're right in a way." She felt as if their love-making had reshaped her. "Belle is a shocking creature. She has dark thoughts and dark needs. Isabella, my real name, the real me, knows nothing of them."

"Isabella. I like it—it suits you. We all have a dark side," Ewan said softly. "It's just that most people do not have a name for it."

"Some abuse it," Belle said with a shiver.

Ewan pulled her close. "Yes, some do. I have seen it in the aftermath of battle many times. But that is not what I meant."

"No, you meant what we have together," she replied with growing understanding. "We clash because it enhances the defeat as well as the victory. Like tonight, there is as much pleasure in submission as there is in domination. Provided we both stick to the rules, of course."

Ewan ran a possessive hand down her spine. "That is it exactly. I knew when I saw you that you would understand me, though, I could not have articulated it so. And you knew, too, you will admit that now?"

Belle smiled into the dark. "Why not? You won after all," she teased.

"Yes, I did. And I am not finished with you yet," he said with a growl, pushing her onto her back.

Afterwards, she slept deeply and dreamt she had been shipwrecked, drifting at sea alone. In the distance, at last, she could see safe harbour.

# Chapter Five

She awoke in the morning alone and feeling strangely contented, as if she had emerged from a dark tunnel into the light. New. Replete. For the first time, Isabella examined Belle cautiously in the light of day, like a scientist surveying a new-found species. Alien but familiar. Part of her, once caged, now set free by this game of theirs. Like an alchemist, Ewan had conjured something new from two separate elements.

Something destined to be short-lived, she realised poignantly. After tonight it was a part of her which would forever go unnourished. Without Ewan, Belle would surely wither and die. The thought squeezed her heart, and she banished it. Plenty of time for pain on the morrow.

After dressing, Isabella found Ewan in the library reading *The Spectator*. He held out his hand in greeting, looking much younger in the daylight, almost boyish. Welcoming. She remembered her dream. Here was a man to keep confidences. A man to trust. A man of integrity, so different from the dark soul she crossed swords with at night. And yet…

Two Ewans; one for Belle, the other for Isabella. Opposite

sides of one coin. Like her. Exactly like her. Like an animal with hibernation in mind, she stored up this comforting crumb for the bleak months ahead.

Wandering aimlessly about the room, Isabella spotted a large map of America laid out on the desk. "Is this the New World?" she asked excitedly. "Tell me about it, Ewan."

He described cities and plantations, a land of contrasts and plenty. "But no words can convey the sense of space the sheer size of it," he said with a sweeping gesture.

Isabella ran her finger over the vast empty space to the west of New England. "The Frontier, they call it. Think what that could mean. The chance to start afresh, without the prejudices and constraints of England."

"That is precisely why the early settlers went there in the first place. But it is a life of hard work and many dangers, too," he cautioned.

"Think of the rewards, though," Isabella said with a glowing smile.

"You are serious," he said wonderingly.

Her smile faded abruptly. "A dream, that's all." She was silent, frowning down at the map. "As a woman, I am allowed no ambitions," she said bitterly. "But you can do anything you want. You are marking time with your hell raising I think, but it does not satisfy you, does it?"

"You're very perceptive. It's not the danger I miss, nor even the battles—it's the challenge, the unpredictability. I had forgotten what that felt like until I met you."

"Your dark side," Isabella said, flushing. "You will need to find another outlet for it after tonight."

He was hurt. "And you, too," he said roughly, testing her reaction.

She shook her head. "Tomorrow, perhaps even tonight if I win, Belle will be gone forever."

"Don't talk like that," he said, putting a hand on her wrist.

She brushed him away. "This is not real life, what has transpired here between us. It is a game. A necessity for me, a diversion for you." She stood, brushing out her skirts, and left the room, seeking refuge in her chamber. She would not give house room to this stupid sentimental feeling the day-time Ewan aroused in her. He was her adversary. For if he was not, then what was he?

The question would not go away. As she bathed and dressed in an evening gown, as dusk fell and night ascended, Isabella and Belle waged war in her mind.

*It's ridiculous to imagine an acquaintance which can be measured in hours could amount to anything important. I hardly know Ewan.*

I know the important things. I have known those since almost the moment I set eyes on him.

*Extreme circumstances brought us together. I am here only to save my brother.*

I came here for Robin but I am staying for my own reasons.

*I am simply in thrall to my own passions then...that is it, surely?*

This chemistry between us is a symptom, not a cause. My passions are the result of my feelings, not the other way around.

*So I am in love with him?*

Yes, I am in love with him. Deeply, irrevocably in love with him. There, it is said!

*I am not foolish enough to think my love returned, though.*

No. And I do not want his pity, either.

*My opponent he must remain then, Isabella said.*

My opponent, Belle agreed sadly.

But by the time Belle faced Ewan over the dinner table, her mood was black. She would be gone in the morning.

She wished she could be sure Ewan would miss her. She wished she did not care whether or not he did. She wished she could stop wishing. She cut viciously into the capon on her plate.

"You have the look of someone with a hunger food won't satisfy."

His words cut into her thoughts. He was not smiling, but he was laughing at her all the same. Pettishly, she pushed her plate away. "You flatter yourself if you think it's you I hunger for," she snapped. "You are a skilful lover, and you have taught me a few tricks, but I am a quick learner. I don't need you. Rather it is you who has need of me."

Her words were meant to hurt him. He knew that, but they hurt all the same. He could not read her mood. When she had left him earlier, he told himself it was part of their game. But she was still angry; so angry with him, and he did not know why. With the curtain up on their final act, it was as if he was in the wrong play. He had not thought of the ending, but he did not want *this* ending. "Isabella," he said urgently, "it doesn't have to be like this, you know."

"Yes, it does," she said at last. "We agreed on the rules at the outset. And you must call me Belle, not Isabella," she added coldly.

As he followed her for the last time to the upstairs parlour, uncertainty made him apprehensive. He had convinced himself that the fall of the dice tonight was irrelevant. He realised he had been horribly wrong. He picked up the ivories. "Three," he called, for the nights of their wager. "No, four," he amended superstitiously, casting the dice reluctantly.

Belle watched unblinking as they landed. Five and six. When it was her turn to throw she looked at Ewan, not the dice. "Three," she called, and three is precisely what fell.

He could not believe it was over. Striding over to the silver salver standing on the table beside the fireplace,

Ewan poured himself a large brandy and downed it in one draught.

"Slowly, take your time," Belle said, in a deliberate echo of his own words that first night. "I would have you sober. You have a debt to settle, Captain Dalgleish."

Ewan looked up. Blue eyes, alight with something. Mouth curled up in a mocking smile, a direct imitation of his own. "But you won," he said stupidly.

"Indeed I did. Which means that I decide what happens." She crooked her finger and swept imperiously from the room.

Ewan followed, his heart thumping with anticipation. By the time they arrived at the door of her chamber he was already hard. Never had he wanted something so much.

"Undress," Belle commanded him, busy rummaging for something in the tall chest of drawers set against the far wall.

He did so. She turned to find him magnificently naked before her. She caught her breath, allowed her eyes to travel slowly over him, from his flaming mane down past the breadth of his shoulders, his chest, the rippling muscles of his abdomen, his powerful thighs, her breath coming shallow and fast as she took in his aroused state. She forced herself to continue down the length of his legs, the beautifully defined muscles of his thighs and calves. Standing thus, there was no trace of the sophisticated gentleman; he was all raw power and overwhelmingly male. Untamed. But not, she hoped, untameable.

She wondered if it was possible to tease a man in the same way as she had been teased. Brought to the brink of pleasure and suspended there, time and again. She was resolved to try.

"Well," Ewan demanded, more aroused than abashed by her scrutiny. "Do I pass muster?"

"You are a fine looking specimen," Belle said dismissively.

He laughed, genuine amusement rippling through his stomach muscles, making his eyes crinkle attractively at the corners.

She could not help it; she returned his smile.

"Come here, Belle."

His words brought her up short. "No! It is for you to do my bidding tonight. Lie on the bed."

A quizzical look, but he obliged. "What do you plan to do with me?"

She looked down at him, trying to etch his image in her mind. Anger gave way to tenderness. Desire, as ever in his company, lurked in the wings ready to take a leading role. "Tonight you are the vanquished. My prisoner. I intend to make use of you. Raise your arms."

Warily, he did so, watching as she produced two silk ribbons, sashes from dresses, he realised, and tied one around each wrist. When she concentrated her tongue peeped out between her lips. He wondered if she knew. He wanted to kiss her. As she tested her knots and began to tie the other end of the sashes to the bed posts, he relaxed. She wanted revenge, but it was not his demoralisation she sought; it was the upper hand. In this dark part of themselves were they not made of the same clay? Tonight, she needed him to resist before he submitted. A reversal of last night. He understood that, too.

Belle surveyed her handiwork with satisfaction. She stood in front of him to unhook her dress, recalling how much he had enjoyed watching her disrobe that first night. How much she had enjoyed it, too. Watching his excitement mount served to increase hers, she had learned. Provocatively, she paraded in front of him, casting silk and lace and cotton and ribbons aside. Naked, she reached up to loosen her hair, stretching her arms above her head to tauten the line of her breasts, watching Ewan through half-closed lids with immense satisfaction. He was positively devouring her with his eyes. A curl of excitement knotted tight in her belly.

Ewan strained at the ribbons. Forced himself to relax.

Belle laughed for the pleasure of it. She climbed onto the bed between his legs. Leaning over him, she allowed her nipples to graze the skin of his abdomen. She shivered at the contact and stooped down to lick him, tracing the line of his rib cage with her tongue. Stopped to watch him.

His eyes darkened with desire. She felt him strain at the ribbons again. "Kiss me, Belle," he whispered huskily.

She shook her head. Leaning over him again, she traced a path with her tongue down his stomach, cradling his length between her breasts, teasing him with her nipples, relishing the feel of their hardness against his silken skin. Down she licked; the inside of his thigh then the other, revelling in the heat and maleness of him, feeling herself tight and wet, aware of his breathing becoming harsh and quicker as she lingered on the crease at the top of his leg.

"Do you like being my prisoner, Ewan?" she asked, her mouth against his skin.

Silence.

Her finger fluttering along the length of him. Circling the tip. Her tongue now, repeating the action, licking her way up, lingering, circling. Ewan groaned.

"Tell me you surrender, Ewan," she whispered.

"No," he managed through gritted teeth, straining at the ribbons.

Belle licked again. More than anything she wanted his hands on her, his lips on her, but that way lay capitulation and she was not ready for that. Not yet. Daringly, she put her lips around him and sucked gently. Silence of a different sort. She sucked again. Breathing so rapid she thought he was in pain. Looked up. Saw his eyes fly open.

"Don't stop."

"Say it," she insisted.

Her lips on him again. He thought he would die with the pleasure. Now butterfly kisses and fingers stroking, her lips again. Now looking at him, demanding. Ewan closed his eyes and looked away, praying she would have pity.

She remembered last night. She could do the same to him. She could have him without allowing him to have her. It was a powerfully erotic image. Ewan was looking at her. She could see the plea in his eyes, though he would not say it. She touched him with her fingers, stroking until she could feel the blood pulse, stopping as it did, glorying in the exquisite pain she could see etched on his face.

She put her lips around him again, drew him in as much as she could hold. Sucking purposefully now, feeling him engorged in her mouth, aware of him straining, breathing, saying her name, but caught up in her own powerful need to control him, feel him, and then he came, and finally she heard him, over and over again, saying the words, *I surrender,* but she didn't care anymore and it didn't feel like a victory; it simply felt right.

She lay on his stomach. She could feel his heart beating hard. She was conscious of her own arousal, and wondered what to do about it. She could make him tend to her as he had last night, but that was not what she wanted. She wanted him inside her. Cautiously, she touched him. Wondering.

A throaty chuckle. "Give me a moment."

She looked up. "Fighting back, Ewan?"

He shook his head. "Simply trying to do your bidding, but I need time to recover. If you untied me, it would help."

But she would not. And it did not take so very long after all.

Lowering herself onto him, shivering as she felt him enter her, satin smooth and hard in contrast to her soft and wet core. Slowly, she sheathed him until he filled her, and she held him without moving.

"Belle," Ewan said urgently. "Belle, untie me."

She shook her head. Even that tiny movement reverberated inside her.

Ewan strained at the ribbons holding him but to no avail. Belle moved again, up, down, slow, too slow, tilting herself forward on top of him, nipples grazing his chest. She was doing something else now, so that he was caught in a vice-like grip inside her. He felt the blood rushing. "Let me go, Belle."

Still she denied him, squirming on top of him, enjoying the friction, enjoying the power she had over him, enjoying the power she had over herself. She lifted herself up again, then down, then writhed.

She could feel herself unravelling. She leaned forward using her elbows for purchase and thrust again. Ewan pushed up to meet her. His eyes on hers, dark amber, watching her, waiting for her, she realised. Finally, she kissed him. Deeply. Passionately. Her tongue hot in his mouth. She thrust, could hold it no longer, came around him, gripping his shoulders, like a complicated knot untying, and felt him climax almost at the same time, so that she was lost, unable to tell which was her and which was he as they fell, glided, and soared.

Little kisses nuzzling her back to consciousness… Abruptly, Belle sat up. Reluctantly, she pulled herself away. She untied him.

Ewan smiled at her lazily. "How does it feel to win?"

"How does it feel to lose?"

"Surprisingly good." He sat up, massaging his wrists.

To her embarrassment, there were red wheals where the ribbons had been pulled too tight when he had strained against them. "I'm sorry," she said contritely. "I didn't mean to hurt you."

He shrugged and pulled her down on top of him. "It's of no consequence."

His hands stroked her back, pulled her close, so close she could hear the thump of his heart. Her head fitted snugly onto his shoulder. How could three days have passed so quickly? Why could not the night last longer? She was dreading daybreak.

"Belle, about tomorrow," Ewan said.

"There is no need to say anything," she mumbled into his chest, unwilling to hear any reminder of their terms or, God forbid, his thanks or his excuses. She would leave without betraying herself if it killed her.

Assuming they were in perfect accord, Ewan smiled contentedly. She was right. There was no need for words to frame something so fundamental. But he would say them all the same in the morning. Unconventional this courtship may have been, but it must be formally sealed. He slept deeply and dreamt of their future together. When he awoke she was gone.

# Chapter Six

"Why did you leave without so much as a word?"

Ewan pushed passed the maidservant and slammed the door of the small parlour firmly behind them. He was clearly angry. It showed in the hard glitter of his eyes, in the rigid way he held himself, leaning against the door, muscles tensed as if waiting to pounce, holding her in a gimlet glare she dared not break.

Isabella shook her head helplessly.

"I thought things were understood between us," Ewan said harshly, pushing himself from the door and closing the distance to her with three long strides. "Last night, you said we need not say anything, I thought you realised—" He stopped abruptly, ran a hand over his unshaven jaw, up to his hair, copper and gold in wild disarray, in tune with his mood. "Isabella, have you any idea how I felt? I did not even know where you live."

She smiled nervously. "We did not get around to such common place information."

"No. What we shared was rather more fundamental," he said, taking her hand. "Luckily, the footman who summoned the hackney for you this morning has an excellent memory."

Hope flickered in her breast, but she could not yet turn it into belief. "We certainly reached a—a frankness in a very short acquaintance which few people achieve in a lifetime."

Navy blue eyes met amber. Each searching desperately for reassurance. It was Ewan who spoke first.

"Two days and three nights that is all, yet I feel I know you. I feel you know me, too."

He was frowning, his mouth a tight line. It was a look which could have been frightening, so fierce it was, but she was not frightened. Uncertainty, need, too, were reflected there. She had never seen him look so anxious. Never heard that note in his voice, not even at the height of their passion. She recognised it all. A reflection of herself.

But still she sought reassurance. "You said last night we had no need for words."

"You thought I meant no regrets," he said, understanding slowly dawning.

She gave a ragged laugh. "I thought you were reminding me of our terms. That you had had enough of me. I could not bear to say goodbye."

A smile lurked at the corner of Ewan's mouth. "Goodbye! One word we will never say. No, it was not that. It was just—something so elemental as we share, it seemed to me sacrilege to speak it."

"Elemental," Isabella whispered. "That is how it felt."

"An irresistible force. We called it a battle, but it was more like an explosion, so powerful it was, that thing which brought us together." He pressed her hand between his, then, knelt at her feet. "We fought for control, when we should have simply surrendered. We are two halves of one being, Isabella. One creation far more powerful than its components. Do you not realise that?"

She knew only too well. *"My face in thine eye, thine in mine appears,"* she quoted softly. "I know that I love you, Ewan, if that is what you mean."

"I look at you and see me. That, my lovely Isabella, is exactly what I mean," he said. "And though our wooing has been rather unconventional, that is what it was after all, a wooing. So I would beg you in the most conventional way to be my wife, for the most conventional of reasons, that I cannot live without you and my life would be empty without you."

She fell to the floor beside him, wrapping her arms around him. "And I must reply in the most conventional of ways that I will, I will, *indeed* I will."

"I love you, Isabella," he whispered into her ear. "A mere three days we have spent together, but we have been meant for each other since the beginning of time."

Finally, his lips met hers. Tongues tangling. Breath mingling. Hot, hard kisses. Arms entwined. Bodies pressed so tight together nothing could ever come between them.

A mere two hours they had been wed. They left on the morrow for the New World.

"You're shivering," Ewan said, running his hands down his wife's arms.

"I'm nervous," Isabella replied. "I know it's foolish, but I feel as if this is the first time."

"It is. Before, we indulged in love-making. Tonight we will be making love. I am as nervous as you are."

Shyly, she untied the fastening of her chemise and let it fall to the ground. She came towards him, white skin, black hair, blue eyes, pink mouth.

"Beautiful," Ewan whispered. "Beautiful Isabella." He ran his hands down the line of her spine to cup the curves of her bottom, pulling her close against him. "My wife. I love you."

"My husband," she whispered, rubbing herself sensuously against him. "I love you."

He kissed her, and his touch sent a jolt of fire through her. Ewan's hair clenched in her hand. Herself pushing, arching her hips into his, relishing the hardness of him against her. He lifted her onto the bed. Touching. Stroking. Licking. Sucking. Her mouth. Her breasts. Down to the heat between her legs. She moaned his name. Began to fall. Then he was on top of her, kissing her, thrusting deep inside her as she climaxed, arching against him, feeling him spill into her at the same moment, kissing, clutching. Calling her name. Calling his name. Drifting weightless, dispersed like a thousand stars into a new sky.

One. They were one. That is how it ended. And that is how it began. In a new world.

\* \* \* \* \*

# THE SAMURAI'S
# FORBIDDEN TOUCH

Ashley Radcliff

## Author Note

Welcome to the opulent world of medieval Japan, where wealth dictates power and social castes are absolute. Here, the land's untamed natural beauty stands in stark contrast to highly ritualized rules of courtship, and an elite few rule the impoverished masses with sword and bow.

In this complex feudal realm blossoms a tenderhearted yet spirited poetess, Miku. Orphaned and alone, she dreams of a love that transcends the oppressive structure of her warlord uncle's luxurious, yet intolerably restrictive, country estate.

Though Miku's journey occurs in a distant land veiled by mystery and beauty, I believe you will find her hopes and dreams intimately familiar. And please join me for future adventures in other equally exotic, sensual locales!

*To my Favorite,*
*who reminded me of all that I'd forgotten*
*and showed me truths I hadn't yet discovered.*

*1183 AD. The windswept mountains of northern Japan. The cultural renaissance of the Heian period is fading as regional nobles, fattened on the abundance produced by impoverished peasants, ignore the growing power of their samurai, hired warriors bound by tradition.*

Miku's breath caught when she realized it wasn't a breeze moving the translucent silk panels that hung across the wide veranda doorway, hiding her chaste beauty from her uncle's garden and the world beyond his opulent estate.

Seated at her low, black-lacquered writing table, she'd first assumed that the shadow moving across the silk *kicho* was merely a wayward cloud dancing in front of the late-afternoon sun. But then the tip of a man's long sword curved against the edge of the elaborately painted golden drapes, and her calligraphy brush hesitated above the scroll. After being banished to her quarters earlier in the day by her enraged uncle, Miku had expected another quiet day writing. But the blade's startling appearance implied something much less predictable—and potentially more dangerous.

Yet danger—as well as love—was something she had only experienced in her poetry. Far from the wanton lifestyle available in the Emperor's glittering court, the cloistered life of an unmarried country noblewoman offered little diversion beyond parlor games. Little diversion for most women, that was.

Miku, however, unlocked her silken cage each day with her calligraphy brush, writing poetry that freed her mind and soul, if not her body. Poetry that stirred her imagination and gave flight to her fantasies. Poetry that her decidedly practical uncle never appreciated—an uncle who now dared to imprison her in her own home for what he called unforgivable breaches of etiquette. Just the thought of his self-righteous pettiness made her free spirit seethe in revolt.

Perhaps soon, maybe even tonight, her dream of a life untethered to the hollow pomp of petty nobility—a life where she was free to be herself, and even appreciated for it—would be fulfilled. Until then, though, at least she had her brush and ink.

But the armed man now standing silently just inches from her was no dream—not even a nightmare.

Miku's mind raced as she contemplated the gauzy screen, her only shield. Her uncle had taken all his servants when he'd left earlier to meet a distinguished—and politically connected—man journeying from the capital city of Heian-kyo. Though he would return the next morning, she was nonetheless alone now as the afternoon shadows lengthened. Alone, except for the single samurai her uncle had left to protect her in his absence. *Or to guard her,* she thought with bitter indignation.

Her uncle controlled hundreds of vassals who worked the wide rice fields surrounding the thick walls of her home. Though lacking the more sweeping national power given occasionally by the Emperor to Shogun warlords, her uncle nonetheless wielded significant local power. And like so many other regional lords, he even commanded a private army of samurai, powerful warriors sworn to do his bidding alone.

The thought of one of these common soldiers lurking so near her private chambers sent a surge of anger through Miku. She had expected the samurai to remain a respect-ful distance from her the rest of the evening, as he had all day—far enough away, in fact, for him not to notice her escape from the manor once darkness fell. But was he now so bold as to step on to her veranda, mere inches from her hidden form?

Miku's eyes fell to the scroll spread open across the lacquered table in front of her. The verse she was compos-ing spoke of cherry blossoms, long considered the most beautiful yet most fragile flower. In her poem, however, one blossom remained open as the first winter snowfall began to drift down, the flower's unexpected resilience against the frost magnifying its pale beauty.

Though her heart thudded wildly, Miku's resolve solidi-fied. How dare this coarse warrior intrude upon her private sanctuary uninvited, regardless of any edict given by her manipulative uncle? All trepidation was now replaced by a sense of smoldering outrage at the armed man's presumptu-ous arrival.

"Speak now, or leave," she said firmly.

There was a beat of silence, and then a low voice growled from the other side of the *kicho*. "I will answer to no one but the Master of this estate."

"The Master is gone, so you must answer to me," Miku said.

"I am aware of his absence and am here because of it."

A chill sharper than the winter's northern wind drove through Miku. So her uncle *had* instructed the samurai to encroach upon her private rooms as dusk fell. She took a deep breath to steady her voice, then spoke again to the shadowy figure concealed by her veranda curtain. "You have invaded the solitude of a noblewoman, and your continued presence is not needed."

A humorless laugh stirred the delicate fabric of the *kicho.* "I will decide what you need."

Any renewed fear the man's words stirred in Miku was quickly burned away by her growing anger toward this insolent stranger who seemed so intent on speaking in riddles. "All my uncle's samurai have sworn an oath to serve him to the death," she said, "and that vow includes protecting me, his only niece. You must therefore guard my virtue as well as my life. And—samurai or not—being this close to me without an appropriate chaperone threatens that honor."

"Your life—and virtue—will both remain in my hands tonight," the samurai said. "Your uncle has commanded that I am not to leave your side until dawn."

The man's uninvited appearance, the unspoken threat of his sword, his unemotional insistence that she had been left at his mercy—all these factors pushed Miku's indignation to the boiling point. Too furious to care that social protocol demanded the thin curtain remain between her, a maiden, and this common soldier, she stood and ripped aside the golden silk. "And I am to have no say in who sleeps in my chambers?"

"I do not plan to sleep tonight," said the man, his dark eyes locking with hers.

The tall, lean form of one of her uncle's finest warriors stood with his back to the setting sun. Though dressed in full military regalia, not even the intricate red lacing and stenciled leather of his plated armor could distract from the man's striking physique. Resting low on the horizon, the sun's fiery orange glow outlined the soldier's broad shoulders and powerful arms. Tightly muscled legs, chiseled as from stone by elite cavalry service, were planted with immovable authority on Miku's veranda. Though he appeared relaxed, the man's muscular power was obviously held at bay only by his recognition of the quiet respect due a noblewoman. This was a warrior, not a gentleman…and his hardened body spoke to years spent conquering and crushing.

As she wondered why a man of his obviously high martial rank would be sent to guard her, the samurai's eyes dropped to take in the white silk *kosode* Miku wore. She wrapped her arms around her body, keenly aware that the flowing, calf-length robe should have been covered with proper outer-garments. *Would have been,* she thought, had she expected anything more than yet another long afternoon sitting alone at her writing bench.

Her skin prickled as the man took in her softly curving frame barely concealed beneath the pale silk. The molten heat of his eyes intensified as they lingered on the exposed skin of her bare ankles, and Miku gasped as a surprising excitement shivered through her body. This man looked upon her as if he owned her, with the bold assurance of a victor in battle assessing the spoils of war.

Never before had a man dared to stare with such unveiled appreciation—and desire—of her physical charms. The realization stunned Miku, leaving her both excited and terrified.

And yet neither had Miku truly felt any of the intense longing her poetry so often described—verses her uncle disparaged as improperly sensual for a noblewoman's pen. Until now…until this handsome samurai's gaze had fallen upon her barely clothed body.

Though intrigued by the surge of conflicting emotions stirred by the man's piercing gaze, Miku reminded herself that he was no elegant suitor, properly versed in the protocol of courtship, for in addition to his long, curved *katana,* he wore a shorter knife at his waist and a bow across his broad back. No, she thought resentfully, this was a hardened soldier trained in warfare. And he had come not to woo her, but to stand guard.

"Why do my activities this evening need special over-sight?" she asked hotly, her suspicions mounting. "You have watched from a distance all day. Why must you stay in my rooms after sunset?"

The man remained silent for a moment as she scanned his jet hair, pulled back from the hard angles of his bronzed face in the formal knot favored by the military caste. He was familiar, she realized. She had caught his brooding, ink-black eyes watching her on previous occasions as she moved about the manor and knew him to be one of her uncle's most trusted warriors, although she had never spoken to him before. He seemed older than her own twenty years, but not by more than another ten.

Her eyes returned to his stoic face, and she noticed the dark shadow of his neatly trimmed beard was softened by a gentle mouth. But his words remained as sharp as the sword that hung across his plated armor. "Your uncle does not want you to forget your place."

"My *place?*" Miku challenged, taking a fearless step toward the armed man. "That is my choice alone."

This self-assured conviction had caused increasing friction between herself and her uncle over the past few months. He had begun to show heightened exasperation at her poetry, with its imaginatively erotic tones. And Miku, in her own right, had started to care less and less about whether her uncle approved of her verses—or that he had recently discovered she'd been sneaking out into the fields and mountains beyond the manor walls. For how else could she be free, even for a few hours, from his suffocating restrictions?

Miku's uncle had accepted the role as her guardian seven years ago with an appropriate sense of familial duty, if not love. But as the months following her parents' death had passed, he had become increasingly strict. Now she hardly dared peek from behind the curtains of his ox-drawn carriage when she traveled to the temple—her only *approved* trips outside of the manor—for fear of his displeased frown. Not that the view of starving, threadbare serfs along the roadside brought anything but grief to her tender heart, knowing she had no power to alleviate their suffering.

Their heretofore quiet battle of wills had come to a head this morning when she'd been caught by her uncle's servants bathing naked in the hot springs of a nearby mountain glade. The old man had exploded with indignant rage and forbidden her from leaving her chambers while he hastily arranged for the visit of an old friend in Heian-kyo, someone Miku assumed would try to convince her of the error of her impulsive, sensual ways.

Yet why would she need such attentive supervision to simply await the arrival of a self-important nobleman to lecture her on the appropriate behavior of a young lady of her standing? An indistinct suspicion crept into her thoughts as she continued to stare defiantly at her captor.

The samurai studied his protectorate carefully, taking in her glossy black hair, loose and long, and her penetrating eyes, sparkling with equal parts curiosity and wariness. On her face she wore none of the heavy white powder favored by so many noblewomen, and her eyebrows had been left in natural arches above her eyes, rather than plucked and repainted high upon her forehead. As he watched her, she impatiently bit a full, unpainted lip with teeth unstained by the black dye strangely favored by other aristocrats for darkening their teeth.

This girl was obviously not just a pampered flower, as he had first assumed. Her independent streak was obvious— and intriguing—and now he understood why the Master had asked him to guard her so closely. He was going to have to be very careful not to reveal anything to her. But it was going to be difficult to hide much from her piercing eyes…and to ignore the thin robe clinging to her body.

"Why did my uncle command such close guard for me this evening?" she quizzed.

"Is more reason needed than the protective love of an uncle for his niece?" he responded evasively.

"More reason may not be needed, unless more reason is being hidden," she replied. If the field of battle were words, Miku knew she could parry anyone, including this mysterious soldier.

The samurai smiled in spite of himself. So this girl was unwilling to let his half answer pass without challenge. Well, her curiosity would have to remain unsatisfied until her uncle's return, he thought.

"My name is Takeshi," he said instead. "Would you prefer that I watch you from here on the veranda, or may I come into the parlor?"

Miku realized that his question, veiled in dignified politeness, actually left little room for true discussion. He *would* be guarding her tonight.

"I prefer that you didn't watch me at all," she said stubbornly, a hand self-consciously trailing across the pale skin at the open neck of her robe, knowing as she spoke that the words weren't completely true. After all, the heat of his gaze had certainly kindled something new within her, novel feelings she might be able to incorporate into her poetry. Why not permit the samurai to stay while she explored these new sensations, at least until she could escape his rigid oversight?

Takeshi smiled again. The Master's niece certainly had more spirit than her repressive uncle. Takeshi had never respected the old man, whose behavior was becoming increasingly despotic toward the peasants who supported his plush lifestyle. And when Takeshi had attempted on several occasions to suggest a gentler approach toward managing the serfs, the Master had dismissed his ideas without discussion.

Although he had the physical and intellectual power to defy the Master at will, Takeshi had not yet done so. Instead, he waited with the patience and strategy of a tiger, knowing the right time would present itself—the time when he would no longer pretend to follow the old man's orders.

Miku glared at Takeshi, his condescending smile of authority again provoking her anger…and suspicion. Something about this samurai's presence made Miku wonder if perhaps her uncle's plans to subdue her included more than just the visit of an aged counselor. Yet while she was certainly no match for Takeshi's brute strength, Miku was still confident that her own wit and cunning would defeat this battle-hardened soldier. And once she had him sufficiently distracted, she would make her escape over the manor wall.

"Perhaps you will join me in a game of shells," Miku said, intentionally keeping her voice light and pleasant. She lowered herself onto a floor cushion behind the *kicho* and indicated he do the same. "My poetry can wait."

If this man must oversee her activities for the moment, then it would be on her terms. He might be accustomed to wholly subjugating all who stood against him on the battlefield, but he had never attempted to bind a spirit as free as hers…and it was a battle Miku felt certain he would not win.

Takeshi moved into the parlor and glanced at the young woman's desk, noting a small scroll embellished with calligraphy. Though he could not decipher the script, the writing revealed an elegant, artful hand. The curving figures flowed down the page in an effortless dance that betrayed her appreciation for freedom and beauty in a way that did not require literacy to understand. This woman was becoming more and more intriguing, Takeshi realized.

"Do not fear being caught playing a woman's game," Miku continued coyly. "No soldiers—save you—remain at my uncle's home tonight."

The taunting smile in her voice made Takeshi look away from the scroll. She lounged gracefully at his feet, her hip-length hair pooling on the floor. Like the swooping calligraphy, the curving lines of her thinly veiled body made the blood within him surge. But admiring her beauty wasn't why he had been assigned to guard her, he reminded himself. In fact, the real reason meant her loveliness would soon be unreachable forever—if he decided not to challenge the Master.

Takeshi slowly knelt across from Miku, setting his sharp-edged *katana* flat on his lap. "It's the most beautiful thing I have ever seen," he said.

Miku blinked, and a pink flush tinged her ivory face. She pushed back a strand of shiny, lacquer-black hair, confused. She had intended to disorient the samurai with her playful banter, yet somehow he seemed to be the one causing her the greater discomfiture.

"The calligraphy," he continued. "It's lovely."

Her eyes opened wide with delight, her plans to thwart his unwanted oversight temporarily forgotten. "You appreciate poetry?"

"I have been told it is the most sensuous art—that it reveals the poet's own soul, laying it bare to be tasted and enjoyed by others."

"Do you write poetry, too?" asked Miku, amazed by how the samurai's words seemed to echo her own deepest musings about the art form.

Takeshi was surprised by how animated the woman had become. She leaned forward now, her face upturned and her lips parted, waiting for his response.

"I am no poet. I have only heard poetry recited and seen calligraphy at the temples I have visited. I cannot read or write," he admitted, wondering what it was about Miku's eager face that made him want to share this secret with her.

Of course, now she would be sure to understand that, like most samurai, he was little more than an armed commoner. While a few soldiers who lived in wealthier urban centers might boast a distinguished pedigree and its accompanying education, he—like most rural samurai—was merely a hired warrior bred for raw strength.

Like the other men in the Master's private army, most of whom were Takeshi's childhood friends, he was simply the son of a local farmer. Takeshi had accepted a martial role instead of following in his father's agrarian footsteps in order to protect his family from marauding bandits who often threatened their fields and homes; his true sense of duty had always been—and remained—to his family and community, not the Master.

But without the approval of the Master, Takeshi would have none of the power and privilege he currently enjoyed. And that approval hinged solely on his ability to swiftly and unquestioningly perform every command the Master gave, regardless of Takeshi's personal opinions.

It was a reality that made him bristle, and yet he had found a way to rein in his own ambitious spirit and warrior's pride—thus far, at least. In due time, perhaps quite soon, Takeshi knew he would move to assert the authority he unofficially held over his samurai brothers, most of whom looked to him—even as they had as young playmates—as their true leader.

And yet unlike the Master, his niece seemed to be genuinely interested in what Takeshi had to say. He was surprised by the twinge he felt in knowing that his illiteracy must disappoint her.

Not that Miku's opinion of him mattered anyway. Not with the plans her uncle had. But not even the cold logic of that truth could douse the growing heat her elegantly curving body and breathlessly parted lips were kindling within him…and the strange desire he had to keep talking with her, to know her better, to learn more about the poetry that moved her so, even though he knew he should be keeping a distance.

"It is of no concern," said Miku, shrugging as if his confession had neither surprised nor dismayed her after all. "There are no words to read in the shell game—only pictures."

She reached toward the clamshells, which were arranged facedown to conceal miniature paintings inside each natural dome. The game required players to match a shell to its second half based only on careful observation of exterior ridges and lines. A correct match was confirmed by the identical paintings of the shells' interiors.

Miku chose a shell and studied it closely, being careful not to turn it over. Her fingers moved above the remaining shells, floating like a small white bird, until she settled on a second shell and placed the two together. There was a small click as the pieces rejoined their original mate. With a smile, she opened the intact shell to reveal matching paintings on both halves.

"Maple leaves!" she said, holding the shell toward Takeshi.

He reached to inspect the artwork. As his rough hand brushed her soft ones, she pulled back, suddenly conscious of his eyes locked on to hers. Though still vexed by his role as her de facto warden, she realized she no longer found his presence undesirable. What was it about this samurai that made her feel an indefinable longing she had never known before, not even in the wild imaginings of her poetry? As a poet, her command of language usually gave her the perfect word for expressing any emotion. And yet now she was left unable to define her feelings, even to herself.

"The play goes to you," she said finally, pulling her eyes back to the shells and trying to still the thundering emotions swirling through her thoughts.

She had written often of love and desire. Although surely this was not what she was now feeling toward a mere soldier—and one sent by her oppressive uncle to guard her every move, no less. No, it must be nothing more than the surprise of his unexpected arrival that made her normally tranquil spirit heave and jostle like the waves on the northern ocean.

Takeshi chose a shell half and rubbed his finger along its outer ridges, carefully feeling each subtle nuance. Then he closed his eyes and placed his hands on the remaining shells, moving across them slowly.

Miku watched as if in a trance as the man's powerful hands glided across the delicate shells, the calloused fingertips seeking out a match. The hands were those of a warrior, hardened and rough, but their movement now was like an artist caressing a favorite sculpture. She was mesmerized by his slow progression across each shell as he gently touched its form before moving to the next.

With his eyes closed and his thoughts focused on the game, Miku realized she had the perfect chance to escape—yet something held her frozen as she continued to watch the soldier. Finally he paused, and his fingers wrapped around a single shell.

He opened his eyes. The young woman was perfectly still, the flick of her gaze from the two shell halves in his hand to his face her only movement. Her breathing had deepened, and a flush had returned to her face. There was a barely audible click as the shell once again became whole, and he slowly held it out to her.

"What do the pictures show this time?" he asked.

She reached for the shell, and, opening it, said, "Plum blossoms."

"Ah, a blushing pink flower against a strong, dark limb," said Takeshi. "Soft and hard, balancing one another."

"You have been dishonest with me," she said, her voice a whisper. "You *are* a poet."

She was leaning toward him, upturned palms cupping his shell. Takeshi reached out to take it, and his hands paused as they covered hers. This time, Miku did not draw away from his touch. So he let his fingers remain.

Her eyes seemed to pierce the depths of his being with their searching gaze, taking in the overlapping tiles of his breastplate, the ridged lines of his helmet and something more—something deeper than his armor. Perhaps this beautiful poet could see what others never had, Takeshi wondered. Perhaps she could look through the battle-forged exterior to the true man beneath—the man he himself had almost forgotten existed, until now.

And without stopping to consider anything further, he bent to kiss her. Her lips received his with a small cry of surprise as she stilled before yielding to his embrace. For a moment, Takeshi's whole world, a hardened landscape of warfare and duty, melted away, leaving only an awareness of the softness of Miku's parted lips and her sweet taste in his mouth.

The skin of her cheek felt like warm silk beneath his rough hand, and he drew her closer to him, pressing her soft body against his armored frame. He tightened a strong arm around her waist, the thin fabric of her silk *kosode* slippery against his touch. Slowly, his other hand ran through her dark hair, gathering it up as his kiss deepened.

Miku trembled as the samurai pressed his mouth against hers, gently at first and then with greater insistence. In all the poetic flights of imagination she had taken at her writing desk and in all her clandestine escapes into the countryside beyond the manor walls, she had never known such a delightful, frightening, all-consuming sensation as the one now tingling through her veins.

He was hard against her, the leather plates of his armor pressing her breasts as his grip around her body tightened. His beard scratched the delicate skin of her face, yet its roughness was softened by the tenderness of his mouth. She felt tiny in the arms of such a powerful man, helpless to fight his passionate advances—yet not wanting to resist, not wanting his kiss to end.

In the embrace of this barely tamed warrior, she suddenly felt safer than she had since becoming an orphan. And yet what more could they ever share than this kiss?

This *forbidden* kiss.

The thought splintered her trance, and she pulled away from him. What had she allowed this samurai to do? Of course her uncle would never sanction such an embrace, Miku realized—but that was of no importance to her. She was not afraid to defiantly take the pleasures he might hope to deny her.

Of much deeper concern was her own choice in the matter. Had she really permitted this relatively unknown man to touch her so freely? After years of being hidden from the world, would she now fall prey so easily to the first man impudent enough to reach for her? Was she not of wealthy birth…and, more importantly, blessed with the richness of a poet's soul? Surely she was not to be so easily had. Her initial anger, which had been melted by the surge of desire his touch brought, was now rekindled.

He watched her in silence now, his eyes pools of impenetrable darkness, but his mouth still moist from her lips. Her hand trembling with both fury and desire, Miku ran a pale finger down the overlapping plates of armor covering his chest.

"My uncle thought he sent a samurai to protect me," she said with an icy stare, "but I see a scaled serpent seeking to devour a caged bird. I wonder that you dare to so boldly approach a noblewoman, the niece of your Master?"

Takeshi had no words for the poet. So he simply stood and, with hands that had just touched her with gentle passion, roughly collected the scroll from her writing desk.

"I thought you could not read," Miku goaded him as she rose to her knees, angry with his impudent kiss—and her own hungry response.

The darkly handsome samurai nodded with a self-assurance she found infuriating and, to her own frustration, intriguing. "You are correct," he said, "but your uncle can. And he has commanded that I not only guard you tonight, but that I also ensure no more poetry is written in his absence. He finds the verses you compose—" his eyes lingered on her lips before returning to her blazing stare "—inappropriate."

"Inappropriate is my uncle's desire to control me," she said. "And inappropriate is *your* desire to…"

Her voice trailed off as a sharp heat burned her cheeks, a blush of anger mingling with the equally consuming flame of her growing attraction toward the stoic soldier. There was something undeniably intoxicating about the samurai's dark, piercing eyes, and she could not ignore the way his powerful body—and equally powerful demeanor—was beginning to make her feel.

The soldier looked down at Miku, his apparent nonchalance in the face of her passionate response belied only by the smoldering depths of his gaze. "Do you truly believe what I want is inappropriate," he asked, his voice a husky whisper, "or merely unexpected?"

Standing above her, his arms crossed with an air of absolute authority, Takeshi held her gaze with the confident look of a man used to complete submission—and one who knew how to enforce compliance when necessary. And yet

Miku's independent spirit was equally unaccustomed to capitulation.

"The life's breath of a poet is her brush," she whispered with quiet fierceness, "and her soul is its ink. You may take my parchment, but you will not control my poetry. And you will never control me."

"That choice is not yours to make," he replied.

Twisting at her waist toward the writing table, she swept up her long-handled brush in one hand. Eyes locked defiantly on her captor, she swirled it languidly in the ink bowl, letting dark paint drip slowly down the bristles of her brush.

Rising to her knees, she turned back to face Takeshi fully. His countenance remained a rigid mask of authority, but she could see his breathing had deepened. Smiling with delighted defiance, she slowly brushed the silky black ink up his bare leg. With a flick of her wrist, she left an elaborately curled symbol on the hardened muscle of his thigh, just below the bottom edge of his armored tunic.

"You see?" she asked, laughter tingeing her voice. "I will continue to create poetry as it pleases me, even if I must replace my scrolls with your bare skin."

His gaze dark and molten, Takeshi flung aside the weighty breastplate covering his torso. His armor gone, the samurai pulled away the light robe that skimmed his muscled body. Unlike the painted shells, the new game Miku had naively instigated was one Takeshi wanted to play—and win.

Miku's brush wavered as she took in his lean form— all of it…battle-sculpted, sun-bronzed and as tense as his war bow. The powerful samurai was obviously not a man to be toyed with. Even without his weapons and armor, Miku knew he was strong—perhaps dangerously so. Yet earlier, his tender kiss and deep-searching eyes had hinted at something much more than just another sword-for-hire. And now he stood before her, waiting.

As Takeshi gazed down at Miku, her brush poised above his naked body, he reminded himself that the embrace of this rare woman could only come at a great price. If he were not careful, he realized, he could risk losing his heart to this willful, poetic beauty—and his life to her uncle, the Master.

But the thought of being touched by that delicate hand, now gracefully wrapped around her calligraphy brush, made his blood surge. The hand that had earlier caressed his face, tentatively at first, then with greater passion as she had returned his kiss. The same hand that, trembling, had traced the pattern of the armor plating his chest…and shielding his heart.

And the look of defiance now smoldering in her eyes stirred his heart even more deeply. A woman of her strength and spirit, one willing to defy the world's standards to suit her own inclinations, excited him, body and soul.

Seeing her breathlessly watch him, Takeshi no longer wished to hinder her poetry. To kneel close to her, yes. To take her fully in his arms, yes. And to allow the stroke of her paintbrush to mingle with the soft caress of her finger-tips on his skin, assuredly yes. To touch and be touched by this perfect woman; to embrace and love her; to subdue her willful spirit just enough to fulfill her deepest desires…this is what he now desired.

Yet doing so would violate his warrior's oath to the Master, who had quite different plans for his niece than involvement with a samurai. Yet did such a petty and tyrannical man really deserve his loyalty? He had never truly felt a sense of duty toward the despicable old man, and perhaps now was the time to cast aside any pretense of obligation.

Takeshi suddenly realized that this maiden's own rebelliousness had already pierced the stoic wall around his heart, the fortress he had thought to be impenetrable. If Miku, a gentle poet, could demand that her will be honored and her desires fully met, then surely so could a worldly warrior like himself.

At once, the thought of even just one night with this alluring poet made the risk of death seem trivial. And one night might be all he could hope to enjoy—for her uncle would surely attempt to demand his life in payment for Miku's chastity.

When he finally spoke, his voice was low and thick with desire. "I will not return your scrolls."

As the sun finished its slow descent beyond the distant mountains and dusk cast a purple glow through the thin walls of her parlor, Miku gazed steadily into the samurai's face. What had started as a game, a way to prove she was in control, had quickly become something far more serious. And far more intriguing. Was this soldier really offering his body—all of it—for her pleasure alone?

With trembling hand, Miku dipped her brush once more into the ink bowl before again tracing it gently up his muscular leg. No longer attempting to write actual characters on his bare flesh, Miku's poetry was now the primal, wordless yearning she felt blossoming within her heart toward this brazen soldier. Though they had just met, she no longer questioned her true desires.

She looked at him fully, her eyes taking in the length of his body above her, savoring the tremulous thrill that tingled through her when she saw him stiffen under her gaze.

Although she had tasted none that evening, Miku felt as if pure saki coursed through her veins. Her skin seemed heated from within, flushed with a growing flame of desire, and her mind swam with a dizzying intoxication more potent than sweet rice wine.

Takeshi looked at her steadily, waiting for her command. Yet who really controlled this moment, Miku wondered?

Their eyes remained locked for a long minute before she lowered her brush from where it hovered above his bare leg.

"Lie next to me," she said, her heart tingling with excitement though her voice remained calm.

She held her breath, wondering if the tough samurai would accept a maiden's directive. But wordlessly, Takeshi knelt, pausing with his handsome face inches from her own. Her breath caught, and she wondered if he were about to kiss her again. She desired his insolence—hoped for a bold and inappropriate act. Yet as she leaned her face toward his, lips soft to receive his embrace, he moved away to recline beneath her.

Disappointment instantly pricked Miku. After boldly stripping away all his clothes, Takeshi would now pretend to be merely an obedient soldier…rather than a man beholden to no one, with untamed desires and dangerous passions? Her disappointment quickly flashed to frustration. How dare this samurai play such games with her?

"I have obeyed," said Takeshi, a knowing smile softening one corner of his mouth, though his eyes remained dark and impenetrable.

"And yet you have not given me what I want," said Miku as she tossed her brush away and glared at Takeshi.

Instantly, his smile hardened into a look of unmitigated hunger. "That is because I am not done obeying," he said, his voice a low with desire. "And neither are you. Remove your *kosode*."

Shocked into capitulation by the abruptness of his command, Miku loosened the silk belt of her gown, allowing the front panels to fall open and reveal her bare flesh beneath. The cool night air from the open veranda skimmed her skin like a dancing koi brushing against a water lily.

"Now show me what you desire," he said, his authoritative tone tempered by longing. The tautness of his muscles as he lay at her knees revealed the depth of Takeshi's inner struggle. Though capable of taking what he wanted at will, he had instead chosen to remain still and wait for her.

Miku leaned down, and, like a butterfly lighting on an upturned flower, her lips gently explored his mouth. Her heart fluttered wildly as she tasted him, the warmth of his mouth a tantalizing invitation to deepen the kiss. And when she did, seeking out his tongue with her own, his mouth responded with a shared passion. Surely, she thought, there could be no greater bliss than the sweet connection of their intoxicating kiss.

He lifted his hands, sweeping them slowly up to her shoulders and pushing back the open robe. Lost in the new delight she had found at his mouth, Miku did not think to modestly resist as her clothing fluttered to the floor, or when his hands moved to cup her full breasts.

No longer was she a noblewoman to give commands. With the sweep of his hands, Takeshi once again captivated his prisoner.

His calloused fingertips began to circle lightly, their touch tracing the outer edge of her breasts. She sighed with delighted pleasure, mesmerized by the gentle brush of his hands across her tingling flesh. And then without warning his thumb flicked across the peak of one breast, releasing sparks of pleasure that shocked her out of her sensual reverie. She felt her nipples tighten and became acutely aware of her position, naked on her hands and knees above him. She realized she could not move her hands to cover her bare breasts without losing her balance.

Suddenly shy, Miku tried to shift away, but Takeshi's grasp tightened around a handful of ebony hair at the base of her neck. He pressed her lips back to his while once more his other hand tickled across the hardened peaks of her breasts. She squirmed with renewed pleasure as he held her in his kiss, unwilling to release his captive. She was his to possess, with no possibility—and no desire—of resistance or escape.

Her eyes fluttered open, and she saw in his gaze a molten hunger. With his unyielding hold on the back of her head, she could not look down at the hand on her breasts but was forced to wait in blind anticipation for the next achingly delicate stroke. She saw heated delight flicker in his eyes each time his fingertips caused a surprised moan to escape her lips.

His fingers continued to tease her breasts, sometimes lightly pinching their peaks until she thought her legs would go weak with ecstasy and sometimes waiting so long between caresses that she would grow impatient and angry, longing for the excitement of his touch. And with each brush of his war-hardened hands, a tingling ache deepened between her legs.

When she had bent to kiss the samurai, Miku had imagined the moment to be hers to dictate. She was the poet, after all, and he a compliant canvas at her feet. Yet Takeshi's firm grip on her hair as he relentlessly consumed her mouth and caressed her hardened nipples told her she no longer controlled this man or what he would do with her. But rather than scaring her, that realization seemed to fuel an even deeper passion. His fingers on her body and his lips against her mouth had unleashed a raw hunger she had never before known.

The ache between her legs was an overwhelming throb now, and, letting her eyes close, she began to slowly roll her hips. Her conscious mind could not fathom what she needed, but her body told her there was a release from the delighted agony she was enduring if only she could open her legs and press her hips against something, against *him*. She stretched her back as her hips continued to sway, giving herself over to carnal instinct as she sought to satisfy her growing arousal. And yet her undulations seemed to only intensify her excitement without bringing any release.

Finally she moaned, her primal sound of delight and frustration a wordless plea to Takeshi. Instantly, he moved his hand from her tingling breasts, wrapped both arms tightly around her and pressed her supple body down to his muscle-hardened form.

Caught in Takeshi's powerful embrace, Miku didn't resist when the samurai rolled her gently onto a nest of silken floor cushions, their kiss never breaking. He was next to her now, his flesh radiating heat as he pressed his torso against her soft skin and slid his hands up the length of her arms, pinning her hands above her head. His grip around her wrists was firm and sure, the touch of a man who knew power and expected submission. It was a warrior's touch, and she had no choice but to surrender to it. Yet the tenderness revealed as his fingertips traced the curves of her palms assured Miku that her lover could release her the instant she requested.

But she did not want him to let her go. She wanted him to possess her, to consume her, to be joined with her forever.

Takeshi's iron grasp on her wrists lightened, and he whispered a gentle warning into her ear: "You will not move. You are my prisoner, and mine to command." Her breath caught as he released her hands, but she obeyed and left them stretched above her, delighting in the intensity of his desire for her.

Takeshi, his black mane of hair falling loose across his chiseled face, slowly slid down her body, his kiss lingering first on her neck, then her throat, and finally taking in the achingly sensitive tip of one breast. She arched into his mouth as his lips closed around her nipple, his tongue flicking back and forth as she writhed slowly next to him in agonized bliss.

As he continued to tease her breasts with his mouth, Miku watched as if in a dream while Takeshi slid one hand slowly around the curve of her hip, down her buttock and underneath her leg, lifting it at the knee and pressing it outward. She was open to him now, and, uncertain of his intentions, she watched as his hand moved to stroke the heated flesh of her inner thigh. Not thinking to be shy, she only trembled with anticipation, awaiting the unfathomable pleasure his next touch would surely bring.

Slowly he released her breast with a lingering kiss and raised his eyes to meet hers. With moonlight reflecting in his dark gaze, he traced the delicate curve of her mouth with his fingertips, their roughness softened by the gentleness of his touch. In instinctive answer to the deep hunger of his stare, she opened her mouth to his caress, her tongue moving playfully across his fingertips as his had just done with her breasts.

His low moan of pleasure told her she had guessed his desires correctly, and she eagerly took his fingers into her mouth, sucking them with a hunger of her own. Finally, with a reluctant groan, he slid his hand away from her lips and down the soft curves of her body. Wet with her kisses, his fingertips lightly caressed a tiny point between her legs. Miku cried out in surprise at the overwhelming sensation that instantly enveloped her.

She pushed up on her elbows, panting with surprised delight, but before she could speak Takeshi once more ran his fingertips across her core. She arched against his hand as sparks of pleasure coursed through her body, then pushed against the silken pillows beneath her as she sought, if only temporarily, to regain control of the explosive desire now unleashed within her.

But Takeshi reached a firm hand around her waist, pulling her back to him. "You are not to move," he reminded her as she struggled beneath him. And despite the gentleness in his eyes, Miku realized he had no intention of allowing her to resist his touch.

She grew still, and his fingers once more traced down her stomach and between her legs. He slid a thumb slowly across her hidden point, the pressure light but unwavering, and she lost the ability—and desire—to fight the intense longing his touch ignited. With a breathless cry of surrender, she fell back to the nest of pillows, the silk cool beneath her heated flesh.

No longer waiting for her to recover from each shock of pleasure his touch brought, Takeshi began to caress her with a rhythmic stroke soon matched by quivering twitches of her hips. Though still gentle, his fingers moved faster and faster until she writhed in abandoned delight beneath him. All conscious thought left Miku's mind as a pleasure more intense than she had ever imagined overwhelmed her. And mingled with that pleasure was an aching need, growing more insistent with each touch.

Whispering into the soft curve of her neck, Takeshi's voice was thick with desire. "Obey me once more, my poetess, and give yourself over to this pleasure."

Miku's lips parted, but she could only moan in response as he lowered his head from the crook of her neck. With a deliberate slowness that caused the ache between her legs to throb, he took one breast into his mouth, his tongue teasing her hardened nipple as his fingertips continued to caress between her legs.

"Obey me," he repeated, and she cried out, abandoning herself fully to the surging waves of pleasure that shattered up from between her legs and washed through her body in a rolling tide of bliss.

She clung to him, desperately afraid that the explosion of sensation would sweep her away. But as the fiery tingle slowly faded to a contented glow, she found herself held tightly as he gently rocked her in his arms. She buried her head against the hard muscles of his bare chest, and he kissed the loose hair that flowed down around her face.

Secure in the protective strength of his embrace, Miku finally stretched and smiled. But when she looked up into her samurai's face, his gaze retained its restless hunger.

"You are not pleased?" she asked, her previously serene face shadowed with confusion and concern.

"A warrior understands the value of patience," he said, stroking her cheek with the back of his hand. "And I must wait a bit longer."

"For what?" she asked, his tender caress causing a smile to blossom on her lips like a lotus opening for the sun.

Takeshi gazed at the poetess in his arms, her naive concern for his happiness piercing the hardened armor of his heart yet again. Was this innocent flower really to be his only for one night? Then it must be a night worth the cost he might be forced to pay. Yet he would take her only when she was truly ready, when she knew the full depths of her own desire. Anything before that would be an assault on the beautiful spirit he had already grown to cherish above all else.

He drew her closer, tipping her head toward the night sky shimmering just past the veranda and open-walled parlor. "A poet should not be concerned with the worries of a warrior. The things of purest beauty, like these stars, are your true focus."

Miku's heart trembled in response to Takeshi's words and to the spangled expanse that enveloped them. How could the night be anything but so perfectly beautiful, she realized, after the moment she had just shared with this brooding yet tender soldier?

As the incandescent moon subdued the distant ocean and drew it inexorably to the waiting shore, Miku knew that she, body and spirit, was being pulled toward Takeshi. And yet, only hours before, he had been relatively unknown to her, merely another of her uncle's sworn mercenaries. Was it something more than fate that had brought them together tonight?

"You have yet to explain why you, the most valued of my uncle's samurai, would be sent to perform such a menial task as watching his insignificant niece?" whispered Miku, her fingertips woven through Takeshi's tousled hair.

"Your significance is greater than you suspect."

Miku's gaze snapped back from the starlit sky to stare into his eyes, surprised. "Explain your meaning."

He paused before answering, and when he spoke his words were measured, the clipped speech of a military officer.

"Your uncle went to meet a man from the capital," he said, his eyes moving from her piercing gaze to the dark shadows beyond the veranda. "An important man. One with many political connections and great wealth. One to whom your uncle plans to give you in marriage. The ceremony will be upon their return in the morning. I am to guard you until that inevitability occurs."

The words bleached Miku's face with shock and disbelief. And then, in the silence that followed his revelation, an angry flush surged to her cheeks.

"Marriage? Tomorrow? When was I to be informed? When was I to meet this man?"

"The Master did not divulge those details to me. He only shared enough to impress upon me the importance of your safekeeping in his absence, and of preventing you from writing any more poetry that might upset your groom's sensibilities. Your uncle's plans for successful political advancement hinge on the felicitous celebration of this union."

But in saying the words aloud, Takeshi realized he could no longer enforce such an edict. He was no longer Miku's guard—for she now held his heart captive. Though tradition dictated he should one day marry a woman of the Master's choosing, Takeshi's heart now acknowledged that his unexpected—yet undeniable—feelings for this maiden might force a confrontation with the old man sooner than he had planned. Before he could speak again, however, his poet sat back, eyes flashing.

"Felicitous?" she said sharply. "There is nothing happy about an arranged marriage to a stranger. A forced alliance with a man I've never met, let alone decided I can love and respect? Never! *I* will decide which man I marry. *I* will decide the man I bed."

She was breathing hard. Anger, shock and defiance surged through her body as she glared at Takeshi, daring him to contradict her.

But instead of demanding her compliance, Takeshi ran a gentle hand down her cheek. She held her breath as his fingertips caressed the edge of her jaw and paused at her throat.

"And who will that be?" he asked, his voice a husky whisper. "Who will you take to your bed as husband?"

Stunned by the directness of his question, she was more surprised to realize she already knew the answer.

Yet while her heart thudded with desire for Takeshi, she also found a growing anger pound within it as well. How could this samurai share such intimacies with her, knowing he must part with her in the morning? Was she nothing more than an evening's diversion, a soldier's plaything to be toyed with before being delivered to the bed of another? Pride filled Miku's heart as she fought to regain control over herself—and Takeshi.

Takeshi watched as a storm of emotions surged through Miku's large eyes before an unexpected detachment seemed to move across her gaze.

"I choose you, of course, my dear Takeshi," she whispered, her words those of love but her voice strangely cool.

"Allow me to perfume my body before I give it to you. I will be but a few moments in my bedchamber before I return to your embrace."

She slipped gracefully from the parlor and into her private chamber, sliding the silken door closed after giving Takeshi one last tempting smile. But the smile fell away as Miku moved quickly toward the room's outer door. Turning back once more to make sure that the samurai had not followed her into the bedroom, she silently slid open its exterior door and stepped out into the dew-wet night—and into Takeshi's waiting arms. Having guessed his prisoner's true intentions, he had stolen out across the veranda and around the side of her suite to recapture Miku.

For a moment Miku's breath caught in her throat, then she fought in vain to escape his tight embrace. "Release me!" she cried, in anger and humiliation. "I will never obey my uncle, or you!"

"I will no longer obey your uncle, either," growled Takeshi, "but neither will I release you."

Lifting her over one broad shoulder, he carried Miku back into her bedchamber and, ignoring her protests, laid her on the sleeping couch. Keeping one arm pressed against her still-struggling form, he reached for several of the silken cords she used to wrap her scrolls of poetry.

"Let me go," Miku cried, unable to pry herself from beneath his grasp. "I will not submit to my uncle's matrimonial plans."

"But you will submit to me," said Takeshi, his voice low and full of authority.

With a deft motion, Takeshi wrapped one cord firmly around her arms, binding them above her head to the top of the couch. Though pulled tightly, the cord's silken texture was soft against her bare skin. Miku gasped in shock, but Takeshi did not pause as he quickly wrapped another cord around her waist. Though her legs remained unfettered, she was in all other respects bound firmly to the bed.

Takeshi looked down at Miku's soft body tied across the silk blankets, her breathlessly parted lips, and her eyes, glowing like fiery embers in the soft lamplight. And in those eyes Takeshi read a burning passion equal only to his own. Pressing one finger across her lips to silence any further protest, he knelt beside her.

"You will be mine as long as I live," he whispered, knowing the words were not the promise she thought them to be, but the ardent declaration of a man who soon might die at the Master's hands.

"I am mine alone to give, not yours to take," she retorted, but the flush spreading across her bare flesh indicated a deeper desire threatened to submerge her anger in a flood of passion.

He pressed his lips to hers, and she fought to move away, but his hands held her face with a gentleness that nonetheless left no room for resistance. With a moan of tormented delight, she finally received his kiss with open mouth, her lips hungry for the taste of him. In her momentary surrender, all thought of the next morning—and the Master's return—faded away from Takeshi's conscious mind.

As their kiss deepened, he caressed her face and ran his fingertips through her dark hair. Miku realized that though he had bound her, she loved this man, and she would joyously now let him possess her completely.

As Takeshi's hands slid across her bare flesh, he moaned with anticipation. He slid onto her, every inch hard and heavy against her soft body. Though part of her willed him never to leave, she still struggled against the cords around her arms and waist, her deep hunger battling with her willful spirit. Though every touch pleased her, she still strained against her bonds, not yet ready to surrender fully.

His tongue curled around hers, and the memory of his

mouth on her breasts made her whimper with desire. An aching desire pulsed through her body, and she instinctively opened her legs, pressing herself against the hot skin of his thigh.

But he slipped away, kneeling again beside her low bed. His lips moved down her neck, delicately brushing the curve of her throat like a calligraphy brush. His tongue traced exquisite characters of his own design, marking her naked flesh as his own. Her skin trembled beneath his touch, and she arched to meet his lips. As he took the peak of her breast into his mouth again, a small cry of delight escaped her parted lips.

He answered her sigh with a teasing flick of his tongue, moving from breast to breast, and her hips tightened in response, the tingling ache she felt increasing with each movement of his mouth. She moaned with desire, her hands clutching at the silk blankets at the top of the bed as she pressed her breasts into his eager mouth. Never had she felt such a delightful anticipation of even greater pleasure. Never had she felt so loved.

His mouth moved lower, tracing the soft curve of her abdomen. She struggled to reach for him, not comprehending anything but her dizzying hunger for his tongue against her breasts, but her hands were stopped by the silken cords. She cried out in frustration, her wordless gasp a plea for his touch. Smiling at her surrender, the samurai pressed her legs open with hands that allowed no resistance.

When his tongue moved quickly across the soft flesh between her legs, she arched back onto the silken sheets, a breathless cry of ecstasy escaping her lips. His tongue flicked across her once more, seeking out her point of profoundest pleasure. She moaned again, this time with greater need. He responded hungrily, tasting and consuming her, his tongue laving across her relentlessly. She was overwhelmed with delight yet sought more, her body and heart his to command.

Sensing her growing need, Takeshi slowed his kisses, lingering so as to bring her to a higher plane of pleasure and desire. Her hips again seemed to move of their own accord, rolling slowly against his hungry lips. With each rotation of her hips and each titillating response from his tongue, a mounting urgency grew within her until she was consumed by its fire. She writhed against his mouth, moaning with pleasure and overcome by his devotion.

Miku's whole world had been distilled down to only the love she felt for Takeshi and that one exquisite point beneath his tongue. And with the realization that his adoration equaled her own, she cried out as intense waves of pleasure shattered through her body.

Takeshi moved quickly onto the bed, embracing her shuddering form in the heat of his arms, pressing her body to him as she trembled and wept, unexpectedly overcome with emotion. As her sobbing subsided, he gently wiped a tear from her glistening cheek with a bow-hardened finger. She turned her face toward his, and he kissed her slowly, each savoring the other's gentle touch.

With a slow sweep of his hand, the samurai ran his fingers up her body, releasing the cord that bound her arms before moving to untie the one about her waist. Then he slid his hand down her body, cupping her hip and pressing her body toward him. Miku deepened her kiss, a renewed hunger stirred by his touch, and he moaned with desire.

She responded by slipping her legs around his waist, pressing up against the erect shaft between his legs. She wanted him all, hardened warrior and tender lover. He moved rhythmically against her, gliding across her wet flesh, and she shuddered with excitement.

Overcome by her arousal, Takeshi groaned as he fought to control his own passion. His hand slid from her hip and moved between her legs. Her body stiffened as one finger slipped inside, slowly and gently. She had wanted to be close to him, as connected as possible, and yet this new feeling was more than she had anticipated. But surely her lover would not do anything but that which brought her pleasure. He had shown her more love than anyone ever had. She would trust him even now.

Gradually Miku's body relaxed as she lay beneath him. Takeshi, his breathing ragged with self-imposed restraint, began to slowly move his finger, gliding it in and out of her body as she grew accustomed to his touch. She felt a new fullness as a second finger slipped inside her, and her eyes fluttered open with alarm.

"This will make what comes next easier," he murmured. She didn't understand his words, but the tenderness in his eyes assured her that his purpose was to cherish her as completely as possible. So she closed her eyes again, surrendering to the mesmerizing rhythm of his touch.

Then in the flickering lamplight, he shifted his full weight above her and, without pause, slowly pushed himself into her, stretching her body as she had not imagined possible. She cried out, struggling to pull away, but his hold around her waist was firm and unyielding as he pressed still farther into her. There was a moment of resistance, of pain, and she gasped and stiffened, her body fighting to accept his full length. And then he was inside of her, filling her completely.

He lay still, kissing her lips and neck and hair, waiting for her trembling to abate. "Two halves of a shell, joined together as one," he whispered, his lips gently tracing the edge of her jaw. "Our bodies are meant to be together." Hearing the poetry that fell so naturally from her untutored warrior's lips washed away any lingering pain and fear as Miku wrapped her arms around Takeshi's neck and pressed her mouth to his.

Slowly, her hips began to move against his. He kissed her more deeply and felt her body relax and open to him.

With increased need, he pushed more deeply into her, her tiny cries of ecstasy captured in his mouth. His rhythmic motion quickened, and she arched against him. No longer able to subdue his own passion, he thrust harder, spearing her again and again with his full length.

She watched with rapt delight as his gaze took in the soft curves of her breasts, quivering with each thrust, and her heart thudded with a newfound pride at the molten desire her body brought to his eyes. The samurai was filling Miku's body and soul, her love and passion heightened by the intensity of his hunger for her. His breath was hot against her shoulder, and she pressed into him, seeking to be filled even more deeply.

The sense of urgent desire was growing once more between her legs, and she opened herself wider. Faster and deeper he moved into her, and she clung to him, ecstatic in his complete possession of her.

Then, with a guttural cry, he stiffened against her, and her body responded with a rushing release of pleasure, the flesh around his throbbing shaft tightening convulsively as tingling waves of delight rolled through her, more slowly than the previous times, but no less intense.

In that moment, Miku realized that the greatest beauty was found not in nature's bejeweled night sky, or even within one of her own artfully wrought poems, but rather in the perfect connection between man and woman, between those who would love each other always. As sated exhaustion quickly overtook them both, not even sleep could remove the smile of exquisite contentment from her face.

She awoke to soft light, cool and pale like oversaturated ink, flowing through the thin silk walls of her bedchamber. Dawn painted the skin of Miku and Takeshi's bare legs as they lay entwined with each other. She pressed herself closer to his bronzed chest, and his arms instinctively tightened around her, his lips seeking out hers.

And then without warning, his mouth was gone from hers. "The *shoko* sounds," he said.

Miku struggled to her elbows, pushing back a thick lock of black hair from her eyes, and listened to the large brass gong that hung at the front gate of her uncle's manor. Its distinctive clang rang through the courtyard, shattering their morning's serenity. Servants were signaling her uncle's return.

Almost immediately, a rumble of footsteps foretold her uncle's imminent arrival at the door to her suite. Before she could do more than hastily wrap a robe around her naked form, the old man and his entourage of servants trampled through her parlor and pulled away the screen that enclosed her bedchamber.

Her uncle stopped abruptly, his irritable instructions to a servant broken off midsentence as his sharp gaze took in Miku's disheveled appearance and Takeshi's sword and bow, abandoned in the corner of the room. Though he'd managed to step back into his short cotton robe, the samurai's shoulder-length hair was loose about his neck instead of tied up tightly in the formal knot required of his military station.

"No attempt to escape was made in the night, Master," said Takeshi, sliding on his helmet and plated armor and calmly moving to retrieve his weapons. But before he could reach his *katana,* Miku's uncle signaled for armed guards to retrieve the blade.

"Yes, I see that my niece is still here, as I commanded. Yet I wonder if she remained truly safe?" asked Miku's uncle, his fury barely contained. "Or was her greatest threat lurking here, in my own home?"

"The only threat I face is from you," said Miku, moving

angrily toward her uncle as his scandalized servants backed away. "I will not—"

"What you will or will not do is *my* decision," snapped her uncle. "Dress in your finest robes and come to the grand hall."

"You cannot force Miku to obey you any longer," said Takeshi, stepping between her and her uncle. "She is no longer yours to command."

Turning toward his private guard, the old man pointed a gnarled finger toward Takeshi. "Arrest this traitor. He will be put to death…after he watches my niece marry another." He rolled an eye toward Takeshi, smirked and said, "You seem to have forgotten that you are not armed."

With a battle cry, Takeshi rushed toward his former Master, but a dozen guards with weapons drawn moved to block him.

"You will follow this sniveling coward?" roared Takeshi, as one soldier pressed his sword to the base of Takeshi's throat while a second wrapped a strong leather rope around his wrists. "Then you are not true samurai—for samurai are men of honor and courage!"

Their faces flushed with anger and humiliation, the two guards pulled the still-fighting Takeshi from Miku's room, their violent exit ripping holes in the delicate silk walls of her bedchamber.

Looking from the tattered fabric to her uncle, Miku trembled with rage and shock. But before she could speak, he snarled, "My request is clear—appear in one hour, or your samurai will die immediately. Your cooperation ensures him at least a few more hours before I end his miserable life."

Now, as she hurried to dress, Miku seethed with barely contained fury. Weighed down by multilayered robes of crimson, green and gold silk, without glancing into her polished bronze mirror, Miku stepped from her chambers and made her way down the long corridor connecting her quarters to her uncle's main house.

Takeshi was unarmed, yet surely he would find a way to defend her—and save himself. But how, she could not fathom. Perhaps such a dream was nothing more than a poet's fancy after all.

Miku stepped into her uncle's large sitting room, her sensuous curves concealed beneath formal robes and her face hidden behind heavy makeup. She had painted her ripe lips to appear smaller, as was the fashion, and her luxurious hair had been pinned back with a golden ornament shaped like a tiny shell. From his position between two armed guards near the Master, Takeshi's heart lurched to his throat as the memory of the simple parlor game they had played pierced through the armor of his heart.

Miku's uncle leaned to Takeshi and in a harsh whisper said, "Do not forget, samurai. You will be killed instantly should you speak to my niece or in any other way acknowledge your...*connection*...with her. Her future husband must not know of this dalliance, at least until the wedding has been completed and the contracted alliance between our families formalized." The old man snorted, then added, "Although, of course, at that point I will have you executed."

"Why are you keeping me alive now?" asked Takeshi.

The old man shrugged with affected surprise. "Why, so that you can watch your beloved poet presented, *body and soul,* to the man of my choosing, of course. When you are put to the blade, I want your last thought to be of her in the arms of another."

Takeshi lunged toward Miku's uncle, but the sharp edge of the other soldiers' swords held him at bay.

"Your prisoner seems quite volatile," whimpered the bloated aristocrat seated nearby, oblivious to the pervious conversation between Takeshi and his host. "Perhaps you should call for a larger contingent of guards? And why is he here, anyway?"

"No reason that should concern you, my honored friend," said Miku's uncle quickly, snapping his fingers to signal for more guards. "The man is merely a wayward peasant who needs my attention after we have concluded these more agreeable affairs. But I will call for additional soldiers as you request, to put your mind at ease."

As more samurai filed into the room, Miku glided forward, stopping before her sharp-eyed uncle and the paunchy man who sat next to him. She knelt on a cushion and raised her eyes, a demure smile on her face. "Dear uncle, your quick and safe return gladdens my heart. The house was quiet without your presence."

At the melodic sound of her voice, Takeshi started slightly. Miku did not look toward him. To express the excruciating emotions ripping at her heart—even with a soft word or knowing glance—would risk his life, so she carefully played the part her uncle expected, even if the old man knew it was all a lie.

"My niece, I have returned with an honored guest and glad tidings. Orochi has come this long way from the capital Heian-kyo, where he serves as an assistant to the Emperor's butler. A very prestigious position, of course."

"Quite impressive," said Miku, nodding stiffly to her uncle's guest. The man wiped his watering eyes and licked his lips in response.

She tried not to shudder as a wave of revulsion swelled within her stomach. Had she not shared the past evening in the arms of another, had she never learned the pleasure that a man's loving touch could bring, then perhaps she would not find this pompous slug so repugnant. But though eminently brave and unquestioningly strong, Takeshi was now unarmed and seemed no match for the army of swords and bows around him.

"I see you are satisfied with this man," continued her uncle. Miku declined her head in forced deference to her uncle's statement. "And he is obviously satisfied with you. But what man wouldn't be, eh?" he asked, poking a pointed elbow into the fleshy rolls surrounding the other man's stomach while sending a goading glance toward Takeshi. "My niece may have an uncomely wildness to her spirit at times, Orochi, but you see that she can be tamed."

The men laughed as Miku caught a look of strangled rage pass across Takeshi's face. Her heart lurched with desperate hope. Was Takeshi going to act? Could she be saved from the revolting fate of sharing a bed, and a life, with Orochi? But her hope withered with the renewed realization that for Takeshi to defy her uncle would be an instant death sentence, carried out at the hands of the other samurai.

"You will wed Orochi," said her uncle slowly, his eyes sharp on Miku's face. "Now."

She kept her hands clenched tightly on her lap and said nothing. Miku well knew the stories of sensuous excess and erotic debauchery that permeated the wealthy elite who lived in Heian-kyo, where monogamy was the exception and multiple liaisons were expected. Though tantalizing for many, she knew such wantonness would only lead to her own heartbreak. How could she expect her new husband to be faithful in a climate such as that? And how could she hope to find happiness when all she wanted was the deep satisfaction that came from being fully known and loved by just one man—*by Takeshi?*

"He will take his wedding night here, in your quarters, and tomorrow you will return with him to the capital." Her uncle poked Orochi in the ribs again and added, "Where she will set aside her poetry and begin giving you many sons and daughters!"

Miku's mind swam with horror as she fought to maintain a tranquil outward appearance. "You show me great love by finding an important man to be my husband," she said finally, choking on the words. "I am not worthy of such an honor."

"True, and yet it is an honor you *will* accept," said her uncle as Orochi leered with watery eyes. "For it is an honor that will grant me favor in the eyes of the Emperor and his court."

Takeshi's bound arms and broad chest trembled with barely contained fury as he looked from Miku to Orochi, his eyes dark and jaw set.

Unaware of the silent drama between his intended bride and her warrior lover, Orochi leaned toward his host. "Yes, the handsome dowry you will send with her to Heian-kyo will go far in impressing His Highness. Your peasants will be honored to know their extra grain is going toward such a magnanimous gift."

Both men laughed as Miku slowly shook her head in disbelief. Not only was she being given to such a repugnant man, but her uncle's serfs would also be further starved to pay her dowry.

"No such dowry will be taken from the peasants, or paid to the emperor." Takeshi's deep voice cut through the room like the blade of a knife. "Now, release me."

Miku's eyes shot to Takeshi and the corps of men surrounding him. Even with arms bound, the strength of his presence, the dark piercing gaze of his eyes and unquestionable authority of his voice expressed more power than any other man in the room. And though ostensibly there to provide extra guard, the soldiers were now instead cutting the leather cord from around Takeshi's wrists and slipping a *katana* into his outstretched hand.

"Stop him," cried Miku's uncle, his voice catching with fear, but the few soldiers who moved tentatively toward Takeshi were quickly halted by the warning snarls and outstretched swords of their braver comrades, now loyal to Takeshi alone.

Takeshi nodded with solemn authority to his men, who acknowledged him with bows of respect, though not so low as to drop their eyes from the two old men quivering at their feet.

"For years, we have followed you with unwavering loyalty," said Takeshi, boldly stepping toward Miku's uncle.

The time had come for him to act, and he was ready. He had always been ready, he realized. It had just taken the fiery temper, gentle touch and courageous spirit of his Master's niece to finally unleash the maverick that had always lurked within his warrior's heart.

"And for years," continued Takeshi, brandishing his weapon, "we have honored our vow to serve you. Yet for years, you have repressed our families and starved our people. You have abused your responsibility toward everyone under your authority." He paused, and Miku's heart leapt to her throat at his next words, spoken in a low growl. "Even those within your own household."

A snarl rumbled through the tightly packed room as dozens of samurai nodded and shifted their weight, as if ready to attack. Takeshi put up a hand, and the murmuring ceased.

"We understand the meaning of loyalty, of honor, of respect. It is you who have no concept of anything more than power and greed and petty lusts. And so it is you who will leave. I will no longer allow you to ravage this land and its people, taking what you want and leaving the peasants to starve. We will no longer permit such injustice," he said, an arm sweeping toward his fellow soldiers. "Rather than bleed the peasants any further, these brave men can swear a fresh allegiance. One to honesty and justice and compassion. One to me as their new leader."

"I thought you were just a peasant," whined Orochi, who

now lay in a quivering pile of robes at Takeshi's feet. "You should be killed for this treasonous act."

"I am no peasant," said Takeshi, "and my actions are not treasonous to the villagers who truly deserve my protection."

"I should not have permitted you to leave my niece's room alive," said Miku's uncle, ignoring the look of confusion that pinched Orochi's face. "Yet as for my niece…"

Takeshi took another threatening step toward his former Master, raising his sword to the man's quivering jowls. "To hear you speak of Miku boils my blood," he bit out, then paused. "But, nonetheless, she must choose her own destiny."

"So you will permit her to leave with me, her beloved uncle?" he simpered. "I need someone to care for me in my aging years, after all."

"I will go nowhere," said Miku, rising from the cushion on which she knelt and moving quickly to Takeshi, her head high and resolve firm. "I belong here, with the man I love."

She stopped before him, looking deeply into his eyes. His desire for her had always been clear, but in his face, she also saw strength tempered with gentleness, passion made complete with love. She now knew he was a man who loved her with all of his being, and whom she loved in return.

"Your niece stays," said Takeshi, putting a protective arm around Miku. "But you will leave at once. My men will escort you on your journey to the capital, where perhaps your would-be nephew-in-law will see fit to put you up in his home and fund your extravagances. For the people of this land no longer will."

Miku's uncle and Orochi, along with the cowardly soldiers who had arrested Takeshi, were dragged from the room by several samurai. Miku turned in Takeshi's arms to face him. "Will the Emperor send troops once word of your insurrection reaches the capital?"

"Perhaps, but I believe the Emperor will be happy as long as adequate taxes continue to flow to his coffers. And that can be done without bleeding the peasants, so long as we samurai and nobility are willing to live more modestly henceforth. My warrior brethren will be in agreement that this shall be so."

"As am I," she said eagerly, her facing shining with adoration and respect. Then, looking deep into his eyes, she whispered, "You have saved the people of this village, and you have saved me."

"If that snake Orochi had laid a finger on you…" His voice trailed off, full of barely controlled rage.

Miku reached up and turned his face toward hers again. "No hands have touched me but yours. And I desire for no other hands but yours again."

Takeshi lifted her into his arms then, and moving through the crowd of milling samurai like a sword parting the mist, he carried her toward her quarters.

"Can it be true that you love me, a mere soldier?" he asked, his voice husky and low as he made his way down the sun-kissed open corridor between the houses.

"You may not come from noble blood," she said, her head resting against his strong chest as he entered her chambers, "but you have nobleness of spirit. How could I not love a man of such conviction and courage?"

"But I cannot read the poetry you write," he said, looking past her to the writing desk, "and poetry is who you are. It is your soul."

She ran a soft finger across his beard, and he looked into her eyes again, an expectant hope softening the hard planes of his face and making her heart ache with tenderness for him. "I will teach you to read," she whispered, "and until then, we will create a different poetry together."

They gazed into each other's eyes for a long moment before he kissed her forehead tenderly and murmured the words she had just read so perfectly in his clear gaze: "I love you, my poetess."

"And I love you."

Takeshi moved through Miku's bedchamber, its silken walls a glowing cocoon in the midmorning sun. Gently seating her upright on the sleeping couch, he knelt before the woman he adored. This free-spirited poetess with a gentle heart and fierce courage. The one person who had finally broken through the hardened defenses of his heart. The woman who had already inspired him to acts of greater goodness and bravery that he could have done before knowing her.

Cupping her face tenderly in his bow-calloused hands, Takeshi pressed his lips to Miku's eager mouth. As her tongue traced the curve of his lips, she ran her fingers through his hair, loosening the formal samurai knot and allowing it to fall to his shoulders in a thick black mane. The warrior who knelt before her was all hard muscle and barely restrained strength, yet his touch remained tender, the gentle embrace of a lover.

Coaxed by his tantalizing kiss and the memory of his more intimate caresses, Miku's body responded with the first throbs of a deeper need. She arched her back and, wrapping her legs around his chiseled waist, pressed herself to his kneeling form. His grip around her waist tightened and his kiss deepened, his tongue piercing her mouth and tasting her fully.

She writhed against his hard, muscled abdomen as sparks of pleasure began to ignite between her open legs. With each roll of her hips, she recognized with growing delight her own ability to control that incomparable pleasure Takeshi had earlier released with his fingertips…and mouth.

At the memory of his hungry tongue against her wet

core, she shuddered with anticipation and leaned back to open herself fully to her willing warrior. Unable to contain his own desire as he witnessed the unfettered abandon with which Miku used his body for her pleasure, Takeshi slid his hands down her back and lifted her buttocks to his mouth. As her shoulders pressed into the soft cushions of the couch, Miku moaned with expectancy.

With an unconstrained hunger, he licked at her wetness, his tongue sliding across her soft flesh to probe deep within her before emerging again to flick repeatedly cross her point of greatest pleasure. She cried out in ecstasy, overcome by the complete control with which Takeshi mastered her desire. Though her lover, he was still a samurai, and she couldn't deny the intensely arousing realization that, although he cherished her deeply, he could still do with her what he wished.

He gripped her more tightly in response to her sighs of pleasure, his tongue relentlessly flicking across her heated flesh as she writhed against his mouth. She was his completely now, with no one waiting to force her into the arms of another. The certainty that he could enjoy her for the rest of his life filled him with a fiercer desire than he had ever known. Not even on the battlefield, when he had parried an opponent's sword and faced down an enemy's bow, had his blood rushed so hot and his vision seemed so sharply focused. All he could see now was Miku, and all he wanted was to please her—and possess her—forever.

With a deliberate motion, he lowered her waist back onto the couch, her legs still lifted in his grasp. Without waiting, Takeshi thrust into her, taking her fully in one swift motion. She gasped as he filled her, then cried out as he pressed into her again and again, every hard thrust penetrating deeper than she had yet imagined possible. He was possessing her, overwhelming her…yet making her pleasure his supreme focus.

Though initially overcome by her samurai's unbridled passion, Miku quickly responded with an equally fiery desire of her own. Her cries of surprise turned to moans of utter abandon as she gave herself fully to his carnal onslaught, each thrust penetrating deep within the slick wetness of her aching arousal. She gripped the sides of the sleeping couch with trembling hands and arched up toward Takeshi, seeking to take his full length with each pounding stroke.

Yet in giving herself over to him completely, Miku realized she was in fact achieving her greatest power. Choosing to accept his undying love, and to give hers in return, strengthened her in a way she could never achieve alone. To love and be loved was stronger than his sword and more beautiful than her poetry.

In that moment of comprehension, Miku's body shuddered over the edge of control. Undulating waves of pleasure exploded from between her legs as she tightened around Takeshi's shaft. He answered her cries of pleasure with his own deep moan, stiffening within her as liquid heat filled her inner core and spilled down her still-lifted buttocks. Then he collapsed onto her, all his furious need replaced in an instant with tender kisses and gentle words of love.

They lay in each others arms, their bodies and hearts entwined, the frantic ecstasy of their shared passion ebbing as a sated joy washed over them. Sighing with contentment, Miku traced a finger languidly across the bronze skin of Takeshi's taut chest, no longer hidden from her by plated armor.

"That tickles." He grinned, capturing her hand in his and kissing her fingertips.

She paused, then smiled. "It is calligraphy."

"What were you writing?" he asked.

Her heart fluttered as she gazed into the inky darkness of

his eyes, so full of love for her. "Your name," she admitted. "Takeshi. It means *warrior.*"

"Yes," he said. "And yet, in finding you, I have begun to discover that there is more to who I am."

"You are a leader, and a poet, and my lover, too," Miku said proudly. "Yet you will always be a warrior. And I love you for that strength."

Takeshi looked into Miku's face, radiating confidence in him. "And I love you," he said, kissing her again.

After a moment he paused to speak once more, his voice low and full of emotion. "Your uncle expected there to be a wedding here today. We will send news to him in Heian-kyo that the nuptials have been consummated after all."

"If that is your will, so be it," Miku said, tenderness coloring her cheeks as she gazed into the dark eyes of the man who would henceforth be her husband. "For you are now Master of this manor."

Nuzzling her long, dark hair, he whispered, "And you will be mistress of my heart forever."

\* \* \* \* \*

# ARABIAN NIGHTS
# WITH A RAKE

Bronwyn Scott

## Author Note

Alex and Susannah's story was so much fun to write! Alex is a rugged intellectual, which gives him a very sexy edge. He seems the perfect comrade for Crispin Ramsden. The idea to set the story in the desert sprang from a remark Crispin makes in his story, *Untamed Rogue, Scandalous Mistress,* about how he acquired his horse. I thought it would be intriguing to use an Undone to explore where Crispin has been during his three-year absence from England. This adventure in the desert seemed ideal.

I hope you enjoy the backdrop for the story. Many of my readers are like me and love to learn something from the books they read. For those folks, here's a great chance to learn about desert life; the *moussems,* the *souk,* the relationship between camels and horses, are all as authentic as I could make them. For history lovers, I based Alex and Crispin's foray into the desert specifically around the events happening after the French take over Algiers. Abd al-Qadir was a real historical figure and was considered a great hero in Algerian history for his rebellion against the French, which was indeed staged from Mascara.

Enjoy, and keep reading!

*Drop by and say hi on my blog*
*www.bronwynswriting.blogspot.com.*

*To all those readers who have taken the time to write and share their enjoyment of the Ramsden brothers over the last two years. And to the fabulous team at Harlequin Mills & Boon whose guidance makes each book shine from the gorgeous covers to what's inside.*

*And always for my family.*

**Look for Bronwyn Scott's**
***The Secret Life of a Scandalous Debutante***
**Coming soon from Harlequin® Historical**

# Chapter One

*Northern Desert of Algeria, May, 1833*

Alex Grayfield unwrapped the long lengths of his turban and breathed a deep lungful of night air, expelling it with a long "Ahhh." On the nearing horizon, the flickering of torch lights illuminated a massive array of tents, a Bedouin village rising from the sands. The faint sounds of music and laughter beckoned welcomingly across the distance. He took another deep breath and closed his eyes in satisfaction. Beside him, Crispin Ramsden's horse shifted on the sands.

"Do you smell what I smell?" Alex exhaled almost reverently. God, he loved the desert. Out here, he was free.

"Trouble?" Crispin gave a low chuckle.

"Women."

"Is there a difference?"

They laughed together in the rising darkness, spurring their horses forward, both of them eager to arrive at the encampment now that the journey was nearly done. Algiers, with its narrow streets and smells of fish and coffee, was two days behind them, the edge of the desert before them.

"You can't really smell them at this distance," Crispin challenged good-naturedly, pulling his horse alongside.

"Can't you?" Alex couldn't resist the gibe. He smiled. "I can smell incense and wine, meat roasting in its own juices on a spit. Only women can conjure such delicious smells."

"Where there's a woman, there's danger," Crispin warned and not without reason. Europe was littered with his bedroom intrigues.

"Well, you would know best on that score." Alex shrugged. "There's bound to be danger anyway, women notwithstanding." Their journey into the desert was no pleasure trip. He and Crispin had been sent to this gathering of Bedouins to take the political temperature of the nomads.

Algiers had capitulated to the French, and Britain wanted to know if there was anything to be gained by supporting the desert rebels rallying against the French occupation. Guerrilla forces under the Emir of Mascara, Abd al Qadir, were already amassed and established after their victory. In November, the emir's army had stopped a French advance into the desert. Buoyed by the emir's success, would others join the fight to liberate Algiers? If so, perhaps Britain might covertly assist in an attempt to offset the growing power of French colonialism. Alex knew as well as Crispin the import of their mission. He who controlled the desert controlled North Africa.

"Do we have a connection or are we just showing up and hoping we aren't killed on the spot?" Crispin turned the conversation toward more serious issues now that their appearance at the camp was imminent. They weren't the first team to attempt to arrive here, although they might be the first team to arrive intact. Six months ago, Lord

Sutcliffe's entourage, including his daughter, had set out from Algiers. But they'd never arrived at their destination. The entire group was presumed most tragically dead.

"Your Arabic is fluent enough to pass," Crispin mused, "but no one would believe I was anything other than an Englishman once I opened my mouth."

"They might think you're French and that would be far worse," Alex joked.

Crispin's French was impeccable and had been immensely useful in the circles they had penetrated in Algiers. But it was Alex's Arabic—compliments of growing up as a British diplomat's son in Cairo—that they'd rely on out here in the desert.

"We have an introduction to Sheikh Muhsin ibn Bitar through my father's connections in Algiers," Alex offered. Beyond that, it was too complicated to explain the circuitous network of friendships so common to the way of life in the Arab world.

Crispin nodded, not expecting more detail. Like Alex, Crispin had had enough experience in this part of the world to know how things worked. An introduction would be all they needed. This gathering was a happy occasion. A *moussem* like this one brought the wandering tribes together for a celebration and the exchange of news. It would be a prime opportunity to hear from many tribes at once.

Truth be told, Alex was looking forward to the *moussem*. There would be food and dancing, competitions and music. They approached the outer circle of tents and Alex smiled. If he was charming and careful, there'd be women too. Ah, life was good.

She would get one chance to escape. If she was over-careful, she'd miss her opportunity. If she was over-hasty…well those consequences were too horrific to contemplate.

Susannah Sutcliffe eased back into the tent, letting the

flap fall discreetly. For six months, since her father's death in a desert skirmish, she'd lived in the awkward limbo of the captive-slave. Muhsin ibn Bitar desired her greatly, which meant she'd not been sorely used in labor. But it also meant she owed him her gratitude. So far, she'd been able to satisfy him with entertainments and sitting at his feet during his meals.

They both knew those acts were nothing more than an extended prelude to his final seduction. He would not be put off any longer. He'd told her as much when they'd set out for the gathering. If she did not please him by the end of the *moussem* she would be given to another. That other was likely his brother-in-law, Bassam.

Susannah shuddered at the thought. Bassam was a man known for his love of diverse pleasures in the bedchamber. But neither did she prefer the company of the sheikh himself, who desired her as an earthly houri. That left only one option—taking her chances in the desert, a most dangerous option in itself. A wrong direction could lead her away from the settlements and caravan routes. It was easy to die in the desert and she would only be able to carry a few days' worth of water at best.

Her plan was simple. She would steal a hardy desert horse or, if necessary, a camel and set out at night while everyone slept. With all the people here for the *moussem*, it would be hours before anyone noticed she or the beast were gone. There would be no margin for error.

She would stake it all on a single action. Camel or horse thievery was a grave crime among the Bedouin. She doubted if the sheikh's desire for her would be great enough to protect her from Bedouin justice. She would live or die on the success of her plan.

Part of her argued against taking such risk. She could stay. Surely there was no shame in pleasing the sheikh. Surely, she could bear it if it meant she could live. If she lived, there might be a better opportunity later. What was it her father used to say? *Live to fight another day?* But he'd also been fond of saying *Never surrender.* She would face the desert and complete her father's mission. When she returned to the consulate in Algiers, she'd have the information her father had been sent to seek.

A girl slipped into the tent, holding a collection of filmy fabrics in her arms. She held them out to Susannah. "The sheikh bids you attend him. I am to wait and help you with your hair."

Susannah nodded. Her knowledge of Arabic had grown enough over the months that she understood the commands. *So the game begins,* she thought as she dressed. By English standards, the garments were scandalous, far more revealing than any good Englishwoman's nightgown. By Bedouin standards, the outfit was sumptuous. The sheikh had spared no expense. Of course, she understood it was important to put on a display of his wealth. She just didn't like being part of that display.

The girl combed out her hair, letting it hang long and loose behind her. A woman entered with a soft bag containing jewelry and placed a small gold circlet on top of her head and bracelets on her wrists. She should be used to the routine by now. This would not be the first night she had danced for the sheikh and his friends. The women who tended her had told her it was a great honor to dance for the sheikh, but she could not dismiss the feeling of being a slave led to market or a cow to slaughter. She'd not been raised to this life. She'd been a diplomat's daughter raised in a proper British household. Never in her darkest dreams had she'd thought she'd end up in a Bedouin encampment, enslaved for the personal enjoyment of a desert chieftain.

The woman held aside the flap. It was time to go, time to set aside any self-pity over her plight. It was time to survive, and to do that, she needed to dance with all the abandon she possessed, to tease and withdraw, to conjure forth every male fantasy in the tent while allowing the sheikh to believe she danced only for him.

# Chapter Two

Alex reclined on the pillows, propped up by an elbow. He reached for another date from the platters laid before them. A relaxed atmosphere permeated the sheikh's tent. The festival had put everyone in a generous mood. Well, almost everyone. Alex amended. One dark-eyed man with a scar on his left cheek sat brooding next to the sheikh. Bassam, Alex thought his name was. The enormous tent was filled to capacity with guests, it had been hard to keep all the names straight. He'd remembered the important ones.

There was a movement at the back of the tent and the sheikh clapped his hands for attention.

"There's to be dancing," Alex translated with a grin for Crispin.

"Did you save me a waltz on your dance card?" Crispin replied drily.

Alex laughed. "It's to be the sheikh's favorite. I do think I prefer this kind of dancing. I just get to sit here and watch. No dance cards, no introductions, no expectations."

"No matchmaking mamas, either," Crispin put in.

"There's a reason I eschew England." Alex had been about to say more but the drums began, drowning out his voice. He doubted he could have spoken anyway. The dancer had carefully navigated her way through the crowd to the open spot in front of the sheikh and even now spun before him in a whirl of turquoise silk, her pale-gold hair as much a seductive curtain as the transparent veiling she teased with.

*Gold hair.*

The sheikh's favorite was not a dark-eyed woman of the desert. She looked English, but looks could be misleading. She might be any number of European nationalities. Alex shot a quick glance in Crispin's direction. Only a slight movement of his eyes gave any indication he'd also noticed. It wouldn't do for them to show any outward sign of curiosity.

The dancer's movements slowed, her hands moving to draw attention to the undulation of her hips, the exposed, sculpted flatness of her stomach; her hands drifted upward, drawing Alex's eyes to the fullness of her breasts encased in a jeweled top. The woman was exquisite, there was little wonder she was the favorite. But with her pale hair and skin, she was decidedly not one of the Bedouin, nor was she Arab.

Whatever and whoever she was, she was positively intoxicating; her subtle scents of sandalwood and roses teasing his nostrils. His body hardened in visceral response to the promise of her sensuality. Her lips parted, a secret smile playing across them, eyes as blue as the Mediterranean met his over the transparent rim of her veils, promising all nature of erotic fulfillment as if she danced solely for him.

Yet there was a provocative innocence in those eyes, creating the impression that this was no jaded concubine expertly tantalizing men but a passionate woman in waiting, perhaps begging to be awakened to love's pleasures. Alex's arousal grew in damning proportions at the prospect, at the fantasy, of taking such a woman to his bed, to teach her, to share with her the exotic mysteries of sex.

Then she was gone, her attentions returning to the sheikh, but the fantasy remained, a potent loiterer in his mind. Later in the evening when the torches burned low and only a few men remained in the tent to discuss news, Alex asked with a feigned nonchalance, "Where did the woman come from?"

"Still in her thrall?" The sheikh gave a commiserating laugh. "She enchants every man, does she not?"

"She is lovely, indeed," Alex agreed, schooling his own features in the dimness of the tent to hide any sign of his own desire. But the sheikh had not answered his question and Alex wanted his answer. "How did you come by her?"

The grim man with the scar leaned forward to speak. "My brother-in-law does not share his concubines. She is not available to you if that's what you're asking."

Alex felt Crispin's languid repose transform into alertness. Alex took the man's measure easily. Bassam was jealous. Bassam wanted the lovely concubine for himself.

"She is a spoil of war, nothing more," The sheikh offered benevolently. "Please, have some more wine."

Englishmen! Englishmen were here, and not just any Englishman, but Alex Grayfield, the Blond Bedouin. She'd only seen him once when she'd traveled to Cairo with her father, but those green eyes could belong to no other. Susannah's heart beat rapidly with excitement, in part over the prospect of rescue and in large part over the presence of a man whose very presence exuded power and sexuality. In the dark privacy of her tent, Susannah gave herself over to the memory.

He'd looked upon her boldly tonight, living up to his reputation. His eyes had answered hers as she'd danced with a message of passion every bit as sensual as the one she was meant to convey.

Her body tingled in remembrance. The sheer male physicality of him had been overpowering even in a tent full other men. Beneath his flowing robes, there'd been no mistaking the breadth of his shoulders or the strength of his body even in repose. Power resided in that body as surely as intelligence lit his mind. There'd been no doubt that his gaze had studied her, his sharp green eyes seducing her. She'd never been more aware of herself as a woman than she'd been in those few moments when she danced before him, their eyes meeting over her veil.

*I want you,* those eyes had said. But for all the ways in which he'd riveted her, she had entranced him as well. A woman did not need to be a whore to know when a man desired her, and now she sought to turn his desire to her advantage.

Alex Grayfield's arrival changed everything. She could avoid the dangers of traveling the desert alone if she could persuade him to take her with him. Providing, of course, she could persuade the sheikh to let her go.

No. The sheikh would never simply let her go. Susannah sank down on the low cot that served as her bed. She had to think. Asking to be set free was far too direct. If asking were a viable alternative, she would have asked months ago. She had to be subtle. She'd learned the value of subtlety during her time among the Bedouin. In the beginning, she'd taken what she'd hoped to be the quickest route to freedom—being so troublesome to the sheikh that he'd let her go out of sheer frustration. But those rash acts had only served to prick his pride and make her situation worse. The sheikh had to be maneuvered carefully.

Susannah absently peeled off her veils, her mind perusing her options. What was it her father had always said about diplomacy? The successful diplomat knew how to play to a man's strengths, how to praise a man's assets. She'd learned, too, that assets weren't always material items but sometimes characteristics.

The sheikh viewed himself as a man generous with his hospitality. And he was, when it came to political generosity. She'd danced at enough of his entertainments to know there was truth in that. He lavished his best food and drink on merchants and their caravans when their paths crossed. In return, she was certain he received the most accurate news and insights the merchants brought with them.

Politics were heating up the desert. This *moussem* was a festival, but it would also be a chance for the remaining tribes to decide if they'd throw in their lots with the Emir of Mascara. There was danger here, too, for the English whether they knew it or not. The sheikh did not support the emir and, by extension, he did not support the English. He would want to determine what the English meant by this visit. To do that, he would court them. But he could not court the English with his traditional largesse of figs and wineskins or the occasional camel. The English had no use for the standard luxuries of the desert.

The sheikh would need a gift substantially more English than that to impress his visitors. He needed *her*. She was the most English gift the sheikh possessed. The sheikh needed to be made to see that returning her out of bondage, and restoring her to her people would be a sign of his 'Western thinking,' a chance to convince the English the Bedouin were not nomadic barbarians, but people of a certain civility who should be left to their own devices.

Susannah reached for a thin cotton shift and pulled it over her head. It was the only truly English garment left to her. Her other clothes had been taken from her that first humiliating day. She wore only what the sheikh provided and at his behest. Putting on her shift had become something of a nightly ritual, a homecoming of sorts, a chance to be an Englishwoman for a few hours instead of this man's fantasy slave.

Making herself a gift was a good idea. It would play to the sheikh's view of himself as a generous lord of the sands. She was astute enough to know the suggestion could not come from her. It would have to come from Grayfield. He had not bothered to hide his interest in her. Such boldness would make his request believable, but it could also be used as leverage against him. He'd best tread carefully lest Bassam and the sheikh see an opportunity to exploit that desire before she could. If she could bind him to her, he would be more likely to take her away regardless of the risk or the permission.

She needed to move quickly. Susannah covered her shift with a dark robe and belted it. She reached for a veil to hide the sheen of her hair. The camp would be busy. With luck she would pass unnoticed, but if questioned, she could say she was on her way to the sheikh's tent. Her decision was made and she did not want to delay. It would be harder to arrange an opportunity to encounter the Englishmen tomorrow.

Susannah took a deep breath and slipped out into the night. She was off to make her "suggestion" to Grayfield, and as with any suggestion, the idea would need to be planted in order for it to take root.

# Chapter Three

Alex was dreaming of houris, or rather of one houri in particular. Even in sleep he did not quite forget that he was an Englishman who favored monogamy. In his dream, he reclined on a couch, pillows behind his head, a goblet of wine at his arm and the woman of his evening fantasies dancing before him. Her hips swayed in a provocative prelude. She came closer, the rose and sandalwood scent of her wreathing him in sensuality.

She bent over him, her long curtain of hair sweeping his chest, her naked breasts brushing his bare skin with dusky-hued nipples. She whispered a throaty promise he couldn't quite hear. If he raised his head just an inch he could kiss those tantalizing lips, and then move on to those delectable breasts.

He levered himself on one arm to cover the small distance, his mouth taking the invitation of her lips. She tasted of honey and surprise, a gasp escaping her in a short exhalation of breath. Instinctively, he reached out an arm to steady her, meaning to draw her firmly to him. He met with unexpected resistance. In Islamic mysticism the houris didn't resist. This was an odd dream indeed.

*Or no dream at all.* Alex's eyes flew open. Oh the woman was very real, that part was in no doubt. He woke to find himself holding the sheikh's favorite about the slender curve of her waist, the fullness of her breasts illumined through the thin cotton of her chemise by the flickering light of the tent's lantern. The deep rose of her nipples had been no figment of imagination either. The chemise offered her very little protection against the proximity of his gaze and the lantern-cast shadows.

The resistance hadn't been feigned either. Her body was tense within his embrace, her eyes questioning and wary. Her plans for him had plainly gone awry. The very thought raised Alex's well-honed sense of suspicion. He hadn't survived this long on luck alone. In his world, nothing was freely given.

Whatever she'd planned, it hadn't been seduction, more was the pity. Alex slackened his grip and she backed away. For a moment, he feared she would bolt. He moved his grip to her wrist, shackling it easily with his hand.

"What are you doing in my quarters?" His voice was harsh, demanding an answer. In the dim light he searched her for evidence of a weapon, to no avail. She was too scantily dressed to conceal anything on her person and her other hand was clenched into an empty fist.

Her gaze shifted infinitesimally to the dark heap on the floor—a cloak most likely, a covering that had been discarded on purpose, leaving her virtually naked to his gaze. Another man might rethink the possibility of seduction, but Alex had been schooled in the Persian world where not all was what it seemed on the surface. His first inclination had been correct. She'd not come to seduce. If she had, she would not have resisted his overture. She would have entered the game boldly with his awakening.

"Release me," she ordered, matching his demand with an admirable hauteur of her own. Definitely an Englishwoman,

Alex decided. He could hear it in her voice and in her defiance. He'd known many women from many backgrounds in his time and had yet to meet any except perhaps the Americans who matched an Englishwoman in boldness when cornered.

"I want answers," he replied. "What have you come here for? Is it the custom of the sheikh to send uninvited women to his guests' tents?" If she said yes, he'd know she was lying. It might indeed be the sheikh's custom; he'd met tribes where the practice was not uncommon as an act of hospitality. But the sheikh would not send his favorite, not after what Alex had witnessed in Bassam's response earlier that night.

She tossed her magnificent length of hair in a haughty maneuver. "I came to talk." She shot her eyes at his hand gripping her wrist.

"Naked? I was unaware of that particular desert custom." She might have been better off with the sent-by-the-sheik defense after all.

Her blue eyes flashed. "It's the truth." She tugged against his grip in her irritation. "I have no reason to lie to you."

"I have no reason to believe you. Perhaps the sheikh has sent you to ferret out my secrets, my reasons for being here. It is convenient for you to come while I'm alone." Alex raised a querying brow. "All the better for conquering and dividing, eh?"

"That's ridiculous logic," she spat. "Why would the sheikh send an Englishwoman to a compatriot? It would be tantamount to asking us to conspire against him."

"Would it?" Alex shrugged with feigned nonchalance, his mind rapidly sorting and discarding scenarios. What did she want that she would steal into a sleeping man's quarters and stand before him virtually unclothed? "Perhaps the sheikh has offered you something of value in exchange for whatever services he's sent you to perform." He raked her body deliberately with his eyes. There was no mistaking what "services" he suspected she offered.

"I'm not here to seduce you." She stammered, her nerve failing her for a moment. Alex watched her realize how exposed she was to his gaze, how little the fabric hid and how much the candle showed. "I'm here to talk."

"Then let's talk." Alex smiled wickedly, rising from the bed of blankets, the coverlet slipping from his body to reveal the unabashed glory of a naked man, aroused and not the least bit self-conscious over it. Indeed, there was nothing to be embarrassed about. His body was tanned from the tawny streaks in his blond hair to the muscled curves of his calves, implying that he engaged in nakedness quite often to have acquired so even a tan. Not even his buttocks had hidden from the sun's kiss. The thought brought a blush to her cheeks.

He stalked her, circling on purpose, with a wicked smile. "Nakedness can be a bit distracting…."

Stopping his pacing, he eyed her critically. "Is that why *you* dressed thus for our 'talk,' my dear? Did you mean to distract me with your charms while you did whatever it was you meant to do? That part of your plan is working admirably, as you can see." He cast an obvious glance downward to his engorged member.

She blushed furiously, desperately. He could see the flush of her skin even in the dim light. The act was entirely winsome and convincingly pure. It kept him unusually off balance. It seemed he'd discomfited the little temptress. Well, good. She needed to know there were consequences for her actions, for her as well as for him. Two could play this enticing game of "naked interrogation."

"Distract you? To what end?" she challenged, finding her wits. "I carry no weapon with which to do you harm." she protested, holding her arms wide from her side. "As you have noted, I have no place to conceal a weapon."

Alex knew the gesture cost her greatly. She knew by now how visibly exposed she was to him, that her modesty had been surrendered from the beginning and he'd made her acutely aware of it. She played the voluptuous, pure houri of the Koran so exquisitely, Alex nearly believed her. He'd seen the same innocence before as she'd danced. But no innocent came so wantonly displayed.

He began circling her again. "No weapon? I beg to differ, my lady. You, in and of yourself, are the most perfect of weapons for driving a man to distraction and much else."

In a swift move, he fettered her wrists in his grasp, lifting them immobile over her head. She gasped, her eyes wide with startled wonder and perhaps a little fear. Had someone threatened her in the past? Alex met her gaze with a knowing smile, recognizing the first signs of her passionate cravings. He was not the only one affected by their game. Desire enlarged the dark pupils of her eyes. Even now he caught the essence of her arousal mingled with the scent of her roses, her wonder winning out over whatever she feared.

"Shall I show you all the ways you distract a man?" His voice was a husky whisper, meant to compel. Dexterously, Alex slid the buttons of the chemise free of their loops, giving his hand access to the warm skin beneath. His hand skimmed the length of her torso, feeling her tremble beneath the stroking caress before returning to cup each full breast, taking them by turn completely in the palm of his hand. He ran the pad of his thumb ever so lightly over the peaks of her breasts, calling them to life beneath his caress.

"What are you doing to me?" she managed, her voice nothing more than a sob of pleasure.

He whispered close to her ear, his attentions turned now to her throat. "Making love to you." His mouth dropped to her breasts, suckling, delighting in her untutored response, part shock at the intimacy of the act and part honest woman enjoying the passion. "A man would do anything to claim this body." God knew he would, was in fact about to do just that no matter the risk. He was blind to all else in these moments but the bounty before him. He was nearly driven to the brink of his control by the firm fruits of her breasts, the scent of her, the innocent responses of her body. Houri, spy, sheikh's tool, increasingly, he cared not.

"Let go of my hands," she begged with a whimper, her desire mounting to the point of insensibility.

He nipped at her neck. "No, I like you entirely at my disposal. You like it, too, your body admits it, your body trusts me, let your mind do the same." He reached around her, drawing her against him with one arm so that she could feel his erection against her bare skin. He kissed her full on the mouth, stifling her pro forma protests as his hand dropped to between her legs. Her mouth opened under his with a silent gasp of pleasure. Christ, she was beautiful.

"'Thus it shall be, that we shall pair, in these gardens will be mates of modest gaze whom neither man nor invisible being will have touched ere then.'" He quoted between kisses, his breathing heavy. There was a reason the Koran equated the houris of Muslim lore with an ecstatic awareness of Allah.

She cried out, taken by early waves of pleasure and Alex knew all resistance had been swept aside in the wake of her passions. He would take her, and they would know mutual fulfillment together this night, whatever other less-pleasant agendas lay between them.

Susannah was oblivious to all else but the feel of Alex's hands on her body, coaxing it to extraordinary levels of pleasure. He covered her entirely, all thoughts of her plans and escapes fleeing her mind in the wake of this new world of ecstasy.

Alex rose above her, golden and strong, his knee parting her thighs with little opposition, the desire in his gaze mesmerizing. Then he shifted, his body lowering, entering her, surging hard into her until she cried out. She was full of him and yet, arching her body wantonly into his, it still wasn't enough. Suddenly there was pain, a shocking realization amid all the pleasure.

She cried out against it, but he was already pressing forward and when the recognition hit him, it was too late. A look of surprise crossed his features, his body stilled momentarily inside her, but passions were too high for them to stop. Even now the pain was subsiding and her body reached for the promise of awaiting pleasure. Her legs wrapped about his waist, trapping him to her. "Please," Susannah whispered.

It was all the invitation Alex needed. His body answered the call to passion, full-sheathed within her, until climax took her and she cried her release into his shoulder, feeling him shudder deep inside her.

# Chapter Four

A pessimist would say she had been carried away. An optimist would argue her plan had succeeded, Susannah mused. Rational thought made a slow return to the dim confines of the tent. Now that she had Alex's attention she scarcely knew what to do with it. Her plan had been based on solid assumptions; he wanted her. But she'd had no idea how far his wanting would take things. Or for that matter, how far *her* wanting would leave her vulnerable to him. Her own responses had been utterly surprising. Alex dozed lightly beside her. Soon, she'd have to wake him. She did not yet have what she'd come to the tent for.

But for now, she wanted to enjoy watching her lover sleep. *Lover.* The term implied that the encounter was more than a physical mating. In addition to his prowess, she recognized in retrospect there'd been an underlying care present in his lovemaking. He'd been sensitive to her needs, wanting her to find her own pleasure, wanting to alleviate her brush with pain. She had not expected that to be the case. Her encounters with the sheikh and with Bassam had suggested the act of sex was solely a male exercise in physical fulfillment at the female's expense. Perhaps that explained why she'd managed to thwart physical consummation for months, and yet had capitulated within moments to Alex.

Alex stirred and woke, taking her in with his eyes, a slow smile on his lips. He traced a lazy line over the curve of her hip and kissed her on the forehead before giving a sigh. "It seems we've done everything but what you came here to do." He sounded regretful to be pulling them back into reality. "Perhaps now would be a good time to talk."

*Talk.* The word struck a chord of trepidation within her.

It occurred to her that she had not told her story to anyone before. The tragedy in the desert had been a grief she'd borne silently these past months. How to unearth all that now and share it with this man who, in spite of their intimacy, was a virtual stranger?

Alex offered a gentle prompt. "Why don't we start with your name. You know mine, but I feel woefully disadvantaged."

Her name would change everything. Clearly, he hadn't known beforehand. He had not come here to save her or to look for her, confirming her suspicion that the British Consul believed her entire party to be dead. It was too much to hope for that anyone had come looking for her. She'd given up on that particular fantasy months ago. It was expensive and risky to send search parties into the desert. Besides, the chances of anyone knowing she was alive were minimal; the sands left no clues, no trails.

There was no escaping recognition. He would know her father's name. On one hand, it would help her cause. The Blond Bedouin would not leave Sutcliffe's daughter in the desert. But it would potentially alter their passion. Would he feel obligated to her? She understood what she'd become in the desert. This interlude, although not of her making, had put her outside English Society. She wanted no man's pity. That was what her logical mind feared. Her heart feared something else: Would he decline to make love to her again out of a retroactive display of old-fashioned honor? Already, her body wanted him again. Once with Alex Grayfield simply wasn't enough.

Susannah swallowed hard and took her chances. "My name is Susannah. Susannah Sutcliffe."

"Ah," came the reply. A small word to carry such import. In that *ah* was the recognition she'd predicted and the dawning realization of what they'd done, of what *he'd* done. He might have been raised in the desert lands, but she could see the English wheels of his mind working in reaction to this latest revelation.

"I know a little of your circumstance," he began. "Sutcliffe's entourage set out from Algiers shortly after the battle in November but no correspondence ever came verifying Sutcliffe's arrival in Mascara. The plan had been to journey from Algiers to Mascara, calling on the tribes that lay between the two cities."

"Is that your mission as well?" Susannah's gaze shot upward to meet Alex's eyes.

Alex shrugged noncommittally. Even now, he did not entirely confide in her. "You will need to trust me before this is over," she said abruptly, picking up the story where Alex had left it. "Perhaps this part of the story will help with that. My father's entourage was ambushed by the sheikh's raiders. You will be killed too if he learns you're here to see if the tribes will join with the emir."

Alex gave no outward acknowledgment of her warning.

"And you? What happens to you in all this drama?" He traced slow, tantalizing circles on her skin. This was her chance. She would never get a more perfect opening.

She leaned forward boldly and kissed him on the mouth.

"Take me with you when you go. I am a slave to the sheikh. Ask for me as a gift," she whispered.

"And if that fails? I do not see the sheikh being eager to part with you."

"Find another way. I understand I ask no small thing." Susannah drew back slightly, meeting his gaze with as much dignity as she could summon while naked in his bed. "Nothing matters except that you take me with you. I did not come to you as a tool of the sheikh's to discover your motives for being here. I have warned you. I might even claim that I've saved your life by doing so and that you owe me a life in return."

"The law of the desert," Alex murmured, the hot emerald coals of his eyes stoked to life. "A life for a life."

"And I choose mine as the price for yours," Susannah answered.

"You shall have it," Alex whispered, his mouth hovering inches above hers. "When we depart the *moussem*, you shall come with us. You have my word on it, my very mouth on it." He sealed his vow with a kiss.

Susannah reached for him, feeling him rise against the contact of her palm. Ah good, his body was in agreement.

Alex made some move to protest, but Susannah hushed him with a gentle finger to his lips and a shake of her head. "I do not want your protestations of honor, Alex. There's nothing to scourge your conscience over." She pulled him to her, her body eager to be claimed. She felt him give himself over to the pleasure building between them. For the moment her absolution was enough. Only a fool would keep Paradise waiting, and Alex Grayfield demonstrated that he was a very wise man indeed.

She would remember that kissing vow, Susannah thought later, slipping out to the privacy of her own tent. There were things more binding than words or contracts. Alex was not alone in his desire. It was something of a surprise that the ties bound both ways. In her naïveté, she had not looked ahead to the potential of forming her own attachment. She had thought to lure him with sex—it was, after all, the only currency available to her in the sheikh's camp. She had not thought to enjoy him in a way that went beyond the sensual. Alex Grayfield had been on display tonight in ways that transcended his naked body. He'd shown her sensitivity where her pleasure was concerned, and he'd shown interest in her thoughts and in her person. He'd asked about her captivity in a way that separated that ordeal from its impact on the political situation. Those lures were, in fact, equally as potent as the temptations offered by his body, and in some ways, more so. In her experience, rare was the man who put others' needs above his own. That was a powerful lure indeed.

She'd known Alex Grayfield's presence would change things, but she hadn't known just how pervasive that change would be. It would be easy to love him. When she'd formulated her plan, such a consequence had been most unlooked for.

Not that it would matter. What man would want a woman who'd danced as she had? She was a suitable companion for a few nights of passion. But a suitable wife? She was realist enough to know those chances were gone. It was a sobering thought.

Soon she'd be free. The desert could be left behind, but the stigma of her captivity could not. She had not allowed herself to think of life beyond the desert. But now she must if freedom was imminent. She could start a new life with the remaining threads of her old one; she had connections, money and her father's name to trade on, but what Society would receive her? Certainly not England's. Whatever new life she cobbled together would have to be far from English shores, and she would most likely have to be alone.

# *Chapter Five*

"The sheikh does not wish to defeat the French?" Crispin rose from his couch, digesting Alex's news the following morning while they broke their fast on yoghurt and dates.

Alex relayed what Susannah had told him the night before. "Sheikh Bitar sees the French as an affront to the traditional way of life. But more than that, Bitar sees al Qadir as a tyrant. Those who do not come to his standard willingly will be subjugated. That makes Qadir no better than the French in the sheikh's eyes."

"But perhaps more resistible," Crispin surmised the implications quickly. "It would be easier to undermine the emir's efforts and take a chance on the French being unable to control what really went on in the desert."

Alex nodded, that had been his conclusion last night as well. "It would be an incredible feat to join the tribes into a unified force. The emir's efforts are unlikely to succeed. The tribes have spent their histories fighting each other and now the emir wants them to be friends."

If the sheikh prevented the English from offering support to the emir, the army he was raising might not defeat the French. There was nothing like defeat to dampen the willingness of men to fight. Without an army, al Qadir was nothing, just a powerless potentate, and Bitar was betting the French would leave the Bedouin alone in the desert.

Crispin sat back down, pushing his hands through his long dark hair. "There's a good chance the sheikh's right. The French can claim to own the territory on a map, but in actuality, it will be difficult to impose rule in such a vast and harsh land. He'd rather take his chances with the French than with Abd al Qadir."

"It's too bad. If anyone can unite the tribes, it's the emir. From what I know of the man, he's a holy man, a decent man. Innovative, too. He's styled his army after the European fashion. He wants his people educated in Western ways. The people who have joined him see the merit of these additions."

"But Muhsin Bitar does not." Crispin sighed. "It would be best if he doesn't suspect our real reason for being here, although two Englishmen wandering in the desert is bound to raise questions." Crispin thought for a moment. "We'll tell Bitar we're horse traders. A *moussem* is perfect for discovering new horses. Perhaps that will give us alibi enough for being here and persuade him we're not politicking."

He winked at Alex. "I do hope to make the alibi a fact in truth, however. The sheikh has a prime goer, the black. The blasted horse sleeps in the sheikh's own tent. Can you imagine that?"

Alex smiled at the look on Crispin's face. "It's because of the camels. Horses can't stand the smell of them, it makes them high-strung, hard to handle."

"Like a woman," Crispin commented wryly. Alex chose to let the deliberate hint slide. Beyond political necessity, he wasn't ready to talk about Susannah and what had transpired last night.

"I must start thinking of a way to charm it out of him,

persuade him to make a gift of it," Crispin mused out loud.

"I think there are better 'gifts' to ask for. It goes without saying that she wants to come with us," Alex interjected.

Crispin fixed him with a knowing stare. "I was wondering when we'd get around to this. Can we trust her?"

Alex shrugged. "Does it matter? She's an English captive being held against her will. But yes, there's little reason not to trust her."

Crispin gave a cynical laugh. "She's a woman, Alex, you can't really trust any of them. But let's hope you've found the rare gem. After all, she knows now that we're here to discover where allegiances lie. All she has to do is tell the sheikh and we're on the run. *And* she'll have whatever it is the sheikh has promised her. Her freedom perhaps?"

Alex bristled at Crispin's implication. "We *can* trust her. She only knew about our mission because it was her father's mission before it was ours. She needs us alive."

Crispin nodded, content to accept Alex's analysis. "Assuming you're right, how are we going to get her out of here?"

Alex grinned. "There're only two options, really, Cris. Either we convince Bitar to give her to us as a gift or we steal her and ride like hell."

"I was afraid you were going to say that. I guess we might as well take the horse while we're at it. In for a penny, in for a pound. Do you think the Crown will ever forgive us for this one? Stealing women, stealing horses. Our skills grow illustrious, dear friend."

Alex chuckled. "Your brother's an earl, they'll forgive you anything. It's me I'm worried about."

"Ha, you'll be the Prince Charming in all this, riding out of the desert with the missing diplomat's daughter riding pillion behind you. It's the stuff of ballads. I can see it now,

'The Lay of Alex and Susannah' sung in all of London's finest pubs."

"Leave it, Cris, she's a diplomat's daughter."

"Being a diplomat's daughter doesn't make her a nun," Crispin countered.

"She is not a houri. She is Susannah Sutcliffe, Lord Sutcliffe's daughter, and I'll thank you to speak about her with respect." Alex bristled.

Crispin looked at him sharply and raised an eyebrow. "Hmm. I don't think I've ever heard you so on edge about a woman. It rather sounds like there's more to you and Miss Susannah than meets the eye."

Alex rose, blithely ignoring Crispin's comment. "I need to take care of some things. I'll see you shortly at the sheikh's tent. I think he has some competitions lined up for today." Crispin and he had worked together for two years. His friend was eminently trustworthy and quite the finest man he'd ever partnered with, but for some reason Alex did not want such crass witticisms slandering his encounter with Susannah.

Alex wandered the *moussem*'s *souk,* pausing every so often to admire the merchant's booths and their goods on display at the fair. He stopped at a booth selling creams and purchased a small pot. The rose scent reminded him of Susannah.

Ah, Susannah. She'd occupied a fair share of his thoughts since last night. Their interlude had been entirely other-worldly, but increasingly it was hard to keep the real-world implications from intruding.

He was on difficult ground. Alex had lain awake long after Susannah had left. He'd meant to spend the night thinking over diplomatic issues, but his thoughts had con-tinuously drifted back to her. When it had been a game of desire, of bodies speaking to one another in the time-less language of seduction, who she was had not been a consideration. She'd simply been a woman, passionate and bold. He'd been a man, answering the lure of her body. It had been simple and primal in the darkness of the tent.

Then he'd asked her name and reality had struck. She was an Englishman's daughter. Not just any Englishman's daughter. There were Englishmen and then there were *Englishmen*. Her father had been of the latter category.

Lord Sutcliffe was no meager player in British affairs. He'd been considered a top-notch diplomat when it came to the Empire in North Africa. Alex's father had met with him on occasion over Egyptian affairs. Alex had admired him as a hero during his years growing up in Cairo. No other man in the Empire had possessed Sutcliffe's depth of knowledge concerning the varied peoples of North Africa.

To be set upon by the mercenaries of Sheikh Bitar was an ignoble death for anyone, particularly one so decorated in life. For Sutcliffe's daughter to be made a captive and subjugated to who-knew-what atrocities was an intolerable slap in the face to the Empire's pride, but Alex's body burned for a personal vengeance against Bitar and Bassam. What had they subjected Susannah to during her captivity? A woman did not have to be bedded to be debased and there'd been a moment of fear in her eyes last night when he'd grabbed her.

Seldom had a woman's attentions claimed him so completely. Alex was struck anew with the power of his desire, his desire not only to possess her but to be the first and only one to do so. That desire brought him full circle in his thoughts.

She was Sutcliffe's daughter and he was an Englishman bound by certain codes of conduct. In the throes of pleasure, he'd taken her virginity. By the nature of her birth and status in society, she could not be like his other casual encounters, enjoyed and cast aside when the excitement ebbed. She would surely demand from him a level of commitment he'd given no other woman. The strange thing was that, for the first time in his life, making that commitment didn't sound like such a ridiculous idea.

A horn blew in the *souk* announcing the beginning of the games. Alex turned his direction toward the big tents of the sheikh, where men were gathering for the traditional competitions. He could see Crispin's tall frame among them. It was time to act. Before he could think of what the future might hold with Susannah, he had to win her first.

# *Chapter Six*

⚜

The activities of the *moussem* suited Alex and Crispin's purposes admirably. Games of skills and other competitions gave them a chance to build a masculine camaraderie with the other men present. They did not hesitate to participate. He and Crispin showed off their talents at knife-throwing. They looked over the horses other sheikhs had brought in hopes of races or trading, bolstering their cover as horse traders.

As night fell and the traditional hookah pipe came out to be passed and smoked in Bitar's tent, Alex felt they'd made good progress in gaining a place of acceptance. Last night, they'd been invited out of courtesy, but tonight they were part of the group, having proven their prowess and their worthiness to be accepted. Alex's mastery of Arabic had made that acceptance easier. That they were dressed in Bedouin robes and speaking the common language of the desert made it harder for Bitar to remember they did not belong. It had been a strategy that had worked well for Alex over the years and he had used it liberally today to gain acceptance for him and Crispin.

Tonight would be the test. Alex knew what the men

should talk about in the tent. They *should* talk politics and the business of their tribes. If they didn't then Alex would know his acceptance was not complete. He reached for a date, using the action as an opportunity to search the tent for Susannah. He had not seen her all day. While that had been disappointing, it had not been unexpected. Her place was in the night. His body quickened in anticipation. He popped the date into his mouth, aware of Bassam's eyes on him. The man had watched him all day.

"The Emir of Mascara has invited us to join him," a man close to Alex said, addressing his comment to Bitar. "Will you journey on from here to Mascara?"

Bitar shook his head and spat, his tone derisive. "No, I will not go to join that infidel dog. He calls this a holy war, but it is nothing more than a ruse to subdue us to his will. He wishes to be more than the emir of a city. He wishes to be a king over all of us."

"Are you not worried about the French? They have taken Algiers," another asked.

Bitar raised his arms wide to encompass the room and the world outside the expansive tent. "What is there to worry about in the desert? The French have no way to impose their law and order out here. Here, we are law and I mean to keep it that way."

Alex nodded along with the other men in the room in a show of solidarity for the sheikh's opinion. He shot a quick glance at Crispin, his nod conveying something entirely different. Crispin nodded back. Susannah had not lied. More than that, she had proven to be resourceful, making the most of her captivity. Her command of Arabic must be better than Alex had originally thought if she'd used her lowly position as a dancing girl to complete her father's mission. His admiration for her increased even further. She'd demonstrated beyond doubt she was definitely her father's daughter.

The pipe came his way and he drew deeply on it, exhaling with fervor. He did not care for the sweet smoke of the pipe but sharing the pipe was a sign of friendship, to refuse would be damning in the extreme. He passed the pipe to Crispin and the drums started. Shouts of approval rose from the men farther back by the entrance and clapping began in rhythm with the drums as the dancers entered the tent.

Alex saw Susannah immediately at the head of the line. Tonight she was dressed sumptuously in red and gold, a belt of coins tinkling provocatively at her hips, tiny brass cymbals in her hands clinking out the beat of the dance.

She was enchanting. Men stared after her hungrily as she passed until she reached the space in front of Bitar. Her hands were mesmerizing, their gestures guiding the men's gazes to her breasts beneath the red top she wore, leaving her splendid stomach uncovered to the collective gaze of the audience. Tonight, her costume left her much more exposed. The gauzy pantaloons rode seductively low on her hips, the delicate bones of her pelvis rising above the coin belt.

She danced as if she were oblivious to the eroticism of her costume, to the fact that her body was on display before men. Before him.

Desire throbbed in Alex. She might be oblivious to the gazes of other men, but he did not want her to be oblivious to him. Primal possession surged. He wanted her to acknowledge him. It was a foolish and dangerous wish with Bassam watching, but he wanted it all the same.

Then she did. She moved slightly to her left and put herself directly in front of him, her hips swaying, her eyes promising. She would keep those promises with him tonight, Alex vowed silently.

There were cards after dancing. For all of his protestations against the inventions of Europe, Bitar had a fondness for cards. Low tables were set up among the groupings of pillows in the tent and the men settled in for a night of cards and wine, some of the dancers staying behind to enliven the games. Alex saw Crispin claim a seat at the table with Bassam and Bitar, and he took his cue to slip out. Crispin would keep the men at the table all night.

Alex slid into the night, covertly grabbing up a wineskin and an errant plate of fruit that had gone untouched. The camp was busy. Other entertainments were taking place in other tents, people eager to impress one another and to make deals while the *moussem* lasted.

He found his own tent and waited. This was the only kink in his plan. He did not know where Susannah was lodged, and he could not go poking about without risk of discovery. But she'd come to him. *If she could.* The very thought of another commanding her to his bed rankled. More than rankled. That was too tame a word. The thought boiled his blood. Of course she'd come. The sheikh was at cards. He would not seek his bed until dawn.

His fears were unfounded. Moments later, Susannah pulled aside the tent flap and stepped inside, her eyes searching for him. She found him and smiled, the hood of her all-concealing robe falling back to reveal her glorious hair. "I can only stay a minute. Did you see today that I was right?" Her words were all business, but she was breathless.

Alex took her hand and drew her to him, inhaling deeply of her rose attar. "I heard the sheikh's testimony from his own lips. He, at least, will not be joining the emir." His words were business, too, but his tone was not. He wanted this night for something more than politics.

"You and your friend believe me then?" Her eyes searched his face. It was touching to know that his acceptance meant so much to her.

"We believe you. I believed you last night." He cupped

her cheek, the length of her hair running through his fingers like gold silk.

"I will not betray you to the sheikh," she whispered, turning her cheek into his hand to nuzzle it.

"I know. Come and eat with me. I have wine and figs."

"I cannot stay." There was regret in her tone. "I only have so much freedom because there's nowhere to run in the desert. But someone may miss me. I never know when the sheikh will call for my services."

"The sheikh will be at cards for hours. Crispin will see to it. He has a penchant to possess that horse," Alex encouraged in low sensual tones. "We have time for other business."

Susannah trembled. This was what she'd risked coming here for. She might tell herself it was to confirm the validity of her information, or to make sure Alex was bound to her, committed to keeping his promise, but deep inside, she knew she'd come because she'd wanted to, regardless of promises and plots. Tonight had only to do with honest want.

Alex led her to his bed and she sat cross-legged, tucking her robe around her. She still wore her decadent dancing costume underneath. She reached for a fig, but Alex forestalled her hand.

"Let me." He took the fig and dipped it in a small pot of honey before feeding it to her. He held it above her lips, dribbling honey on them and she licked them, her heart fluttering faster in her chest, warmth pooling between her legs.

"Tease," Alex whispered hoarsely.

She bit into the fig with a small moan of delight.

"Temptress," he growled and she laughed, amazed to find she had such power over him.

"I had not known eating could be so enjoyable." She bit into another offering of fruit.

With an oath, he set the tray of food aside and came up over her, covering her with his length. He kissed her full on the mouth and she reveled in the taste of him, the sweet flavor of honey and wine from the sheikh's feast lingering on his lips.

He explored her mouth with his tongue and she responded with passion, her body urging him to taste all she offered, proving last night had been only the beginning. His hands moved beneath her robe, stilling when they met with evidence of her costume. "No chemise tonight?" he asked quietly.

She stiffened. "I didn't have time to change." She hesitated. "Does it repulse you?"

Alex sat back on his heels and studied her face. "You could never repulse me. I only dislike that he parades you in front of others as a sign of his hospitality." He was kissing her again, trailing little kisses down the column of her throat, causing her pulse to race at the base of her neck. He spoke between kisses.

"When I saw you tonight, I wanted you to dance only for me. I wanted my eyes to be the only ones that watched you. I wanted to rip Bassam's throat out for seeing you dressed like that. I wanted to carry you out of that tent and ravish you straight away."

His hands were at the skimpy top she wore, working the clasp at the back to free her breasts. He kissed her bared nipples and she shuddered in delight. His lips traveled downward toward her belly, stopping to kiss her navel, his hands intimately and possessively framing her body at her hips, his thumbs resting on her pelvis.

Slipping the gauzy pantaloons from her legs, his hands returned to their original positions at her hips, his chin resting lightly at her belly as he looked up at her, his green eyes dark and intent. His thumbs massaged gently as he spoke. "I mean to worship you, my beautiful Susannah."

He did not wait for an answer but reached for the wineskin, spilling some on her breasts and her belly and suckling deeply. Susannah cried out, helplessly aroused at his audacity, acutely aware of his breath warm on her, his mouth bent to the heat at her core. Her hands tangled in his thick hair, clutching for balance, as he brought her to a shuddering wave of pleasure. She had not thought her body possessed the ability to claim such gratification.

Alex was moving over her now and she spread her legs instinctively to welcome him. Her arms twined about his neck, her legs about his waist, claiming him as her own, pushing him forward into her. She rose against him, her hips meeting his, urging him deeper. Then it began, truly began. All else had been a precursor to the great joy that awaited her. Alex drove her there and joined her, their bodies exploding together, the warmth of him filling her with great pulsing throbs as he emptied his body into hers in the most intimate of communions.

# Chapter Seven

"Is it always like this?" Susannah's question was whispered in awe, an eternity later, once their bodies had settled and she lay securely in his arms.

How was he to answer that? It had never been quite like this for him either. "It can be. Sometimes it is less." *Much less,* Alex thought to himself. He was beginning to see how his prior encounters had been limited, nothing more than a physical function of the body that brought temporary satisfaction. *This* was something else entirely. But he could hardly explain that to Susannah when he could barely explain this new wondrous thing to himself.

Susannah nodded against his shoulder, her hair tickling his nose. "I didn't think it would be like this. I didn't think lovemaking could be for me. I thought it was really only for the man. The sheikh…" Her voice broke off and she squirmed uncomfortably against him.

"The sheikh what?" Alex probed softly, his prior fears of what she might have endured in captivity rising to the fore. She might have come to him a virgin, but there were other ways… "Tell me, Susannah."

"It is nothing, now. You've proven it can be otherwise

and that's all that matters. I won't have you doing anything rash. What's done can't be undone."

"That's not the most compelling argument, Susannah," Alex said grimly. "If anything, it makes me even angrier. Tell me. I am not prone to rash behavior, I can give you my word on it."

She drew a deep breath and slowly began to spill her tale, the tale she had not shared with him last night when he'd asked: how she'd been brought before the sheikh, spared in the ambush because the captain of the raiders thought Bitar would fancy her gold hair. Bitar had indeed fancied her. He'd cleared the tent of all but his physic and ordered her to strip. It had been the last she'd seen of her clothing, and Bitar had gazed upon her naked form, lust evident in his eyes for what seemed an age. "Let us see if she's a houri in truth," he'd said, submitting her to the most personal and invasive of examinations, his delight bordering on ecstasy when the physic confirmed her purity.

Alex breathed deeply beside her when she finished. "The sheikh has debased you and is responsible for the death of your father. I will kill him for you, if you like." He would, too. Life and death had different meanings in the desert, and there was a part of him that was far less English than the other parts. He had killed for honor before with just cause and was not afraid to do it again should right demand it, should this vibrant woman in his arms demand it.

"I want only to put all this behind me," she answered.

His kiss was strong and firm on her neck. "Then let me love you tonight and erase those memories. The sheikh meant only to humiliate. I mean nothing of the sort." He pulled her to him and whispered out loud the litany that had run through his mind all day. "You're mine, Susannah, and no other's."

As he joined with her for a second time that night, reaching once more for ecstasy, Alex knew he wanted her in ways that transcended this bed. He wanted Susannah for her passion, for her intelligence, for her courage and strength. He wanted her forever.

*You're mine and no other's.* The words dared her to hope as Alex helped her into her clothing. Dawn was approaching and she could not risk staying a moment longer. The sheikh would be ending his night of cards.

"Soon, Susannah, we'll be away from here, free to make our own plans," Alex promised, settling her robes about her.

*Our own plans.* How nice that sounded. But she had to be fair. "You are not obligated, Alex, just because you're the one who found me."

Alex tipped her chin up so her eyes met his. "Finders, keepers, isn't that how it goes?" he teased lightly.

*For how long?* she wondered. He might keep her in Algiers as a mistress perhaps, visiting her when his work brought him in from the desert. Would that be enough for her? Surely, he would not offer her more. Once he saw how Society would treat her, he would understand he could not be so gallant with his intentions.

Still, the last two nights had proven how wonderful it was to be loved by Alex Grayfield. It was more than a physical experience. She'd felt cared for, cherished in his arms. She knew enough now to confirm what she'd expected earlier. Her feelings for Alex had grown beyond the physical. For better or for worse, she had traveled far and fast down the path of love.

She reached up to his face and kissed him softly on the lips. "Thank you for everything, Alex." It was as close as she dared come to saying "I love you." Then she was gone, slipping out into the camp, hugging her hope as she went, Alex's words a mantra in her mind. *You are mine and no other's.*

# Chapter Eight

"He covets her, Muhsin. And I think she is not indifferent to the Christian dog." Bassam took a sloppy sip of wine and reclined against the pillows in his brother-in-law's tent. They were alone in the quiet part of the afternoon and he was free to speak his mind at last. "You have lost your prized horse to the one. If you are not careful, you will lose your houri, too."

The sheikh shrugged his shoulders in a gesture of nonchalance. "The blond one is cognizant of our ways. He would not dare to intrude in that domain."

Bassam narrowed his eyes in thoughtful contemplation. "Beneath his robes, behind his flawless command of the language, he is an Englishman. That is a fact best not forgotten." He studied Muhsin. His brother-in-law was much taken with the blond newcomer and with his dark-haired companion. It was making him careless.

"The *moussem* will be over soon and they will go their way," Muhsin reasoned.

"With your favorite horse."

Muhsin laughed. "Do you think I'd be sitting here so calmly if I meant to let them actually take the horse?"

Bassam relaxed slightly. That sounded more like the brother-in-law he knew. "And your English houri? Will she stay behind, too?"

Muhsin's eyes darkened at the mention of his latest acquisition. "I have told her my patience is up. After the *moussem* she is to be mine in truth. She is an untouched gem, all that a virile man desires."

"Like the houris promised by the Koran in the afterlife," Bassam mused. "Modest, voluptuous and untouched by another, her body without the blemishes of childbirth." He eyed Muhsin speculatively. "What if she's been touched by another after all?"

"She has not. My physician has vouched for her chastity," Muhsin contested.

"That was months ago." Bassam played idly with a cluster of grapes. "I did not exaggerate when I said you stood to lose your horse and your houri. Last night, she went to the Englishman's tent while his friend kept us at cards. She was there a long while."

The sheikh's face darkened with anger. "How do you know this?"

"I saw the desire in the Englishman's face the first night she danced. I had her followed, for her protection, of course, in case the Englishman forced his attentions upon her," Bassam said slyly. "But last night, there was no forcing. She went to him."

Bassam watched the implications become clear to Muhsin. After a calculated silence, Bassam spoke. "She has abused your generosity and patience. She has shamed you by giving herself to an infidel."

The English bitch had shown him nothing but disdain since her arrival in camp, Bassam thought. A woman in her precarious position should have welcomed the bargain he'd been willing to make her. But she'd shunned him just as she'd shunned his powerful brother-in-law. She would soon learn her place. She would soon see that the power of her wiles extended only so far, and that the real power over life and death, freedom and captivity, lay with him. She would regret her choice to go it alone.

Muhsin's anger grew. "She favors the Englishman over me? She favors a meager *horse trader?*"

"It is perhaps more than that," Bassam insinuated. The seed of doubt had been planted and he nurtured it with his other suspicions. "The two newcomers are more than horse traders, don't you think?"

He had all of Muhsin's attention now. "What do you suspect they're hiding?"

"They've come for her, perhaps? Maybe they have been sent to find out the truth about the entourage that disappeared in the desert? Perhaps they've come to finish what the entourage started? They've come to ferret out alliances and see where the tribes will side?"

"Spies? Is this what they do in exchange for my hospitality? I have welcomed them into my tent and shared the hookah with them."

Bassam nodded solemnly. "They have misused the hospitality of the desert quite horribly. Punishment would not be out of order. The *moussem* ends tomorrow, it would be a good time to make an example out of them, to show the tribes what it means to defy Sheikh Muhsin ibn Bitar."

Muhsin was thoughtful. "Yes, I think you may be right about that. I will start with the captive tonight."

A wicked gleam lit Bassam's eyes. "She can be used to draw the Englishman out and force him to perjure himself. If she is known to be in jeopardy, he may show his hand."

Something was wrong. Susannah stumbled in the sand, fighting against the strong grip of Bassam's hand about her wrist. He was angry. This was no polite escort and she could only speculate why.

She had danced tonight for the sheikh, as always, had pleased the audience. It was the last time she'd have to dance in that manner. Tomorrow she'd be free. Alex would make his request tonight as the men sat and talked. Had he already made his request? Was that why Bassam had come for her without warning?

"You have defiled yourself with an Englishman, without permission. Now, you will pay." Bassam jerked her to an abrupt halt outside the sheikh's tent. His face was close to her. She could smell the residue of spices on his breath, the gaminess of the roasted lamb. She fought the urge to cringe. She could not afford to show weakness in front of Bassam.

He forced himself upon her lips, his mouth demanding she open to him. She struggled against him, twisting her head to avoid contact. She kicked out with her foot, but Bassam was too swift. He pinioned her against him. "You're a feisty one, and I find I am less discerning than my brother-in-law. I do not care that I have not had you first, only that I have you next and last. I can still save you. Remember that before you lash out." He bit at her ear, nothing like the loving nips Alex had showered her with. She stifled a yelp against his harsh methods.

Where was Alex now? She hoped he was safe. Somehow the sheikh knew what they had done. Had Alex made his request yet?

Bassam pushed her inside the tent and she scanned the interior rapidly. Alex was there, seated across from the shiekh. He was alone. Crispin was not present. Alex sat erect, his body hard and alert. He was aware that the situation had become hostile. But even so, his presence buoyed her hope. She took courage from his cool assurance as he eyed the sheikh unflinchingly. Alex would not fail her.

"Is this how you treat your guests? I have come to barter with you honestly for a lowly slave in your possession," Alex charged, taking the offensive as she was thrust into the center of the conversation.

She met his eyes with a quick glance, but he shifted his gaze away. Probably a smart choice. Susannah averted her own eyes to the floor, unwilling to give away more emotion than she wanted. Her freedom lay in the balance, dependent now upon the wits of Alex Grayfield. A wrong glance from her, a wrong word, would seal not only her fate but his. They were now irrevocably linked together.

"You have taken her without my permission. You've lain with her and befouled her."

"And I am willing to do my duty by her," Alex replied evenly, showing no agitation at the harsh words meant to provoke. "I will take her from your sight."

"That is not all." Muhsin held up a hand. "She has committed an act of defiance against me. I have it on good authority that *she* went to you, she sought your bed willingly." He gave a manly shrug. "If it had been simply a matter between men, we could have settled it between ourselves," he said benevolently, although Susannah doubted it would have been as simple as he made it sound. "But a woman's dishonor combined with a slave's disobedience must be accounted for lest others find me weak and seek to try me in kind."

The look Muhsin cast her chilled her in spite of the tent's heat. She heard the implicit deal Muhsin was willing to contract with Alex. She would be made to pay most horribly. If Alex confessed she'd come to him, he could pass unscathed as long as he left.

Alex said nothing, and Susannah breathed more easily. She wanted to trust Alex, but the offer had to be tempting. The sheikh spoke again. "You have in your possession a horse I admire. Relinquish the horse and that would cover any misunderstanding between us."

Again the implicit opportunity to deny her, to lay the blame entirely at her feet; she had seduced him and he had not understood the inappropriateness of the seduction. Susannah clenched her hands to keep them from trembling. Surely Alex would not betray her? He'd promised. But what did she know of the man? Was he a man of his word or would he seek to save himself at her expense? Her mind warned that she knew nothing of him, a man who had wandered in from the desert two days ago.

But her heart argued otherwise. The man so concerned with her pleasure, who worshiped her body so reverently, was a man of sincerity and honor. Whatever he did with her afterward, he would not leave her here to face a cruel fate at Bassam's hands. She knew what awaited her if he denied her—public punishment and the private humiliations Bassam would heap upon her. She could imagine, too, what awaited Alex if he did not deny her. At the very least there would be trial by fire, the Bedouin tradition for truth-telling, at the worst he would be ruined as a man unless she could intervene.

"Will you play me for her? She is not one of you. Your codes are not her codes. Whatever she has done, let me at least play for her. I fancy her and, unlike you, I am not repulsed by her sin," Alex said with cool casualness.

"No cards." The sheikh laughed, warming to the idea of a competition. "If you're as good as your friend, it is hardly fair."

"Weapons then. We are all fair hands with knives," Alex suggested. "You and Bassam against Crispin and myself."

"It is dark."

"The tent is large. We can set targets at the far end," Alex countered.

The sheikh glanced at Bassam. "What do you say?"

Bassam grinned. "Take the challenge. If they win, they may take the girl. If they lose, they will leave camp before sun-up, happy to be alive and praising the sheikh's generosity."

Susannah fought the urge to seek out Alex's gaze. Her fate balanced literally and metaphorically on the point of a knife, and she, a woman used to taking care of herself, could do nothing about it but watch and wait.

## Chapter Nine

It was to be a private competition between the four of them, but it was no less tense for the lack of spectators.

Alex critically watched the targets being prepared by a trusted relative of the sheikh. He resented being unable to go to Susannah, who'd been manhandled roughly to the side to sit under guard.

She'd borne up stoically under the crass negotiations. She'd kept her eyes modestly downcast throughout the transaction, but he knew she'd heard the unspoken messages as well. As Sutcliffe's daughter she would have been trained to read between the lines. He'd feared at one point she would protest and give herself up out of some misguided effort to save him. Such a sacrifice might have momentarily cleansed the conscience but it would have done little to alter the situation. She'd shown great insight and understanding to know enough to withhold her reaction.

"Is she worth it?" Cris spoke in low tones at his ear, passing him a throwing knife. Crispin Ramsden was a saint among men, Alex thought, a tarnished saint to be sure, but a saint all the same. He'd come without question ready to defend Alex's interests. Alex knew no finer gentleman than the rough-edged brother to the powerful Earl of Dursley.

"Yes," Alex replied. Everything was in that answer. He hazarded a glance at Susannah. He had not imagined himself to be a man open to love at first sight. In that regard, he'd believed himself to be much like Crispin, a cynical lover of women, quick to take pleasure but less hasty to bind himself to one in any permanent fashion. Yet a woman like Susannah demanded more, and he found he was more than willing to give it.

She was beauty personified with her pale gold hair and houri curves. But she was more than beauty. Her blue eyes were windows into mystery and intelligence. Without him realizing it, she had become an essential part of his plans for the future.

"We have to get out of here alive first," Crispin commented. "You're already planning your life together. Let's work on the present."

Alex laughed. "My apologies for being so transparent."

"A man in love always is." Crispin hefted a knife, testing its weight and balance. "I've seen it before. When my brother fell in love with Tessa, it was fast and deadly."

"You talk about it as if it's a disease, spreading like cholera."

"Well?" Crispin challenged.

"We'll find you a woman next."

Satisfied with their weapons, their talk turned serious in the moments they had left. The targets were nearly set.

"What's the plan if we lose?" Cris inquired, baring his teeth at a glaring Bassam across the tent.

"The same as if we win. It won't matter to them. They're not letting us go easily."

"Is this the ride-like-hell option you spoke of earlier?"

"Yes. Any chance our horses are close?"

"The black is outside. The sheikh thinks I've brought him to return him. The other two horses are in the rope pen behind the sheikh's tent where we left them when we rode in."

Alex spoke rapidly. "Susannah and I will make for the horse pen. You take the black and ride out. Don't wait for us."

Crispin nodded, understanding the necessity. If he rode out on the prized horse, he could be a successful diversion. "I'll see you in Algiers then, my friend."

All was ready. The targets were at thirty paces, a distance that would require a strong arm as well as accurate aim. Additional torches had been brought to the tent to ensure quality lighting. The flames also increased the temperature. Alex could feel sweat beading his brow in response to the additional heat.

The rules were simple. Each of them had four throws. The best combination of throws would determine the victor. Bassam threw first, two of his knives finding purchase on the second ring of the target, one of them on the outside ring, the final knife successfully finding the ring closest to the center.

Crispin tossed the man a look of disdain as if to say, *Is that the best you can do?* He stepped up to the line and sighted his target, throwing methodically, his arm in a guaranteed rhythm. Three of his knives gained the closest circle from the center, making the one knife of Bassam's look like a lucky strike compared to the expert accuracy of his. His fourth knife fell short of excellence and joined Bassam's in the second outer circle, but he'd still bested the sheikh's brother-in-law.

Alex gave Crispin a grateful nod. Cris had not failed him. They were ahead, three knives to one. But the sheikh remained. Alex had taken his measure carefully during the competitions the day before. Muhsin ibn Bitar was a fine knife-thrower; no one but himself had matched the sheikh. Even then, their competition had been a draw.

Undaunted by Crispin's excellence, Muhsin toed his mark and sighted the target. He threw slowly and with deadly accuracy. His first knife hit the bull's-eye and he cast a mocking glance at Susannah. His second knife sliced the ring closest to the center where most of Crispin's had fallen. But his last two throws were devastating, both of them hitting the center target.

So be it. Susannah was pale on the sidelines. This would be difficult indeed. The problem with throwing last, Alex thought, was that he would know if he'd lost after he'd thrown two knives. If at least one of them was a bull's-eye, he was still in. If neither hit a bull's-eye, the other two throws mattered not at all. Alex drew a deep breath. He had his methods and it would not do to deviate now.

Susannah held her breath, marveling at Alex's calm. In his turban and robes he might be one of them, so seamlessly did he fit in. Only the sharp green of his eyes and the sun-streaked hair that she knew lay beneath the winding wrap of his turban betrayed him as belonging to another world. She tried not to think of that world. It was a world in which she was no longer sure of her place.

Her renowned father was dead. Would she be welcome in his circles abroad? She could perhaps see herself making a quiet home in Italy or in Cairo where her experience in the desert wouldn't matter as greatly. Or would she be forced home to England and her mother's people? There would be pity there but no acceptance. They were strict people, doggedly adhering to the moral codes of Society. A Bedouin captive, a woman who'd lived without chaperone in a society they'd deem as immoral would not be suitable to their world. But all that remained to be seen, all of it resting on Alex's broad shoulders.

He stepped to the mark and stared hard at his target for long moments. All four knives were in his belt and he pulled forth the first one now and tossed it lightly in his hand. The wait was maddening. Without warning, he threw the first one, hard and sure toward the target. In rapid succession he drew the other three. He fired without hesitation. His movements mesmerized. He threw quickly and without thought, unlike the others, who'd deliberated before each throw.

There was no time to think, to register the landing of the knives. Later, she'd realize he'd planned it that way. He'd guessed all along that neither victory nor defeat would matter. The sheikh would not simply let him leave with her if he won. Neither would Alex simply walk away without her if he lost.

The speed of his throws was utterly distracting. He'd moved to her side before anyone realized it. The man in charge of the targets was busy tallying the scores. But Alex was pushing her toward the tent entrance behind them.

Crispin was already there, arms crossed and legs spread, ostensibly awaiting the pronouncement of victory.

Alex had just gently shoved Susannah into the darkness outside when the cry inside erupted.

"We have won, have we not?" Alex heard Crispin's challenge. "We're free to go."

There were harsh words and the commotion of a fight. Alex was torn between the need to go back and assist Crispin or to stay with Susannah. Crispin could handle himself in a fight. His sacrifice would be for nothing if he and Susannah did not get away.

"Quick, the horse pen." He ushered her forward in the dark, holding her firmly when she stumbled.

In the end, there wasn't time to get both horses. The animals were skittish with the camels so near them and

Alex had trouble calming his stallion down long enough to throw Susannah up. A challenging neigh in the darkness warned Alex Crispin had made his getaway. He swung up behind Susannah and kicked his horse into organized motion, leaning sideways and slicing an exit in the rope pen with a knife he'd secreted up his sleeve. He'd never, ever intended to fight fairly.

The opening in the pen full of camel-skittish horses had the desired effect. The animals spilled out into the camp in a rampage, taking the revelers unawares. But the distraction did not entirely ensure their escape. Bassam sighted them and raised the alarm.

Alex kicked his horse into a gallop, taking his chances with speed. If they could clear the camp, they would make it. But he needed a lead in order to get to the cache he'd stashed earlier in the day. Without those supplies, the desert would finish them off as surely as Bassam's knife.

Luck was with them. They cleared the camp and the rampaging horses ensured that no one had the speed to follow them into the desert. With more luck, the sheikh would assume they had no supplies, that their flight was precipitous and poorly thought out, and he would leave them to their demise.

Alex spotted the formation he'd used to mark his cache. He pulled the horse to a halt and slid off. "We made it." He grinned up at Susannah, pale but game on the back of the stallion, her hair a tumble of gold in the moonlight. She'd never looked lovelier to him.

"We won't survive without water. It's days back to Algiers," she said matter-of-factly.

Alex's grin widened. "I left supplies here today, in anticipation of our flight tomorrow. It's a good thing I plan ahead." He dug in the soft sand until he came up with wineskins and saddlebags of food. He passed them up to her and watched her settle them across the horse's withers.

She smiled, and he noted her tension had seeped away at the sight of water. Alex swung up behind her, ready to ride again. There was still distance to put between them and the camp. "Once we're safely away, I have some other plans I've made for you," he murmured in her ear.

She pressed her back against him and he savored the feel of her body nestled against him, close and intimate, her buttocks to his groin. He felt himself harden instinctively, but that would have to wait.

He urged his horse to a trotting pace. If they traveled by day they'd have to walk to save the horse from sweating too much, but in the cool of a desert night, they could manage the speed and right now they needed it.

"Will Crispin be all right?" Susannah asked when it became apparent he wasn't joining them.

"Crispin's always all right. He has a stash, too. He'll see us in Algiers," Alex answered confidently.

She sighed, her head moving sleepily against him. "You won, you know. All four knives were bull's-eyes."

She drowsed against him and Alex welcomed her weight. She was his. Just as soon as they reached Algiers, he'd make it legal.

Somewhere between the last of the night and sunrise, he found a cave with enough room for the horse to be comfortable during the hot day. It would do, for his horse and for him. The excitement of the evening's events and the woman he carried with him still fired his loins, seeking relief.

Inside the cave, he made their meager encampment, laying down a blanket for their bed. He laid Susannah gently upon it and she stirred at the movement, looking up at him through sleepy eyes. She reached for him. "Come to bed, Alex."

Four simple words, and yet the most powerful aphrodisiac he'd ever experienced, the words of a woman inviting a man to bed.

In a swift movement, he shrugged out of his robes and fell naked beside her in acceptance of the invitation. She snuggled beside him, her sleepiness disappearing. "You saved us, Alex." She kissed him hard on the mouth, a hand dropping low between them.

Alex groaned appreciatively. Her hand moved to stroke his length, massaging, arousing, if it was possible to be aroused further. Suddenly, she rolled over and straddled him. "I was thinking about this as we rode tonight," she whispered, letting her hair fall forward and tickle his nipples. "I was thinking that I could ride you like a horse, like a stallion."

"You could." Alex grinned as she teased.

"And I was thinking," she continued, bending to kiss him on the mouth, "that while I was up here, I could do… other things.…"

Alex's reply was hoarse. "You could," he managed. But his permission was hardly necessary. She'd already started the journey downward, trailing kisses down his chest, her breath feathering his navel, her lips pressing either side of his thighs and then finally reaching their destination.

She tested tentatively at first, her lips a mere flutter on the sensitive head of him. Then firmer as she took all of him, sucking and licking until Alex cried out into the night. This was an ecstasy beyond words and he reveled in her boldness.

When he could stand it no longer, he urged her head up and pulled her above him, letting her take his length inside her and begin to ride toward fulfillment. As the sun rose outside the cave, Alex took them both to completion, her body collapsing against him, satiated.

They spent the day in the cave. The sun was too hot to

make travel worthwhile. There was little to do but make love and talk, not that Alex minded. When he was with Susannah, he was discovering he wanted to do little else.

"Where will you go when we reach Algiers?" Susannah asked, playing idly with the flat of his aureole.

"Cairo. My family lives there, and you'll want to meet them. But there will be reports to make in Algiers. We'll be there awhile."

"We?" Susannah lifted her head, her sea-blue eyes curious.

"Us." Alex smiled softly. "I plan to marry you once we reach civilization. If you'll have me?" He levered up on one arm. "Susannah Sutcliffe, will you marry me? I cannot guarantee a life rich in wealth, but I can promise a life rich in adventure."

She laughed, but turned her gaze away. "The sun has touched you, Alex. You hardly know me and you must know that no one will consider me suitable. I'm damaged goods."

Alex snorted at that. "And what am I? I am no lord's son. I'm the son of a diplomat, who hopes to be a diplomat himself. Perhaps we've got a viscount grandfather somewhere in the family tree, but it's a tenuous claim to Society at best, and it's not a connection I trade on." Then he sobered, another thought striking him. "Perhaps you do not wish to marry me?" He had not anticipated her refusal. He was not a man who dwelt on failure. He had not thought of losing the knife contest just as he had not thought of losing her. They were both impossibilities to him.

She smiled softly. "I do not wish to hinder you, Alex. I recognized at once that first night I danced before you that you were a man of honor…"

Alex was in no mood to talk about his honor. "I want you, Susannah. Your intelligence and your courage. You are an incredible woman, and I want you to be mine." He reached for her, a hand behind her neck, pulling her to him for a kiss that spanned the chasm of her doubt. "Magic like this doesn't happen every day, Susannah," he whispered into her mouth. She stared at him, searching his eyes and slowly a smile of pure happiness spread across her face. He actually looked nervous. It had seemed impossible, but it was true. She was loved.

"Yes, Alex," she whispered back, her body molding to his as he rolled her beneath him. "Yes, I will marry you and be yours."

Glowing with relief, Alex moved to claim her, rising above her in man's age-old possession of a woman, a possession as ancient as the desert itself. He thrust deeply, finding his homecoming in her warmth. "Mine."

Ah, but he loved the desert.

# Epilogue

*A few months later, Algiers*

"I am told I must call you 'sir' now." Crispin sighed dramatically. He leaned on the rail of the little balcony of Alex's apartments looking out over the bay. A fresh wind blew off the water as the two friends said their farewells.

Alex nodded, smiling. "It was something of a surprise. London moved pretty quickly." He shot a sidelong glance at his friend. "I wonder if your brother had something to do that."

Crispin made a noncommittal gesture with his shoulders. "Maybe. I happened to mention something to Peyton about your latest exploits in my last letter home."

"Well, thank you. Susannah and I will be moving to the consulate in Cairo in a few weeks. It will be good to be home and among my family," Alex confessed.

Crispin elbowed him good-naturedly. "I told you you'd come out of this like a hero."

"What about you? How will you come out of this?" Alex asked.

"I'm headed home, by way of Greece. But headed home, nonetheless. It's time."

Alex nodded. Crispin had received news of an inheritance a while back and had dawdled over claiming it. There were issues to settle with his brother, Peyton, and issues to settle within himself that had delayed his going home. Cris didn't talk much about it, but Alex knew he struggled with his own sense of identity. A man couldn't wander alone forever.

He knew that better than anyone now that he had Susannah. The sun sank low over the harbor and Crispin turned from the railing. "I'll go now and leave you to your lovely wife."

They embraced as brothers and Alex saw him downstairs, laughing when Crispin mounted up on the "stolen" black stallion. "Did you ever name the beast?"

"I named him Sheikh. Seemed fitting." Crispin winked and set off down the street.

It would be the last time in years that Alex would see Crispin. But his future lay upstairs in Susannah's arms and he took the steps two at a time.

Susannah waited for him, listening for his footsteps on the stairs. He would be lonely when he returned. But she would see to it that he would not be lonely for long. In his absence, she'd lit candles in the bedroom and unbound her hair. She slipped on a dressing gown of thinnest linen, knowing full well the effect of the material in the candlelight and the effect on him.

She heard him enter the apartments and call her name.

"I'm in here, my love." Susannah moved to the doorway, her hands outstretched, reaching for him. He was handsome in the flickering light, the candles illumining the leonine hues of his hair. She felt her need for him rise. In the months since their marriage, the hungry edge of their passion had not ebbed as she had thought it would, nor had it mellowed with the ordinary pace of days.

She took his hands and drew him to her and through the door to their bedchamber. She was fast learning there was nothing ordinary about life with Alex Grayfield. In bed or out, he was an extraordinary man with whom she'd found a passionate and intellectual partnership.

"Come, I have wine and cheese." She pushed him gently down to the big bed and shrugged provocatively out of the dressing gown, letting it slide down the length of her body, reveling in the naked desire that sprang to life in her husband's eyes.

She came to him, straddling him, stripping away his garments until his body was bare before her. Susannah reached for the decanter of wine. Alex raised his eyebrow in sensual query. She smiled in answer. "Wine is good for other things than drinking." She poured out a bit onto his body and bent her head to him, loving him the way he loved her—the way everyone wants to be loved in their life.

\* \* \* \* \*

# COMING NEXT MONTH FROM

# HARLEQUIN®
# HISTORICAL

## Available April 26, 2011

- **HAPPILY EVER AFTER IN THE WEST**
  by **Debra Cowan, Lynna Banning, Judith Stacy**
  (Western)

- **HOW TO MARRY A RAKE**
  by **Deb Marlowe**
  (Regency)

- **THE GAMEKEEPER'S LADY**
  by **Ann Lethbridge**
  (Regency)
  First in duet: *Rakes in Disgrace*

- **CLAIMED BY THE HIGHLAND WARRIOR**
  by **Michelle Willingham**
  (Medieval)
  *The MacKinloch Clan*

HHCNM0411

# REQUEST YOUR FREE BOOKS!

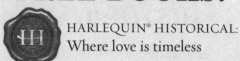

HARLEQUIN® HISTORICAL:
Where love is timeless

## 2 FREE NOVELS PLUS 2 FREE GIFTS!

**YES!** Please send me 2 FREE Harlequin® Historical novels and my 2 FREE gifts (gifts are worth about $10). After receiving them, if I don't wish to receive any more books, I can return the shipping statement marked "cancel." If I don't cancel, I will receive 6 brand-new novels every month and be billed just $4.94 per book in the U.S. or $5.49 per book in Canada. That's a savings of at least 18% off the cover price! It's quite a bargain! Shipping and handling is just 50¢ per book in the U.S. and 75¢ per book in Canada.* I understand that accepting the 2 free books and gifts places me under no obligation to buy anything. I can always return a shipment and cancel at any time. Even if I never buy another book from the Reader Service, the two free books and gifts are mine to keep forever.

246/349 HDN FC45

| Name | (PLEASE PRINT) | |
|------|----------------|---|
| Address | | Apt. # |
| City | State/Prov. | Zip/Postal Code |

Signature (if under 18, a parent or guardian must sign)

Mail to the **Reader Service:**
**IN U.S.A.:** P.O. Box 1867, Buffalo, NY 14240-1867
**IN CANADA:** P.O. Box 609, Fort Erie, Ontario L2A 5X3

Not valid for current subscribers to Harlequin Historical books.

**Want to try two free books from another line?**
**Call 1-800-873-8635 or visit www.ReaderService.com.**

* Terms and prices subject to change without notice. Prices do not include applicable taxes. N.Y. residents add applicable sales tax. Canadian residents will be charged applicable taxes. Offer not valid in Quebec. This offer is limited to one order per household. All orders subject to credit approval. Credit or debit balances in a customer's account(s) may be offset by any other outstanding balance owed by or to the customer. Please allow 4 to 6 weeks for delivery. Offer available while quantities last.

**Your Privacy**—The Reader Service is committed to protecting your privacy. Our Privacy Policy is available online at www.ReaderService.com or upon request from the Reader Service.

We make a portion of our mailing list available to reputable third parties that offer products we believe may interest you. If you prefer that we not exchange your name with third parties, or if you wish to clarify or modify your communication preferences, please visit us at www.ReaderService.com/consumerschoice or write to us at Reader Service Preference Service, P.O. Box 9062, Buffalo, NY 14269. Include your complete name and address.

*With an evil force hell-bent on destruction,
two enemies must unite to find a truth that turns
all-too-personal when passions collide.*

*Enjoy a sneak peek in Jenna Kernan's next installment
in her original* TRACKER *series, GHOST STALKER,
available in May, only from Harlequin Nocturne.*

"Who are you?" he snarled.

Jessie lifted her chin. "Your better."

His smile was cold. "Such arrogance could only come from a Niyanoka."

She nodded. "Why are you here?"

"I don't know." He glanced about her room. "I asked the birds to take me to a healer."

"And they have done so. Is that *all* you asked?"

"No. To lead them away from my friends." His eyes fluttered and she saw them roll over white.

Jessie straightened, preparing to flee, but he roused himself and mastered the momentary weakness. His eyes snapped open, locking on her.

Her heart hammered as she inched back.

"Lead who away?" she whispered, suddenly afraid of the answer.

"The ghosts. Nagi sent them to attack me so I would bring them to her."

The wolf must be deranged because Nagi did not send ghosts to attack living creatures. He captured the evil ones after their death if they refused to walk the Way of Souls, forcing them to face judgment.

"Her? The healer you seek is also female?"

"Michaela. She's Niyanoka, like you. The last Seer of Souls and Nagi wants her dead."

Jessie fell back to her seat on the carpet as the possibility of this ricocheted in her brain. Could it be true?

"Why should I believe you?" But she knew why. His black aura, the part that said he had been touched by death. Only a ghost could do that. But it made no sense.

Why would Nagi hunt one of her people and why would a Skinwalker want to protect her? She had been trained from birth to hate the Skinwalkers, to consider them a threat.

His intent blue eyes pinned her. Jessie felt her mouth go dry as she considered the impossible. Could the trickster be speaking the truth? Great Mystery, what evil was this?

She stared in astonishment. There was only one way to find her answers. But she had never even met a Skinwalker before and so did not even know if they dreamed.

But if he dreamed, she would have her chance to learn the truth.

*Look for GHOST STALKER by Jenna Kernan, available May only from Harlequin Nocturne, wherever books and ebooks are sold.*

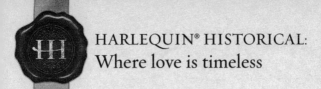

# HARLEQUIN® HISTORICAL:
## Where love is timeless

# *Claimed by the Highland Warrior*

### FROM FAN-FAVOURITE AUTHOR
# MICHELLE WILLINGHAM

## *SCOTLAND, 1305*

Warrior Bram MacKinloch returns to the Scottish Highlands to retrieve his bride—and the dowry that will pay for his brother's freedom.

His wayward wife, Nairna MacPherson, hopes for an annulment from her estranged husband who has spent most of their marriage in prison.

But the boy she married years ago has been irrevocably changed by his captivity. His body is scarred, nightmares disturb his sleep, but most alarming of all is *her* overwhelming desire to kiss every inch of his battle-honed body....

### Available from Harlequin® Historical
### May 2011

*Look out for more from the MacKinloch clan coming soon!*

•

# Harlequin Desire

ALWAYS POWERFUL, PASSIONATE AND PROVOCATIVE.

*USA TODAY* BESTSELLING AUTHOR

# MAUREEN CHILD

**BRINGS YOU ANOTHER PASSIONATE TALE**

# KINGS *of* CALIFORNIA

# KING'S MILLION-DOLLAR SECRET

Rafe King was labeled as the King who didn't know how to love. And even he believed it. That is, until the day he met Katie Charles. The one woman who shows him taking chances in life can reap the best rewards. Even when the odds are stacked against you.

*Available May, wherever books are sold.*